PRINCE
of CHRISTLER-COKE

NEAL BARRETT, JR.

GOLDEN GRYPHON PRESS • 2004

This is a work of fiction. All the characters and events portrayed in this novel are either fictitious or are used fictitiously.

Parts of this novel appeared in different form in *Slightly Off Center*, Swan Press, 1992, Copyright © 1992 by Neal Barrett, Jr., and in *Ten Tales*, James Cahill Publishing, 1994, Copyright © 1994 by Neal Barrett, Jr.,

Copyright © 2004 by Neal Barrett, Jr.
LIBRARY OF CONGRESS CATALOGUING-IN-PUBLICATION DATA
Barrett, Neal.
   Prince of Christler-Coke / Neal Barrett, Jr. — 1st ed.
     p.   cm.
   ISBN 1-930846-28-2 (hardcover : alk. paper)
    1. Consolidation and merger of corporations—Fiction. 2. Corporate culture—Fiction. 3. Social classes—Fiction. 4. Corporations—Fiction. 5. Prisoners—Fiction. 6. Escapes—Fiction. I. Title.
PS3552.A7362   P75   2004
813'.54—dc22   2004000970

All rights reserved, which includes the right to reproduce this book, or portions thereof, in any form whatsoever except as provided by the U.S. Copyright Law. For information address Golden Gryphon Press, 3002 Perkins Road, Urbana, IL 61802.

First Edition.

IN LOVING MEMORY
OF
LORI WOLF

Thanks for all the
smiles, all the laughs you left for me.

PRINCE OF CHRISTLER-COKE

~ ONE ~

The afternoon sun painted flat panes of gold across the porch, danced in the fountains on the lawn, and warmed the marble columns of Iacola Keep. This white and dazzling stone, to Asel's eye, seemed pure and lightly veined as a Chek maid's thigh, a counterpoint to bright dabs of color gathered round him on the porch, on the steps, on the verdant lawn itself, the gay robes of lords and ladies of noble corporate mien.

Every hue and tone was there, every variegate and plaid, each Great House here to witness somber rite and occasion most high, here for merriment and drink, for sly misdeeds and shady deals, mischief and scams of every sort.

Asel found his mother in the crowd, amid House troops clad in blue and white, found his brothers and his cousins and his ants, found the tall and hungry form of Uncle Hal. Found the portly House Bishop half asleep, found the pale and brooding Lord of SEC.

Poor Ducky Du Pontiac-Heinz rambled on, droning through his toast, apparently intent on self-flagellation to the end. Asel risked a glance at Loreli. Not the thing to do but he did. The girl seemed detached. Not completely focused on the day. A nice nose, and a rather pouty mouth. If she heard Ducky's speech, Asel couldn't tell.

Asel felt more or less compelled to smile. If Ducky Du Pontiac-Heinz could make an ass of himself in front of everyone at Iacola Keep, then Asel had the grace to watch him squirm. Oh, how it must be ripping old Duck inside! Anyone could look in those gray septic eyes and see a man who dearly wished to die. Yearned to vanish quietly in the earth.

The thought struck Asel with a surge of dark intent, an image sweet as choclit in his head. It seemed too much to ask, that on a day that was truly Asel's own, Ducky might strangle on his drink, turn some sordid shade of green, and expire upon the lawn. And this, only moments before sweet Loreli's Peek, which of course is what Ducky came to see, knowing in his cold Duck heart that was *all* of Loreli he'd ever get.

A little, dark-haired flunk offered a sweet to Asel's lips. Asel waved her off, and gestured for his glass. Ducky seemed nearly done, coming to the end of this farce. Coming unraveled at the seams. Seeming not to care at all, Asel allowed himself to hear a word or two:

"*Time to put aside . . . corporate malice and regret . . . friendly competition . . . bile and enterprise . . . capital gain and grief . . .*"

Ducky, so resplendent in manly spangled green. Ducky's smile sewn tight with the cords of absent joy.

"*Time to toast a dear friend . . . twenty-one this day . . . named Prince of Christler-Coke . . . the lovely Loreli . . .*"

Asel could stand no more. The words just came, without due reflection or thought. With scant consideration for corporate manner and tact. A reproach from Uncle Hal. Stern disapproval from the Lord of SEC.

"Oh, *urpo*, Ducks," Asel said, "that's quite enough. We're all going to be simply *ill.* . . ."

Stone-dead silence, then a flutter of applause for Ducky's toast —mostly from the back, from the marginally affluent, the hungry and intent. More restrained from the titled and secure.

Ducky turned a deep shade of red that clashed awfully with his suit, then forced a hearty laugh. A flunk raised a crystal to his lips, a rather pretty creature, Asel thought. From Toonisha, or somewhere about, one of those dreadfully dreary spots over *there*, Ducky being prone to dusty skin, girls with oddly tilted eyes.

His own flunk, a demure little Britt, raised Asel's glass as well, and Asel took a sip.

Well-wishers and other parasites circled Ducky with respect.

"Nice speech, Ducks," said Harry Chase-Breck, who had little need to toady up.

"Good lad," said the ancient, near destitute scion of Kimberly-Kraft.

"Goddamn fine," said the squat and portly Jackie Cee of Disney-Dow. "Damn fine indeed."

Asel's mother wasn't near, but her keen and practiced North

Virgentle ears, bred to catch transgression and offense, picked up Jackie's words at once.

"Suh, you are in *East* America now," she chided. "We ah most religiously inclined and we do take affront in such mattahs as foul and vulgah tongue."

Mother gave the youth a gentle smile, but there was nothing so forgiving in her eyes.

"Your pardon, Lady," said Jackie Cee. "Very deep regrets." An abject bow, formally correct. But Asel saw the scorn in froggy eyes. Saw coastal dreams of elderly assault.

Serves the scalawag right, Asel thought. Califoggy State had sent this pissboot from Disney-Dow as a gesture of contempt, a slap as clear as bogus bonds. A bold reminder of their long and scarcely legal love affair with the House of Du Pontiac-Heinz. Father had told them to toss the bastard out, but Asel intervened. Said rejection, after all, is recognition of a sort.

This, the first time Asel had spoken out in a truly business sense. Well, of course, the first time he *could*. Asel had scarcely noticed at the time. It seemed the thing to do. And Father had readily agreed. As if Asel made decisions every day. When it dawned on Asel what he'd done, he felt a sharp, intense little thrill of corporate repute, and a very nice erection as well.

The little Britt popped a sweet in his mouth. Asel bit down on something hard.

"That's a nut," Asel said. "There's a nut in there."

"Oh, dear!" The flunk looked contrite. "*Terribly* sorry 'bout that."

"I don't like nuts of any sort."

"I forgot."

"Well don't."

Asel spat the offending goodie in her hand. Noted a nice, gold bangle on her wrist. Assumed he'd awarded it for carnal enterprise, but couldn't really place her at all.

Loreli's Peek seemed to go quite well. Her mother's flunk made a speech:

"*Two great Houses joined together* . . . *blah-blah-blah family pride* . . ."

Loreli stood. Her mother's flunk drew white silk aside to reveal the bridal breasts. Quite enthusiastic applause.

Nice pair of whoopers, Asel thought. But his eyes were on the Duck. Disappointment in the cesspool eyes, but not enough. Not at all what Asel had hoped, which was more like rage and despair. Spasm and lament. Dire affliction of every sort.

Ah, but wasn't that a trace of a smile? Asel felt better at once. If Ducky was smiling, he was dying inside. Watching his dreams disappear. Ducky Du Pontiac-Heinz could get all the lovely honkers he desired, but this pair was forever out of reach. Wedding bells would ring. The two great houses of Christler-Coke and Pepsicoma-Dodge would be one, and the Duck would be doo-doo out of luck.

With a household trooper on either side, Asel rose to meet his bride to be. Mother joined him for the short, formal walk. Soft family carpet underfoot. Since early childhood, Asel had believed that Mother was entirely composed of air. A trace of lavender and rose. A whiff of angelkake. So delicately bred, so refined, she lacked the shame of inner parts.

The two mothers faced each other in ritual array, as if they'd never met before. As if they hadn't been plotting this day since Asel and Loreli were born. As if a hundred lawyer earls on either side hadn't sealed and secured the nuptial stock.

A reader flunk spoke for the mother of Loreli:

"*I give my daughter blah-blah . . . godly communion . . . dividends for all . . .*"

"*Hearty issue and bliss,*" answered Mother's flunk. "*Love and municipal bonds . . .*"

Asel's Uncle Hal stepped up, a corporate flunk by his side. The flunk read the bloodline for the House of Christler-Coke:

"*And Anheuser-Tusch*
begat Canon-Cadillac,
begat Kodak-Smack,
begat Pfizer-Kaiser-Nizer,
begat Motorolacola,
begat AT&Me,
begat Hershey-GE . . ."

The flunk had a very nice voice. If you liked, you could hum right along. He seemed to go on for some time. Then Hal stepped back, and Loreli's uncle took the floor. His flunk had trouble with his t's, and appeared to be slightly off key:

"*And IBhim*
begat Montgomery-Sears,
begat Playtex-Rears,
begat Brut-of-the-Loom,
begat Tylenol-Doom,

begat Volkshaagen-Dazs,
begat Bigg-MacIntosh . . ."
All this came to an end. Mothers and uncles smiled. White silk passed from flunk to flunk; bridal breasts were concealed once again. Viewed from mere inches away, Asel felt they were a very nifty pair. Worth, he supposed, in the abstract sense, perhaps eight-point-two zillion each, depending on current market trends.

Applause, then Asel's little Britt joined hands with a distinctly Sweedish flunk of Loreli's, and the four strolled down the steps onto the lawn in the traditional nuptial walk. Past the fountains, down the path. Past the formal garden resplendent with white and crimson rose. Past the neatly sculptured shrubs and the busts of business kings.

"Well," said Loreli, "it's real nice to meet you, okay?"

"My pleasure," Asel said, and wondered if this were so. The girl seemed less than astute. In the afternoon light, certain blemishes appeared.

"I guess we'll get along," said Loreli.

"It's difficult to say."

"You like riddles?"

"I absolutely loathe them."

"I got a real good one."

"Keep it to yourself."

"The wedding was swell."

"I'm afraid I didn't notice at all."

"Your mother's sure pretty, you know?"

"Yours, if I may say, is somewhat rotund. I do hope tubby genes are not dominant in your line."

"Oh, they're not. Mother has a weakness for sweets. Noogut cremes. Choclit buhnies. Poork in any form."

"I don't believe that's a sweet."

"Mother doesn't mind."

"I think we'd best be getting back," Asel said.

Loreli sneezed. Her flunk whipped a hanky to her nose.

"God bless," said Asel's Britt.

"Thank you," said Loreli's Sweede.

~ TWO ~

The remainder of the walk passed in blessed silence between the two. Asel enjoyed the scenery on every hand. Beyond the tall helms that lined the drive, his great-grandfather had artfully contrived a stand of moors, patterned in the rude Scodish mode. Gray spires of rock, aged by chemical design, burst now and then through rolling hills. Asel had always found them rather disturbing to the eye. A bit of bold savagery, unexpected and abrupt.

Past the moors was the river, and some sort of mountains after that. Father and Uncle Hal had chided him more than once about lolling around this one small corner of the grounds, and never even looking at the rest of the estate. Hal said Vermint and New Yuk were very nice. There were two or three Virgentles to the south, that Mother had brought to the House. And of course, Asel thought with some irritation, now there were all those places of Loreli's he would have to remember as well.

I'm of age, and it won't do any harm to take a look. I might take a honeymoon trip. Find out where Loreli's going, of course. Don't want to end up there....

It was getting rather hot. Asel gestured and the Britt produced a fan. On the far pale horizon, beyond a bank of windswept clouds, he saw several dark specks against the sky. Some sort of byrds. Byrds were nice to watch. Apparently, there were several different kinds. He might have a flunk learn their names.

Asel's cousin said Uncle Hal was most anxious to see him. As ever, Reynard seemed slightly discomposed.

"They're in the study," said Reynard. "Your mother is in an absolute snit. Asel, she is *not* going to do it. I simply knew this would happen."

"She will and that's that," Asel said.
"I love the new you. There's power in your stance."
"Forget it, Reynard."
"I sense this aura of command. How's the new bride?"
"Utterly absurd."
"She seems awfully sweet."
"I don't care to talk about this."

Asel left Reynard and cut through to the sunroom, ablaze with gaudy light. The little Britt trailed along. The high glass walls revealed merrymakers dining on the porch. Seating had been carefully arranged, in tune with net worth and family line. Flunks popped goodies and wynes in noble mouths. Biff, the gouty Duke of Seagram 7-Eleven. Boarson of Calvin-Neutraswine. The crafty Lord Bill of Nabisco-Shell. Each, to a man, intent on executive plunder and rape. Swindle and trade. Larceny and shifty enterprise.

And where was good Ducky, the disappointed Duke of Du Pontiac-Heinz? Too sick to eat, Asel hoped. Pining for the wealth and fine melons of the lovely Loreli.

Mother was indeed in a snit.

She wandered about the study, darting here and there and back again. Short Rushin flunks tried to follow in her wake. One offered tissues and salts. Another jasmin ti.

Uncle Hal collared Asel at once. "You talk to her. That woman won't stand still."

"I thought we settled all this," Asel said.

"It's not settled now."

"Yes it is. Father simply cannot appear. What would everybody think?"

"Tell *her*. She'll listen to you."

Asel had doubts about that.

"Look. There's something else," Hal said. "The market's on a spree. You father wants to see you right away."

"What's wrong with the market?"

"Up and down. Unsettled and confused. Irregularities and tics."

Asel looked from Mother to Hal. "What am I supposed to do first?"

"Everything at once."

"I don't much care for your advice," Asel said.

Hal didn't seem to hear. He left Asel standing in the center of the room and disappeared into the hall. Asel guessed his mother's dizzy course and tried to cut her off.

"Mother, we simply must go through with this. There is nothing else to do."

"You have placed yoah self in my path," Mother said.

"I want you to sit."

"You are sayin' simply awful things about that puhfectly lovely girl. Ah will *not* have that, Asel."

Reynard, Asel thought, visions of torture and abuse in his head.

"We are not discussing Loreli. We are discussing something else."

"A dahlin girl. Unquestioned family line."

"Mother. These people came to see Father. They didn't come to see me. They must be assured the House of Iacola is intact. He cannot go out there looking like *that*."

Mother seemed aghast. "Theah is nothin' wrong with yoah father."

"Absolutely everything is wrong with Father."

"He is simply undah the weathah."

"It's safe to say that."

"Asel, I will not do this." Tears filled Mother's eyes. "The very idea is appallin' to me. I cannot tolerate the presence of a mechanical puhson in this house. It is against God's will."

"Five minutes," Asel said. "Maybe three. It says hello and that's it. Mother, stand still."

Mother faked Asel out. Darted to the left, then the right, leaving flunks behind.

Uncle Hal reappeared. "Don't like this at all. We've got intruders on the screen. Over the estate. Choppers from the SEC."

Asel looked startled and alarmed. "They can't do that."

"Go outside and see."

"I feel you saw some byrds."

"Asel, I know a chopper from a byrd. Have you seen your father yet? No. Go and do it now. Don't delay. See him at once."

Hal vanished again. Mother continued to wail and move in quick, erratic arcs. Asel's head began to hurt. He felt confused and out of synch. This entire Prince thing was a pain, right from the very start.

"A drink," he told the Britt.

"Coke? Brandi? Ti? Graype? Salmonade—"

"Damn it all, you decide. Do I have to do everything around here?"

The light in Father's den was subdued, pale as dawn except for one small corner where blue screens chattered and chimed, blipped and beeped, clinked and hummed in some order or disarray. Bells rang and buzzers buzzed. Clever Swizz doctor/business flunks padded silently about in white athletic shoes. Holo banners of violet and pink seemed to race across the air, vanish and appear, revealing the megabuck traffic of the day.

Asel stepped across a serpentine coil, thick strands of copper and gold, silver and brass, bundles of clear plastic tubing that rushed vital nutrients in and sucked the waste out of his father's chrome encapsulated chair. Asel shunned the tubes with some distaste. It would seem—well you would think—they could make the things opaque.

"Uncle Hal says you wanted to see me," Asel said. "I hear the market's gone astray."

Father blinked and clicked, gave a pulmonary wheeze. Varied parts appeared to move, vague and indistinct under frosty silver glass, but scarcely indistinct enough.

"BUYOUTS,....,TEMPO-RARY SURGE," Father said, in fairly clear metallic tones. "FELONIUS ASSAULT,....,ILL-EGAL ENTER-RISE,...,"

"Okay, what do you think is wrong?" Asel said.

"WHAT WE GOT HERE, SON, IS ......UNDER-HANDED ACTION IN THE WORKS,....,CRISIS UNDEFINED,....,MAJOR BAD NEWS,...,CHRISTLER-COKE AND PEPSICOMA-DODGE ....,DOWN 3 AND A HALF,....,FALLING FASSSSSSST,...,"

Asel was taken aback. "But that's not possible. I mean, the wedding and all. Our stock ought to be *up*. Even I know that."

"BUY AMERICAN DOG,....,HUSHPUPPY-LEAR,....,"

A flunk went into action at once.

"SELL,....,ATLANTIC KATZ & MYCE,....,DEL MONTE-SKAG,...,"

"Father, just listen a minute. Uncle Hal says the SEC has choppers in the air."

"WATCHED YOU ON THE,...,TUBE,...,THAT GIRL'S GOT BOOBERS OUT TO HERE,...,"

"I guess she's all right. I guess she'll have to do. Look, what do you want me to do? I could use a little help right now."

"THERE WE GO AGAIN,....,DOWN 4 AND AN EIGHTH,.... 4 AND A HALF,....,"

Asel tried to follow purple numbers in the air. Nothing made any sense at all.

"BOTTOM LINE, BOY, WE'VE GOT FRAUD AND DE-CEIT,..,UNDERHANDED SHIT OF EVERY SORT,......VANDALS,

SCALAWAGS......RAMPANT THIEV-ERY AND TRADING ON THE SLYYYYY......"

"But—what's it all *mean*?"

"BUY PROCTOR AND GUMP.......SELL REEBOK-KNOPF......BUY SWIFT-PANAM......SELL PRUDENTIAL STRIFE......BUY CADILLAGAA-FAGGA-BAGGA-ZLIIIIIIIIIK!"

"I don't know what he's trying to say. I simply have no idea. We're in deep trouble, I think I got that."

"Your father has insight and zeal," said Uncle Hal. "Uncanny knack. Get-up-and-go. Greatest business mind of the age."

"Well I'm not," Asel said. "I just started today and I haven't had lunch. Father says *some*one is trying to screw Iacola House. I don't know any more than that."

"I'd say he's right. We're up to our noses in it, lad."

"What about those choppers?"

"I am trying, with no success, to find the Lord of SEC. I've got flunks out searching everywhere. Don't think he wants to be found, you ask me. Your mother is being an absolute pest, Asel. She will not stand up with your father's faxx. I have been so informed, in no uncertain terms."

Asel moaned. "All right. I'll go out there myself. Do I have to *do* anything?"

"Fully programmed. Just stand there and smile."

Asel wanted more help than that. Hal always seemed to sense the right moment to walk away.

Outside, the tables were deserted but there was still food about. The Britt fed him cream lahm sandwich and pengwin ti. Asel thought he saw Ducky in the crowd or maybe not. Peter Dee of Betty Cracker-Nash wandered by. Ruby denim tux. Green lamé shorts.

"Asel, you simply must come along," Peter said. "Robbie's bought Spayne. He wants us all to go and see."

"Can't," Asel told him. "Got a bunch of business stuff."

"Oh, you old tycoon." Peter gave him a sly and wicked wink. "You are not going to be any fun now, are you?"

"I guess not."

A House trooper came to Asel's side, and guided him quickly to the outer hall. Asel gave a start. Father's faxx looked remarkably real. Certainly better than Father had looked in years. Silver hair and ruddy cheeks. A sparkle in the azure plastic eyes.

Asel saw a flunk nearby, holding a tiny, black box.
"What's that?"
"Remote control, sir. Very compact."
"I thought this thing was completely programmed."
"Yes sir, it is. The remote's in case something goes wrong."
"Something just better *not*."

Guards opened the grand entry doors. Asel stepped out on the porch, the faxx by his side. It seemed to walk quite well. Asel detected a nearly imperceptible whir. Uncle Hal had told him the faxx would be credible at eight-point-seven-two feet. At precisely this distance, velvet ropes had been draped across the porch.

Seven flunks raised trumpets to their lips. Nobles and their ladies offered cheers and hurrahs.

Father's faxx raised its hands. "I bid you welcome to Iacola House . . . splendid occasion . . . God bless you all . . . friend and foe alike . . ."

More applause. The faxx sounded perfectly fine. Asel waited. Apparently, this was all his bogus father had to say.

"Prince Asel," a man shouted from the crowd. "President Flick and the First Lady would like a picture with you and your father. They'd be most grateful for that."

"Yes, very fine, piss off," Asel smiled and waved. "Thank you very much."

The faxx turned, and strolled back through the door. Asel watched it go with great relief. Some small device seemed out of synch; the azure eyes kept blinking on and off, and something sizzled in the fine silver hair. . . .

~ THREE ~

Uncle Hal was waiting just inside. "Get that thing out of here," he said, frightening Asel's flunk. "Asel, come with me right now. I've got that swine Lord Pierce cornered in the sunroom. We've got trouble here, boy."

"Did he say exactly what?"

"Won't say a thing. Wants to talk to you. *And* your father as well."

"He certainly will not."

"Right. You tell him that."

The Lord of SEC seemed to Asel akin to an upright roach. Dark and dissolute, thin and slightly stooped. Bad breath and some vague imperfection of the soul. An appalling lack of taste in his attire.

"Sir," Asel said, "I understand you wish to talk. I don't wish to listen to whatever you have to say."

A bow in Asel's direction, half an inch short of respect.

"My sincere congratulations on your princely elevation, on your lovely wedding day—"

"Never mind all that," Asel said sharply. "What's going on here, Pierce? Your people have choppers over Iacola Keep. You'd better call them off."

"Just a formality, sir. Nothing to cause alarm. Routine in, ah, matters such as this."

Asel exchanged a glance with Hal.

"Matters such as what?" said Uncle Hal.

Lord Pierce seemed to hesitate. "Investigations of a sort. Some question of family defect. A possible, ah, blemish in the line."

Asel exploded. "Damn you, fellow. This is absolutely vile!"

Hal turned to a flunk. "Get the bishop in here. Right now."

"You had best explain yourself at once," Asel told Lord Pierce.
"I find you impertinent and rude. Your clothes are out of style."

The man dared a yawn. "Perhaps we should talk to your father."

"Absolutely not."

"As you wish, then."

"Listen. I find you unwholesome at best."

"This is terribly embarrassing for me."

"Oh, I'll just bet."

The bishop appeared. Obese and out of breath. Hal jabbed a finger at the Lord of SEC. "Tell this *person* the family line is pure. Set him straight at once. He has alluded to a blot."

The bishop looked stunned. "There is no flaw whatever in Iacola House. What an appalling thing to say."

"There is certain evidence to the contrary," Lord Pierce said. He looked directly at Asel. "Your marital blood test reveals a rather clear ancestral fault."

"This is insane," Asel said.

"Nevertheless. There is obviously a stain. An extra little chromosomal blip where none should be. Quite possibly a stenographic gene." Lord Pierce raised a sympathetic brow. "On your mother's side, it seems."

"Oh, dear." The bishop brought a finger to his lips.

"*Mother!*" Asel was consumed with sudden anger and disbelief. "I can assure you that no one in Mother's family has ever—*worked* a day in their life. This is totally obscene."

"And this just now coming to light, of course," Hal said, a nasty edge to his voice. "On Asel's wedding day. When two great houses come to merge. My, what an odd conjunction of events. To have this *fault* appear at such a time."

The Lord of SEC showed no expression at all. "Sir, if that is an implication of any sort, I take offense."

"I want you off my grounds and out of here at once," Asel said.

"There are certain formalities to attend."

"Well, attend to them somewhere else."

The bishop closed his eyes. "And Anheuser-Tusch begat Canon-Cadillac, begat Kodak-Smack, begat—"

"Shut up," Asel said.

A flunk gestured Uncle Hal aside. Asel looked past the sunroom windows to the lawn. The crowd seemed somewhat thinner than before. As Asel watched, several nobles took their leave with great haste.

"Get me a drink," Asel told the Britt.

"Kawfee? Ti? Sider? Nuttermilk—"

"Damn it, whatever. All right?"

Uncle Hal returned. His features showed pallor and alarm.

"We've got more air action, boy. Whole squadron coming in. SEC Mark IXs." He looked coldly at Pierce. "Three of *our* House choppers are down. You've got some explaining to do."

Pierce spread his hands. "I regret any loses due to, ah—defensive action on the part of our craft. It is the policy of the Commission, of Securities Exchange—"

"My *father* put you where you are today," Asel said heatedly. "You are *not* a real lord. You seem to forget that point."

"I derive my authority from the entire Board of Business kings," Pierce said with a haughty air. "*You* seem to forget about *that*."

"I want him flogged," Asel said. "Hal, stay here with this toad. I'm going to see Father."

Asel stopped, as a great noise seemed to consume the very air. The windows in the sunroom shook. Shadows appeared on the lawn. Choppers descended like a blight, ugly as earwigs and lice, black as centipedes.

"Now this is intolerable," Asel said. "Remove those things at once!"

"There is absolutely no cause for alarm," said the Lord of SEC. "There will merely be a slight occupation. Until the investigation is complete."

"This is an outright invasion is what it is." Hal grabbed a passing flunk. "I want every House unit here at once. Pencilvainy Armored, Ohiyo Assault—"

Automatic fire began to chatter on the lawn. A House soldier sprawled on the porch. Asel's flunk cried out in alarm as red-clad troopers swept into the room.

"I will not have this," Asel said. "Leave. All of you. Right now."

A trooper poked a slightly mauve weapon at Asel's chest. The barrel seemed plagued with copper warts.

"Leave him," said the Lord of SEC. "Take the others out."

Asel started to protest. The weapon seemed effective and complex. The bishop and respective flunks left at once. Even Asel's Britt disappeared.

"I'm sorry for any inconvenience," Pierce said. "We'll try to clear this up."

"I plan to have you boiled."

"Sir. Let's try to get along."

"Let's not."

Pierce swept his cloak aside and sat. Apparently, a deliberate affront. "A charge such as this takes time. Hearings, studies, that sort of thing. I expect you'll feel some discontent."

"I'm not listening to this. What kind of discontent?"

"Relocation of a sort. Possible restraint. Incarceration and proper penal care."

Asel was stunned. He could scarcely get a breath. "Don't be ridiculous. That is totally out of the question."

"I'm afraid not."

"I might stay around the grounds a day or so. I might agree to that."

"Oklahomer comes to mind."

"What's that?"

Pierce stood. "You can go outside if you like. Don't wander off. We'll need to talk."

"I hardly see the point."

He wondered what he ought to do next. He needed to talk to Hal. Nothing seemed to be going well at all. He might take a nap. Hopefully, Hal would clear the whole thing up quite soon. He was very good at that.

All the guests were gone. Loreli too, he supposed. White cloths fluttered about on empty dining tables on the porch. Black choppers squatted on the lawn. Asel was pleased they had carefully avoided Mother's garden. Her prize roses were windblown but intact.

After a while, Hal found him by the trees along the road. Uncle Hal looked tired. His face seemed to sag.

"This has not been a very good day," Hal said.

"It started off rather well. Things seemed to go downhill."

"Sorry to see you lose Loreli."

"The girl's defective, Hal."

"Fine knobbers, though." He looked at Asel. "This is not simply a SEC thing. I'm certain that bloodline business was a ruse. This is a takeover bid is what it is."

Asel frowned. It was difficult to consider all this. "You think we've been had?"

"Good lad." Uncle Hal seemed proud. "Ducky Du Pontiac-Heinz and his crowd, you ask me. And that lout, Jackie Cee, from Disney-Dow. They had some help, too. Some of our people. Those ships got through unopposed. I'd guess your cousin Reynard. That boy is devoid of family pride. I expect he's into dope and hard aerobics."

"I never liked him at all," Asel said. "How's Mother taking all this?"

"Dead. Had a flunk do her in."

"I suppose that's best. Has anyone told Father?"

"No need for that. I fear he is rather deceased. Someone chopped his lines. Awful mess in there. Reynard's people, I suppose. It's clear we had several clerk snipists in our midst."

Asel fell silent. A tablecloth blew across the lawn, impaled itself upon a shrub.

"I think they're going to send me to Oklahomer, Uncle Hal. I don't much care for that."

"Shouldn't think you would. You're an Iacola, Asel. You'll come through fine."

"What about you?"

"I've had it up to here," Hal said. "Got me a pill from one of those clever little Swizz. Guess I better lie down. Best of luck to you, boy."

"Thanks, Uncle Hal."

Asel watched Hal walk unsteadily toward the house. He wondered if he should get a pill, too. On the other hand, how bad could Oklahomer be?

Asel's little Britt came out across the lawn.

"I've been greatly concerned. Are you all right, sir?"

"Of course not."

"I can't go with you, you know."

"Who told you that?"

"They said you couldn't have a flunk."

"That's ridiculous."

"Well, I'm sure you'll be fine."

"I'm sure I'll be nothing of the sort."

Asel had nothing more to say. After a moment, the flunk wandered off. Asel listened to the wind in the trees. In spite of the waning sun, the day was quite hot. A jacket was too much. He waved for someone to take it off. Remembered there was nobody there. He moved one arm, to see what that might do. Nothing. He shook his shoulders hard, hoping the thing would fall down his back. Finally, he bent down until his hands touched his toes. The tail of the jacket slid off across his head.

"How utterly absurd," he said aloud. "I simply *cannot* put up with all this."

He stood on the lawn and watched the sun disappear past the trees, past the moors, past the mountains and the river, and whatever sort of world might be beyond that. . . .

~ FOUR ~

Asel dreamed of Iacola Keep. Dreamed of the broad, green lawns and marble halls. Dreamed of noble statuary and artful filigree. Richly polished wood and fine carpet to the knees. Dreamed of fluted glass and plates of gold. Wyne and jellied lahm. Slick eel sandwiches and klams. Dreamed of perky servant flunks from overseas. Leggy Hunns and Britts. Chesty Lahps and Sweedes. Woke to the awful sound of Hank Jockey-Visa throwing up.

"Hank," Asel said, viewing this scene with displeasure and alarm, "stop that at once. Right now. What a revolting thing to see."

"Can't help it. Awfully sorry 'bout that." Hank looked at Asel with terribly hollow eyes. His face was white as sauce. Asel couldn't imagine what the fellow could possibly find to retch. He had scarcely eaten a thing in five days. Still, Hank had clearly found *something* in his craw.

"Well, cover it up," Asel said. "Do something. Don't just leave it there."

Asel got out of his bed and made an effort not to breathe. The small compartment was cramped beyond belief. The AC was faulty at best. Asel sensed a different rhythm underfoot and raised the window shade. The morning sun hurt his eyes; the scene outside did little to soothe his growing irritation of the day.

"Appalling," he said. "Absolutely drear."

"What is it?" Hank asked.

"Oklahomer, I should guess. I fear we have arrived."

The prison train slowed. The countryside was flat and unappealing; ochre seemed to dominate the land. Everything in sight was a dull and somber shade of brick. Asel squinted and tried to find a tree.

"Oh, *God!*" Hank looked past Asel and sank back to his bed. Moaned and covered up his eyes.

"I cannot go through this, Asel. I simply cannot."

"I suppose we must, Hank."

Hank turned away and curled into a ball. A man and a woman stood beside the tracks. Asel watched them as the train lumbered by. Both were short and fat. Their clothing was completely out of style.

"I intend to kill myself," Hank announced. "Hopefully, before we leave the train. I've watched you, Asel. You are a very strong person. I'm not. I don't intend to live like this. I don't suppose you have a knife. A fountain pen would do."

Asel sighed. "There is no reason we will be ill-treated, just because we're going to prison. I'm sure our accommodations will be quite nice."

Asel didn't believe this at all, but it seemed like the right thing to say. Hank Jockey-Visa was a complete and utter bore, tiresome to a fault. Asel tried to be polite, but couldn't quite recall where he'd met the fellow before. He recalled one or two of the others, but Hank simply didn't come to mind.

Still, the fellow's loathsome behavior seemed to bolster Asel's own waning courage. The more Hank whined and threw up, the more Asel vowed he would not bring himself down to that. One did, after all, have standards to uphold. Even if one did, on occasion, pee in one's pants at the thought of southwestern penal life.

He scarcely had time to dress before the guard stuck his head in and rudely called them out. His arms got caught in his coat. His feet became entangled in his pants. Asel cursed his clumsy hands. Getting dressed alone was a problem he had never imagined in his happy, former life.

Hank looked awful. Totally deranged. Buttons and collars and cuffs in disarray.

"I could use a little help," Hank said. "Where do you suppose this hand's supposed to go?"

"That's entirely up to you."

"I've considered broken glass. Some sort of potion or drug. Asphyxiation might do. I can hold my breath for some time."

"Give it a try," Asel said.

Breakfast was a most unpleasant affair. Aigs ill-timed, likely with intent. Tarnished silverware. Jam of some crude, commercial grade. Jooce barely chilled. Asel felt this was an omen of things to come. Hank didn't eat at all. Asel felt he had to keep his strength. Prisoners were taken directly from the dining car and shuffled off the train. The guards were only semi-alert. There were three in Asel's group besides Hank. The twin Lords of Wrigley-Keds, feeble and subdued in aqua tennis shoes. The Duke of Sexxon-Apple gave Asel a scathing look, showed Hank a lazy smile. Asel felt Hank shudder by his side.

"I absolutely hate that person," Hank said.

"I suggest you stay out of his way."

Hank looked appalled. "How am I supposed to do that?"

Asel didn't know and clearly didn't care.

The heat was intense, the scenery grim and bare. Asel saw no sign of buildings of any sort. After a moment, the train creaked and began to pull away. As it passed, Asel glanced into a second-class car. Sober, desolate faces passed him by, Slaavs and wily Terks, Greiks and Levenknees, low-management flunks caught in some petty theft or misdeed, caught at trickery and guile, caught taking pencils home.

Behind them, a car full of stenos and clerks. Guilty of filing crimes, secretarial sin. Some were quite attractive, Asel thought. Some made lewd remarks. Asel wondered where they were being taken now. Perhaps they'd be close by.

A lone bus appeared. Asel had never seen one before. Dusty, battered, its windows blurred by the sun, it seemed some relic of an age long past.

"I absolutely refuse to ride in *that*," Hank said, "I simply will not."

"No talking!" said the guard.

"Did you hear that, Asel? Did you hear how the wretch spoke to me?"

"Yes, Hank, I did."

Once on the bus, the Duke of Sexxon-Apple sat directly behind Asel and Hank.

"Bertie, go away," Asel said.

"I can sit anywhere I like."

"Yes, I suppose that's true. Still, if you insist on bothering us, I will be compelled to say I find you totally offensive and rude. Without taste of any sort."

"I don't care if you do or not," Bert said.

Nevertheless, the rebuke seemed to work. Bert kept his silence after that. Hank remained stiff and ill at ease.

A line of trucks passed the bus going west, stirring up dust. Asel saw nothing but scrub oke and dirt. Everything looked extremely dead. He was certain the long road stretching out into the heat went absolutely nowhere at all.

After a nearly insufferable hour and a half, a cluster of buildings appeared ahead. A very large and rusty sign tilted by the side of the road:

WELCOME TO THE
NATIONAL EXECUTIVE REHABILITATION FACILITY
(NERF)

"Oh my *God!*" Hank cried. His features seemed to crumble and fall away.

Bert gave a most unsavory laugh.

Asel turned on him at once. "I'm glad you find this amusing. Especially since you appear to be on this bus as well."

Bert sniffed at that. "I do not intend to stay. Lawyers are on the move. Certain high people will be informed. Dire measures are in the works. I am wrongly charged and falsely accused."

It was Asel's turn to laugh. The Wrigley-Keds twins joined in. Even Hank risked a smile. . . .

~ FIVE ~

Asel could see no walls or fences, no gates of any sort. The bus turned down a narrow street. Asel stared at very ordinary shops. Tacky stores and chintzy boutiques. The bus stopped. A guard ordered everyone out.

A tall, scarecrow of a man stepped up to greet them. His blue uniform had shrunk, leaving patches of doughy white at his ankles and his wrists.

"Gentlemen, I'd like to welcome you to the National Executive Rehabilitation Facility at Dry Rock, Oklahomer. You will be treated fairly. You will receive medical care if so required. You have the right to sing and dance. You have the right to carnal fun. You will be assigned a job. You will be happy in your work.

"You will not abuse, mutilate, or destroy sports or recreational equipment. You will not urinate in the pool. You will now form an orderly line and choose your E-1 clothing allotment from the store directly to your right. Leave your present garments, shoes, and underclothing in the sanitary booths provided. You will not, I repeat, *not*, take said garments with you when you leave.

"Your E-1 clothing is specified as follows: Two trousers, casual wear. Two shirts, sport or recreational style. One suit. One jacket. One tie. One pair of shoes, dress. One pair of shoes, work. One pair of shoes, hobby or play. No sandals or boots. Three pair of socks, white. Two pair of underwear, white. One pair of pajamas, with string. One jogging suit and appropriate shoes. Work wear will be issued at your assigned job. Gentlemen, you have ten minutes. Report back to me. Do not loiter or wander aimlessly about."

The man was clearly practiced at his chore. Asel couldn't recall a thing he'd said. Nevertheless, he made his way toward the store, Hank whining at his heels.

Asel was appalled. He had never even dreamed of such wear. Who in God's name *wore* this sort of thing? Hawahyan shirts in pyneappul prints. Double-knit pants. Jackets with checks that hurt his eyes. The store was a Polly Hester hell.

Everything smelled old, and Asel suddenly understood why. These garments had molded in a warehouse somewhere, possibly for several hundred years.

Asel was weary, more or less resigned. He shed his blue lame tights and silken shirt. Left his plumed hat behind. Tossed away his sable tie. Traded soft kid boots for leather shoes as hard as steel. The stranger in the mirror was a man he didn't know. Common and base. A person without a trace of noble mien in a leisure suit of awful powder blue. A tie with slightly walleyed malerds in flight. Maybe Hank was right. Death was an alternate way of life.

Hank was in tears. Seersucker jacket and red bow tie. Rayon pants and white shoes. Outside, he searched the sidewalk for bits of broken glass.

Asel had to laugh. Bert, the Duke of Sexxon-Apple, was a symphony in lime. Bert gave him a killing look and refused to meet his eyes. Each of the Wrigley-Keds twins wore polo shirts with a horse sewn on the front. Matching pants of horrid red. Elevator shoes.

"This buckle is rather sharp," Hank said. "I feel I could open up a vein."

"Good luck," Asel said.

"Back on the bus," said the scarecrow man. "We haven't got all day."

"On your left, you will find your basic penal units. This will be your new home. Maintenance is required. Garbage days are Mondays and Thursdays. Take pride in your quarters, gentlemen. Snap inspections will occur at any time. Number Seven-Oh-Two." The bus stopped. "That's you, mister."

Bert stepped off without a backward glance, tried to walk with noble stride.

Two blocks later, the twins were gone as well.

"Number Seven-Oh-Five," the fellow said, and nodded Asel's way.

"Oh, we're together," Hank said, jumping to his feet.

"*Sit.*" The man in the bad uniform pointed a bony finger at

Hank. "I will not put up with your fancy ways, you'd best remember that."

Hank looked forlorn, totally impaired. "I won't be seeing you again, Asel. I have some ideas. There might be a tub. I can fashion some device."

"Find something high," Asel suggested.

"Thank you. I'll give it some thought...."

~ SIX ~

Asel stood on the sidewalk and inspected his new home. After the clothing store, he was hardened to surprise. Two-story townhouses out of the past, jammed, crammed, slammed together wall-to-wall. Powndkakes of architectural hash. Georjan. Kolonyal. Quaint Englesh thatch. Pseudo-Gothal, with imitation turret and vault. Number Seven-Oh-Five was Early Rowmen with plastic gingerbred.

After several faulty tries, he learned to turn the knob. The door opened easily enough. The scene inside was bizarre. Sofas in garish color prints, manic parruts, and mukaws. A wagonwheel chandelier. On the wall, velvet paintings of tawny Taheati girls. Tin swords and rusty mail. A clock that wagged its tail.

He passed a stairway and walked into a gloomy hall. The hall ended at a door. Asel stopped and sniffed. Horrid smells filled the air. The door swung open and nearly knocked him back. "Hey, come on in, man," a voice said. "Fellow said you'd be along."

Asel was too stunned to move. The man grinned from the far side of the room. Broad features and a thin mustache. Purple Dacron pants. A shirt with a female mouse in yellow shoes. Solid as oke, close to six foot eight. He held some kind of cooking utensil in his hand.

Asel simply stared. "My heavens," he said at last, "correct me if I'm wrong, but you're a colored person, are you not?"

"Sort of Alybama beige. Cocoh, tohsty. Mister Sypi *au lait*."

"Please don't think I'm ill-bred in any way," Asel said, for he hadn't missed the disapproving glance. "Truth to tell, sir, I have simply never seen one before."

"One what?"

"Why, a person of the darky persuasion. Spaydes, shades, Famous and Handy. Marty Luther and the Pibbs. I am quite well schooled, don't think I'm not. Our House did business with the South. Textiles, two-tone shoes. Shrymp and marmahlade. Say, how does it feel to have peculiar pigmentation of the flesh?"

The man studied Asel for some time. Appeared to decide between violence and accord. Seemed to realize Asel was simply dense, that he lacked the basic tools for insults and affronts.

"You came in today."

"That's correct," Asel said.

"On the morning train."

"Yes, with considerable discomfort and regret."

"And which House is that, the one you saying did business with the South. Just who you supposed to be?"

"Asel Iacola. Prince of Christler-Coke. Or I was. I don't appear to be now."

The kawfee-tinted man was clearly impressed. "That's you? Say, you own about all America East there is."

"Did," Asel said. He looked soberly at a kookoo clock on the wall. Simulated wood. Oke leaves and akorns entwined. Foliated growth without end.

"These people knew exactly what they were doing," Asel said. "They mean to break our will. Everything here is cunningly conceived. Insidious and sly. Deliberately middle-class from an age gone by. Ah, no offense, by the way, but what are you doing in my house? I'm certain I got the number right."

The man with the permanent tan seemed to hesitate, as if translation was in the works. Then, he suddenly laughed aloud.

"Absolutely," he said, displaying quite alarming teeth. "You got the right address. Mine too."

"That is patently absurd."

"Tell me about it." The fellow stuck out his hand. "I'm Sylvan Lee McCree. Former High Earl of Dixie-Datadog. Sometime Duke of Georgie-West. Kaintucker, and New Whoreleens."

Asel looked at Sylvan's hand. "I don't do that."

"Got you, friend. Problem with the hands. Don't know quite what to do. Took me six whole weeks to learn to brush my teeth. Cook an aig, tie a shoe. I sure do miss those fine little import gals."

"Saucy Dayns and Phinns," Asel said.

"Honky Poals and dusky Polly Knees."

"Husky girls from Khuba and Peroo."

Asel sighed. "I simply cannot tolerate this. I'll never make it here."

"Yes you will. It takes awhile, man."

"I fear Hank was right. Self-destruction brings instant relief."

"Hank who?"

"I am absolutely starved. What time is dinner served?"

Sylvan wondered how to handle this. "I've got a bit of bad news, Ace. On top of all the rest. That thing I'm holding is a pan. That room back there's called a *kitchen*. Doesn't anyone work here but us."

"Please don't jest," Asel said. "I have no sense of humor at all."

Sylvan grinned. "All right, Ace, no use putting you in culinary shock. Your first night here, we're eating out."

"That is Asel. Definitely not *Ace*."

"Love that tie. Those ducks look as natural as can be."

Asel didn't care for Sylvan's shirt. A raht in polka dot seemed wrong for dinner wear.

Sylvan didn't miss the look. "You're new in town. What we have here is your semi-formal going-out dress-up attire. Be good if you'd start fitting in. It doesn't get much better than this. . . ."

~ SEVEN ~

Asel had heard about restaurants, but had never actually been to one before. Growing up in Iacola Keep, there was simply no reason to imagine dining anywhere else. Every possible delight was right at hand. One only had to ask, and a dusky flunk from Sansabar would place some morsel in your mouth. Live troute soup. Kwail konsue-mae. Appul badjer pye.

Such wondrous foods were very much on Asel's mind as he tried to manipulate a fork by himself, tried to force creamed chipped mohle down his throat. He dropped the clumsy tool in disgust.

"My God, Sylvan, what kind of place is this? I seem to have sewage on my plate. Offal on toast."

"Cafeteria," Sylvan said, filling his face with something grim. "Lots of other places in town. Most of 'em worse than this."

"I find that hard to believe."

Sylvan poked at his plate. "That's why I mostly eat at home. Everybody learns how."

"What a ghastly idea."

"You like this stuff?"

Sylvan clearly had a point. Still, the thought struck Asel like a blow. Preparing one's meal! He wondered if Hank had discovered this. If he had, he'd surely found some way to do himself in.

"Now that I am here," Asel said, "I'm quite sure Mother and Uncle Hal were aware of Oklahomer. They must have known what it was like. No one told *me*."

"They both deceased?" Sylvan seemed to sense this was so.

"Fortunately, yes. Father as well. Only Father didn't have to kill himself. A clerk-snipist did that."

Asel looked at his koal slaw and wondered what it was. "It all happened so terribly fast. And it was such a lovely day."

"Always is," Sylvan said.

"Everyone was there. Business nobles came from far and near. I think we served a lot of lahm. Or lampree, I can't quite recall. I married Loreli. Attractive girl, but dumb as a stone."

"Still, that's beside the point. Mother was very pleased. It was really quite a coup—the son of Christler-Coke and the daughter of Pepsicoma-Dodge. And then it all fell apart. I was Prince for an hour and a half."

"Uh-huh." Sylvan pushed his tray aside. "Caught you right flat. Took it *all* away."

"A perfectly savage corporate raid. Ducky Du Pontiac-Heinz and that sneak from Disney-Dow. A very tacky thing to do."

"A little sly intrigue," Sylvan suggested. "Money changes hands. Stock finds a pocket or two."

"Ducky bought off the SEC. Uncle Hal explained that, just before he took the pill. Ducky has Loreli now, I suppose. Well, he's certainly welcome to that . . ."

Asel paused, and looked curiously at his snuff-colored friend. "Correct me if I'm wrong, but you seem to know how this dreadful thing occurred. I think you'd best explain that."

"Always happens the same way, Ace." Sylvan looked tired. "You get too big, someone pulls you down. I was doing fine. Got the greeds, and just had to go and buy Mechsyko. Bought Eata-Fajita, Inc. Bought PanElectric-Goat. Bought Petro-Tacosex. *Friends* of mine on the Karoliny Coast set me up. Charged me with bond manipulation, first degree. Security assault. Now I'm sitting here eating pigg shit pye. Let's get out of this place. Head back home and find a drink."

Asel stood and followed Sylvan out. Dreadful odors seemed to cling to his clothes. Dinner moved about inside at a most alarming pace. Asel felt completely unsound. As if he might unravel on the spot. He kept his eyes ahead, tried not to look in the windows of the shops. . . .

~ EIGHT ~

By the time they reached home, the day was fading fast. The sun disappeared without effect, an underdone aig fading quietly out of sight.

"That's your room," Sylvan said, "at the head of the stairs, door on the right. You not going to like it 'less you got a thing for boats."

Asel didn't. The bed, the dresser, and table were a cheery mapul hue. There were knobs to great excess. As if the wood might have swallowed, then failed to digest, a number of tennis balls. The wallpaper depicted sailing boats and matched the spread. The lamp pictured colorful signal flags. A ship's wheel adorned the foot of the bed. More opportunities for knobs.

Asel was too tired to care. There was little more anyone could do to offend. In spite of the décor, he fell asleep at once. Woke with a start. Glanced at the tacky little clock with an anchor on the face. It was well after three, and he knew he would never sleep again.

He was up with the sun, a moment he had seldom shared before. He had eaten very little at the place where food came on a tray, and he felt quite empty, dizzy in the head.

Padding downstairs, he made his way through the living-room maze. Past a pride of plastic chairs, a lamp shaped like a kat. A picture of a clown about to cry.

He found the room Sylvan had described. A switch brought antiseptic light that hurt his eyes. At least, Sylvan appeared to be neat. There were glasses and plates, each in their proper place. Across the room, he opened the door of some device. Another light inside. Everything cold to the touch. There was nothing that looked like anything to eat.

He turned to a cabinet on the wall. A shelf was filled with cans. There were brightly colored pictures on the fronts. He recognized karuts at once. Pees next to that. He examined the cans with care. There was clearly no opening of any sort. He put them down with disgust, turned off the light and walked back up the stairs.

Sylvan was obviously asleep. It didn't seem right to wake him up.

"Sylvan. I hope you don't mind."

Sylvan gave Asel a bleary eye. "I don't mind, Ace. What the hell you want?"

"I wish you wouldn't call me that."

"You waking me up to tell me this?"

"Of course not, Sylvan. I simply want to ask you a question. I will not take much of your time."

Sylvan blew out a breath. "You and me going to have to make some rules."

"I just want to know," Asel said. "I want to know how *long* we have to stay."

Sylvan sat up. "You're serious about this, right? Yeah, I can see you are. Ace—Asel, you've got constipation of the head. I'm talking major neglect."

"I don't care for your attitude at all."

"I don't guess it's your fault. You're new at chicanery and business enterprise. Didn't get the chance to learn a man's got to get himself some drive. Got to grow and survive. Which is what this Ducky did to you. I've sent a few folks here myself and you can bet your ol' daddy did too. That's what Oklahomer's *for*.

"Friend, there isn't any *how long*. You come to this place, you come to stay. What you and me are doing is *hard time*."

Sylvan was prepared for surprise and alarm. Anger and cardiac arrest. Asel, though, showed no distress at all.

"Thank you," he said. "I certainly appreciate your help."

"You like some choclit mylk?"

"I don't believe I do."

"You can have your own mug. It's got a picture of a dawg."

Asel didn't answer. Sylvan watched him walk back across the hall to his maritime bed. . . .

~ NINE ~

"They've got the molds over there," Sylvan said. "This plaster shit goes in the molds. Looks like rock but it's not. The goop gets hard. The molds come off. A bunch of little statues come down the belt. We put 'em in a box. Twelve to every box. Stack the boxes over there. Trucks pick 'em up, take 'em out of here."

"What for?" Asel asked.

"What you mean, what for?"

"What for? Why do we want to do that?"

" 'Cause we got to, man."

"Well. I'd just as soon not."

"I'd just as soon not too."

"Fine. Let's do something else."

Sylvan considered. Fear seemed the answer. Reason, with Asel, was a dead-end street.

"Ace, we don't work they're going to take the TV. They will come and get the buoze. You go to check stuff out they'll give you bad tennis balls. Make you wear lace-up shoes. That's why we got to do what we do."

Asel was appalled. "That is blatant use of force. Coercion and constraint."

"There you go."

"I will not be a party to this at all."

"Good. You want to pick up or pack?"

Asel learned several great truths about work. It wasted a good deal of time, and seemed to have no purpose he could see. Still, it required little thought. If you liked, you could easily consider something else.

He was somewhat curious about the others who worked in this place. Deposed business kings, princes, and counts. Dukes and corporate earls. Men of quality and taste, yet they didn't seem to mind this inane and meaningless pursuit. They went about their tasks in atrocious jumpsuits of rose or pink without complaint.

It's a lot like being a servant . . .

His stomach turned over in a lurch, and he thrust the thought quickly aside.

Asel questioned Sylvan over lunch, which Asel couldn't eat. Imitation lemynade. A sandwich on cadaver-white bred, the filling made of nuts, crushed into a horrid, sticky paste.

Sylvan Lee McCree tried his best, though his patience was wearing thin.

"What do you mean they don't *mind*? 'Course they mind. What a fool thing to say."

"No, they don't. They appear quite content."

"You've got an awful lot to say for a man's only been here half a day."

"Well, do *you*?"

"Do I what?"

"Like packing little statues in a box."

Sylvan looked perplexed, annoyed, and ill at ease. "I have been here three years, friend. Going on four. Every day, right here. I don't like it at *all*. So what am I going to do if I don't?"

Asel didn't answer. He might be somewhat slow, possibly dense, but he knew it was time to leave Sylvan alone.

Asel couldn't find Hank. He spotted Bert, Duke of Sexxon-Apple, and one of the Wrigley-Keds twins. Bert offered his usual sour grin, a condescending eye, the boorish air that had made him so insufferable on the train.

And how long would Bert's spirit hold? Asel wondered. Everyone else had apparently set their pride aside. Former lords of industry and trade now behaved as foreign flunks, content to spend their days making plaster statuettes.

Asel was more than a little puzzled. What were these absurd things *for*? Had anyone ever asked? He was already weary of the statuette's deep and brooding eyes, the heavy somber brows. The features mirrored gloom and discontent. Disaccord and doubt. Constriction of the bowels seemed a clue to dark distress.

As the plaster figures lumbered down the belt, Asel turned one over and studied the base:

***SAN CLEMENTE SHRINE ***
SOUVENIR OF CALIFOGGY STATE

No answer there, but Asel wasn't surprised to learn where the statues went. Nothing good ever came from the West, from the land of Disney-Dow. Land of the insufferable Jackie Cee, who had insulted Mother to her face. Mother, of course, was gone, but Asel would never forgive the offense to the House of Iacola Keep.

What Iacola Keep? There's no such thing anymore . . .

He tried to set the thought aside, but it lingered dark and heavy on his mind.

Late in the afternoon, Asel heard cries of alarm. Inmates and guards rushed to the far corner of the factory, toward the big plaster vats. Word spread at once that someone had done himself in, performing a nice two and a half, and sinking to the bottom at once. Long poles were used to probe the depths. Finally, a body was retrieved, a man encased in imitation stone, curled in a final, fetal attitude.

Inmates and guards crowded close about, wondering who the victim might be. Asel, though, didn't have to ask. He knew poor Hank had found a way home. . . .

~ TEN ~

Sylvan cooked a stew. It appeared to contain whole onyuns and taytoes, and anymal bits that liked to float. Asel yearned for poached newt. Whoopie krane pye. Foxx flambe. Still, he was hungry enough to eat. Sylvan made an effort to be friendly and polite, to set aside their differences of the day. He knew Asel was thinking about Hank. Sylvan figured the fellow was doomed from the start, but it was no use telling Asel that.

Asel tried to be civil as well, but his heart wasn't in it at all. Sylvan left him alone. Asel stared at his food and retreated to his room. Tried the TV. Sat by the window and watched the dreary day fall away.

Asel found thinking difficult at best. Uncle Hal did it; Father had done little else. Asel had given it a try once or twice, and found it caused severe aggravation of the head.

Still, it appeared to be something one couldn't control. Bothersome thoughts kept popping in and out. Some seemed frightening at best. Others seemed lucid and remote. Veiled and crystal clear. No matter how he tried, the process wouldn't go away. Asel gave up, sat on his bed, and resigned himself to mental enterprise.

Something brought him up out of sleep. Music. Girlish laughter. Stomping about. Asel blinked at the clock. Saw it was half past two. He dragged himself out of bed, walked down the hall, and knocked on Sylvan's door. Minutes passed. Sylvan greeted Asel with a scowl.

"I'm sorry," Asel said. "I suppose you have company in there."

"She's gone. Ace, you going to do this every night?"

"No. As a matter of fact, Sylvan, the problem won't arise. I've come to say goodbye."

"You came to do what?"

"I've been thinking about it, of course. I guess I kind of decided on the way from my room to yours. I simply don't like it here at all. Penal life is not for me. I find it quite tedious at best."

Sylvan gave him a wary look. "Ace, you can't do that."

"It's Asel. And why not?"

"Because you can't."

"Yes, I can, Sylvan. I have seen no barriers of any sort. Those trucks leave the factory night and day. I don't know how to make one go, but I suppose I could learn. I don't believe anyone will notice that I'm gone."

"They will, you don't show up for work."

"Yes, I suppose that's true."

Sylvan ran a hand across his face. "Asel, you are flat out of your mind. You know what they'll do when they catch you and bring you back? No women. Not that you know any yet. No volleyball. Nothing to drink but light bir. You want that?"

"I am twenty-one years old. I have made perhaps two decisions in my life. I feel it's time I made another. I do not intend to end up in despair. I will not let myself become like the others I have seen, devoid of any spirit or pride. I do not intend to leap into plaster like Hank."

Asel sat, and looked intently at Sylvan Lee McCree. Persons of a darker persuasion no longer tended to offend.

"Do you know why they have no fences or gates in this place? Do you know why, Sylvan? They know we won't leave. They don't think we can. No offense, but I can see what's happened to you, and everyone else. You cling to this deplorable, middle-class existence because you're afraid to lose the few, small privileges you have.

"I simply cannot tolerate this. I would rather lose everything now, than learn to live in fear of losing cream-chipped mohle and discount athletic shoes."

Asel stuck out his hand. "I have never made this gesture before, but I would like to try it now. We have only known each other for a day, but I think I consider you a friend."

Sylvan took Asel's hand in a firm grip. He didn't speak, but there was sadness in his eyes. Manly affection. Honor, and noble brotherhood.

"Asel—"

"Goodbye, Sylvan. I wish you luck in your incarceration here."

"Ace, there isn't any place to go," Sylvan said, as Asel started for the door. "You can't go home, and you sure don't want to go west."

"Then I shall find some other direction," Asel said. "There are three I haven't tried."

* * *

He walked outside into the dark and sultry night. Several lights were still on: beacons, perhaps, against condo oppression and regret. Argyle socks. Rubber shower shoes.

There was fear in Asel's heart, but pride had a place there as well. Maybe Sylvan was right. Maybe they would catch him and bring him back. And, if they did, Asel knew he would get away again. The thought cheered him on and brought a lightness to his step.

A voice called out in the dark, and Asel turned. Sylvan ran toward him down the street, stuffing his shirt in his pants.

"Ace, I am a bigger fool than you are," he said, "we're never going to pull this off."

"Yes we will, Sylvan. And let me say I'm delighted you have decided to come along. I sense far better days to come. I feel a certain freedom in the air."

"I feel I am stepping in a whole lot of shit," Sylvan said. "But I can't see you doing this alone. How you figure on working a truck?"

"A truck is a device like any other. Certain laws of science apply."

"And you know what they might be?"

"Don't be absurd. Do you know how the bathroom works? Do you know the laws of TV? No. But you use them, right?"

"I see you've given this some thought. What color do you think? They got bile-green trucks and some reds. A real bad off-tangerine."

"I don't suppose it matters," Asel said. "Don't you see, Sylvan? That's why we *have* to go. Penal life violates every sound principle of taste. There is absolutely no accord. Nothing seems right. Nothing goes with what you wear."

"You got that right, man."

Ahead, in the dark, the long line of trucks came into view, true colors thankfully muted in the hours before the dawn. Asel felt a familiar fear tug at his chest, but he quickly shrugged it aside. He thought of Uncle Hal, Mother, and Father unplugged by callous hands and left to drain away.

Freedom is the heritage of noble men, and even lesser folk deserve certain rights in servitude. They should not have to wear tacky clothes, or eat chipped mohle . . .

It was quite a deep thought for Asel, but he felt good about it, and it didn't hurt at all. . . .

~ ELEVEN ~

Half an hour down the road from NERF, in the last dark hours of the night, Asel discovered the truck clearly had no interest in his needs, no desire to help. No hum, no buzz, no happy blinking lights, simply a device that depended on manual persuasion to do anything at all. You had to tell it where to go, or it would take off blindly to the left or to the right. You couldn't eat or take a nap—if you did, the damned thing would veer right off to the side. In the second place it was night, which didn't help, as neither he nor Sylvan could find any knob that would illuminate the road.

It didn't take Sylvan long to insist on relieving Asel at the wheel, and Asel quickly agreed.

"It's not that I couldn't if I wanted to," Asel said. "But I don't, and see no reason why I should."

"Right. I do the driving, you keep your eyes open. Can't tell what you might see."

"Like what?" Asel had been on edge since their escape, and Sylvan's words alarmed him no end. "What did you have in mind?"

"I don't know. I'm just saying, we are escapees driving a tangerine truck. Can't anybody see us at night, but the sun is coming up in Oklahomer, same as anywhere else. Can't hardly *miss* us then."

"We haven't seen a soul," Asel said. "I don't think there's anybody here. Which makes sense to me. Who would want to live in such a place? It's hot, dusty, and I doubt there's anywhere to eat."

"Got to be someone. Never been anywhere there wasn't."

Asel squinted at Sylvan McCree. "I'm recalling my lovely ride on the train. What I saw out those filthy windows were louts, beggars, people in terrible clothes. That's who's out here. No one of gentle birth, no one we want to see."

Sylvan had several things to say, but he'd learned it was no use arguing with Asel. Asel had no respect for anyone's opinion. He had made up his mind about everything, and didn't need to hear about anything else.

Still, Sylvan had to admit, it was this self-centered, overbearing, totally repulsive attitude that drove Asel to ignore all reason and common sense and forge blindly ahead because he simply wanted to.

Like deciding he wouldn't stay at NERF. Some sly mogul takes away your marbles, there you were. Period. No other count, no other duke, had ever imagined getting away. It was simply something you didn't do.

Including me. And I am sure I'll pay dearly for following this damn fool before we're done. . . .

Asel would never admit it, but dawn, so to speak, shed a different light on the concept of freedom as a nobleman's heritage and right. The sun seared his eyes, and the air was too hot to breathe. The road ahead wavered, shimmered in the heat.

Asel followed Sylvan's advice to keep his eyes open. Still, there was nothing out there to see. Red dirt and dead weeds. A rusted, burned-out truck by the road—older, even, than the one they were driving now.

At noon, a great column of dust appeared, not a hundred yards ahead. It hovered and swayed, writhed and trembled like some monstrous worm, then moved off slowly to the left and vanished out of sight.

Sylvan said he had seen one in the South. They were some device of nature, harmless unless you got close. Asel, until that moment, had harbored only vague religious thoughts of any kind. Now, he was not sure the thing was harmless, or natural at all.

"I wish I had some idea where we are," Asel said. "We've escaped incarceration, but we need to have a goal. Somewhere to go. Driving is hot and boring, and I don't see any destination ahead, simply more road."

"If it helps," Sylvan said, "we're going sort of southwest."

"It doesn't at all. Anything with the word *west* in it concerns me a great deal. West is Califoggy, and that means Jackie Cee of Disney-Dow. He and that bastard Ducky stole Iacola Keep and killed Father and Mother and Uncle Hal. I believe I told you that. A clerk-snipist got Father, and Mother did herself in . . ."

"Yeah, I recall you telling me a couple of times before."
"Loreli had nice bumpers. But she had a tendency to zits. You could look at her mother, and see where that might go."
Sylvan sighed, and wiped a mauve hanky across his face. "I'd help on this direction thing, Ace, but we only got four, and none of 'em looking too good. East is where we came from, cross that one out. West is no good for you, and I can't show up down South. North, far as I know, isn't much of anything there."
"Four directions seems a bit stingy to me. I can see more than that from here. Are you sure about this? Did you read it somewhere?"
"I went to Floriday U." Sylvan's voice seemed to take a sharper tone. "I know how many directions there are, I'm telling you there's four."
"Floriday You."
"That's an education institute. A school."
Asel sighed. "I thought you were a duke. You never said you went to school."
"What's wrong with that?"
"Nobody *I* know did."
"Yeah, well you know someone now. And don't start that noble shit with me. I got as much as you, which, at the time, is nothing but fond memories of flunks and shrymp and import shoes—"
Sylvan stopped. Not because he had no more to say, because he did. He stopped because the truck had made a sound like a gasp, like a rattle, like a sigh, and come to a halt in the middle of the road. . . .

~ TWELVE ~

Asel moved into the driver's seat, while Sylvan stepped down. Even if the thing wouldn't go, it seemed one should stay in control. And, there was simply no reason they should both get out. Neither were of the mechanical persuasion, or had any notion of moving parts.

Though Sylvan appeared to do nothing at all, Asel admired his posture, his stance, his inquisitive attitude. As he walked around the truck, he frowned, kicked at the wheels, and looked frightfully intense. Had he somehow learned some mythic truth, found some secret that would make the thing go?

It hardly seemed likely. Still, Sylvan had admitted attending a school of some kind.

"Whatever one did at such a place," he muttered to himself, "they would hardly teach a person of gentle birth about *trucks*."

"You say something, Ace?"

"No, nothing, really." Asel had been so immersed in his thoughts he hadn't noticed Sylvan had slid in beside him again.

"I looked the whole thing over, best I could. I regret to say I didn't find a thing. Whatever quit working, that's what it's doing now."

"I'm sure it's something quite outside of our experience. You would think when they make things, they'd try and make them right."

Sylvan shook his head. "Kind of folks do crafts and stuff don't think about you and me, just think about themselves."

"How very true *that* is. And how true it has ever been." Asel felt a touch of irritation—irked, vexed, annoyed at those who served their betters with little pride and a shitty attitude. How much nicer it would be if they just found joy in the things they had to do . . .

Asel nearly jumped out of his skin as the truck abruptly came to life. Something in the bowels of the thing began to fret, clamor and whine, then settle into a pleasant hum.

"What'd you do?" Sylvan asked. "How'd you do that?"

"I didn't do a thing. Didn't you?"

Sylvan gave Asel a thoughtful look. "You got it started once. You remember what you did then?"

"Nothing. I simply got in. In a moment, the device began to go."

"Huh-unh. Didn't, either. You did something to it."

Sylvan looked at the panel of wood set behind the wheel that made the truck veer in one direction or the next. There were switches, little glass buttons, and knobs.

"You touched somethin' up there. I'm sure you did."

"And I'm just as sure I did not, Sylvan. What would I touch? This is all totally foreign to me . . . What? Do you find that amusing? I certainly do not."

Sylvan wiped a hand across his grin. "You bumped it, Ace. Bumped it with your knee. Bumped it then, like you did just now."

"I think I would know if I did something like that."

"Yeah, but you didn't. The one you punched, it's the shiny thing right there. . . ."

Before Asel could stop him, Sylvan reached out and punched the button again. The truck sighed, and died on the spot.

"Oh, well now look what you've done."

Sylvan punched it again. The truck came to life.

Asel laughed. "Wonderful! Punch something else. There might be water, food of some nature in here."

"What kind of fool you think I am, man? Push your luck with heavy machinery, it's going to push you right back."

"Perhaps you're right. It's best we simply get on our way again. If NERF is on our trail, they'll employ some sly, clever fellows who can manage a truck quite well. . . ."

~ THIRTEEN ~

Little changed as the day wore on. The land got flatter, the sun got hotter. If there was a knob for AC, they hadn't found it yet.

Asel's shirt stuck to his back. Sweat poured down his face, down his chest, down his crotch, leaving him dizzy and out of sorts. Sylvan sweated too, and the mixture of the pair was toxic, disgusting, and embarrassing as well. Still, they were both of noble birth, and pretended nothing was amiss.

For the first time since their escape, other traffic appeared on the road. Four kars. The cramped, tacky Linkuns driven by the marginally secure. One truck. A small vehicle piled high with dead wood, going the other way. A raggedy bunch walking on foot. Another after that. Asel and Sylvan were concerned, but no one even looked their way.

Finally, the sky turned purple, and, as it will in such a clime, night rushed in with no warning at all. One moment Asel could see the road ahead, the next it was gone. He flipped the silver switch, and the truck came abruptly to a halt.

Sylvan had been dozing in the heat. He sat up quickly the instant Asel stopped.

"What you doing? What you stopping for?"

"Perhaps you didn't notice. It's dark out there."

"Gets dark every night. Put the lights on, man."

"What lights?"

"Shoot, you got me woke up for this?" Sylvan poked buttons and knobs on the wooden panel. Nothing happened. Outside, in the black-black night, something rustled, something sniffed, something scuttered all about. Asel didn't care for that.

Sylvan felt around on the floor, on the door, and, finally,

reached under the panel itself. At once, harsh and dazzling light covered the road ahead. Another, dimmer light left the inside of the truck in a warm and friendly glow.

"All right," Asel said, "how did you do that?"

"Trucks all got lights, Ace. Everything you ride in has got a light."

Asel was somewhat annoyed. "If you knew how to do it, why didn't you do it before?"

"Wasn't dark before. Isn't any need to find lights, got the day out there. Come on, my throat's dry as dirt, isn't getting wetter sitting here. Let's go and find something to drink."

"And where do you intend to do that?"

"Now how would I know? I didn't stop here, you did. . . ."

Asel looked up at the night. Leaned back against the wheels, which were still rather hot. "I'm thinking aigplant shake," Asel said, "big dip of perch ice cream."

"Cold badjer ti," Sylvan said.

"Mewl ade, add a sprig of mynt."

"Huh-unh, sinnyman. Just a little hint."

"Thistleberry wyne."

"Percolated swyne."

"Dolfenburger, eel fryes on the side."

"Labster eyes and llamah beens—hey, man, we were doing drink. Now you're into food."

"We're not getting anywhere on drink. We might do better on food. You people of the darky persuasion, what do you eat down there?"

Sylvan gave him a look. "I expect we eat as well as milkface, lily-white, bleachbutt folks up your way do. Choclit soo-she on a stick. Marroe soufflé. Bald eegul pye."

"I never acquired a taste for the ethnic dish of any sort, but I guess I'd try one now."

Asel sighed, and peered off into the dark. There was nothing there to see. There were grunts and snuffs and rustles now and then, and he wished they'd left the lights on in the truck.

Twice, since they'd stopped, other trucks had whined by— trucks very much like their own. Asel was glad they'd pulled well off the road. NERF would surely have the word out now.

His trousers itched. The cheap shoes from NERF didn't fit. He thought about his perky little Britt at Iacola Keep. She could rub and she could knead, she was awfully good with feet.

Did well with other parts, too, but that wasn't on his mind now.

"There is nothing out here, Sylvan. If there was, I feel we would have come upon it now. My throat is dry and I'm hollow inside. We must find water, or we'll perish out here."

Sylvan sighed. "I got to tell you, Ace, if I hadn't been to Oklahomer, someone'd told me 'bout it, I'd say it was a lie." He kicked at something in the dark. "Shit, man, this isn't any place Sylvan Lee McCree ought to be. Ought to be looking for those bastards from Karoliny stole all my stuff, got me sent out here."

"There's little use in musing about the past," Asel said. "Frankly, I have little hope of regaining America East. What's gone is gone, and I'm thirsty and tired, and I think we could both use a good night's sleep."

"Uh-huh. How you plan on doing that?"

"I'm beginning to think we should keep on the road. I doubt anyone will find us in the dark. Those other machines come from somewhere, Sylvan. We might find a decent place to stop, get a good meal, get a little rest. I *have* to clean up and get out of these filthy, middle-class clothes. And I must have proper shoes."

Sylvan groaned. "What's the matter with you? I feel you've lost control. I feel you're only partially intact. You're the one just said we got to put the past behind. Now you got it in front of us again."

"Perhaps I was hasty. The lack of food and drink has sapped my strength, clouded my sense of reason. I'll be fine when we're on the road again. . . ."

"Asel? Where you going now?"

"What a peculiar thing to ask. Where would you imagine I was going? I am going to the truck, of course."

"Truck's the other way."

"I think not, friend. I have an uncanny sense of direction. Mostly from Mother's side. Her family was very good at that. If you want to go and get it, fine. I'll wait here and—*whuuuup!*"

Asel hit something hard, something big, something dense, something unyielding that knocked him flat on the ground. He shook his head, dazed and out of synch, came up on his knees.

"Asel? Where the hell are you, man?"

"I'm over here. I think I have suffered an injury, Sylvan. I feel I have bruises, severe lacerations, and cuts. I have no medical experience, but I'm sure I've broken something else."

"*Hey, he is t'inkin' he broke somethin', Pete, what you t'ink a' that?*"

Pete, and a number of other persons somewhere in the dark, broke into laughter at this remark.

Asel was seized with apprehension, frozen with fright. He needed to run, find his friend and flee. Before he could move, the darkness was filled with blinding light, a light that revealed a dozen squat, bearded men in gaudy, Karobean shirts and tattered straw hats. Each, Asel saw with alarm, were armed with long-barreled Yamaha-Eights, a weapon no longer in style.

And, though he could scarcely believe his eyes, these louts stood before a wall of sandy-colored stone nearly thirty feet high, a wall that seemed to stretch out forever on either side.

"We're travelers," Asel managed to say, "and if we've intruded on your territory, we do apologize and we'll be on our way."

One of the unkempt fellows, clad in baggy pants and a tasteless flowered shirt, stepped up to Asel and showed him a mouthful of mossy-colored teeth.

"You're intrudin', all right, mister, but you ain't likely bein' on your way." He paused, something went *clickety-click*, and he pointed his outdated weapon at Asel's head.

"Where you are is at the West Oklahomer Wall, buster, in the legal custody of the 16th Armored TechsMechs Rangers. You got a religious persuasion of any sort, you might ought to mumble somethin' now. . . ."

~ FOURTEEN ~

Perhaps, Asel thought, it might have been best if the brutish Rangers had carried out their threat, and slaughtered them on the spot. It was clear he and Sylvan were in the hands of a savage crew, who took great pleasure in kicking and poking at their prisoners every chance they got.

Asel had imagined confinement at the National Executive Rehab Facility was crude and unrefined. Still, he had never dreamed of the conditions he encountered at the hands of the Rangers. The tiny cell he shared with Sylvan was scarcely more than a closet with an unswept floor—no table, no chairs. Wallpaper in a horrid floral print.

Nevertheless, both of them had slept, a-shiver in the cold night air. Asel had terrible dreams, in which Ducky and Jackie Cee committed unnatural acts upon the lovely Loreli. Worse still, Loreli seemed to respond to these attentions quite well.

When he woke, the morning sun was ablaze through a narrow window high up in the wall of their room. At once, the dawn disappeared, and the room became an oven. Asel could scarcely breathe. Sylvan was awake, bleary-eyed, sad, and, Asel noticed, still quite dark. Asel wasn't sure he'd ever get used to that, and wondered if Sylvan had similar thoughts about him.

"Wasn't the finest night I ever had," Sylvan said, "though I'm trying to think of something worse. There's insect life here, Asel. Creatures of every sort, and many of them bite. This environment is out of control. I'm not sure our captors did us any favor, allowing us to live through the night."

Sylvan's words mirrored his own first thoughts upon waking in a hostile atmosphere.

"This simply won't do. We will talk to these wretches at once, whoever they may be. There has clearly been a misunderstanding —nothing we can't sort out, I am certain of that."

"I'm guessing these folks are better at the brutal arts than they are at talking," Sylvan said. "That's what I'm seeing so far."

He was leaning against the wall, sweat making dirty rivulets down his face. He had taken off his shoes and his shirt, and was rubbing the shirt between his toes.

"For God's sake," Asel said, "don't *do* that, please."

"Why not?"

"Because it's disgusting, that's why."

Sylvan looked up a moment, then went ahead with his task.

"I figure you noticed, they haven't sent a perky little Britt in to fill up a tub, give you a rub. Didn't bring you clean underwear. Didn't bring you any clothes. Didn't even bring a wyne list, Ace."

"I am not a child. I'll thank you not to treat me like one."

"Just making sure you got the picture."

"I've got the picture. That doesn't mean I intend to sit here and —play with my feet and feel sorry for myself. I got out of NERF— and got you out too, if you'll recall—and I further intend to get us out of here."

"Shit, Asel, you don't have to be reminding me of that. You're a credit to your race, far as I'm concerned. Still, I *do* believe it wouldn't damage your *h*eroic spirit if you let a little reality creep into your thinking now and then. I know that's asking a lot, but won't kill you to try."

"Oh, well . . ." Asel was somewhat taken aback, but not at all shaken in his determination to take a stand. He stood, feeling every bruise, every kink, every kick.

"You've had your say, Sylvan, and you're quite entitled to that. Still, I see nothing wrong in putting a positive face on what, at first thought, may seem a disastrous, hopeless situation. We shall get through this, I assure you of that."

Sylvan showed him a weary grin. "We will. We will surely do that."

He stuck out his hand. Asel kept his at his side.

"What?"

"You've been touching your feet. There was dirt and stuff between your toes. Now it's on your hands. As there are no facilities here, I think we can skip the obligatory gesture this time."

"Good point. I got no idea what you been touching either, man. . . ."

~ FIFTEEN ~

Somewhere close to noon, the door of their small room opened, letting in a fearsome, blinding light.

"Look here, fellows," Asel said, coming to his feet as quickly as he could, "you will go at once to the person in charge of this filthy, lawless band, and tell him we demand to be—"

The door slammed shut. Asel blinked at the bright after-image of men in ugly hats.

"He heard what I said. We'll get some action now."

Sylvan didn't answer. He was looking at a broken crock of water just inside the door, a bowl of black beens, a melun that was clearly overripe, and some sort of bred that was thin and exceeding flat. He sniffed at the water, reached in and held something up to the light.

"It's a myte of some kind. It swims quite well, and there are other things floating about. I don't imagine you'll want any, Ace, it looks awfully bad."

"I'm on to your sly, darky ways, Sylvan, give that thing to me."

Sylvan tried to jerk the crock away. Asel wrenched it free and drank until water dribbled down his chin.

"You're right," he said, "it's awful," wiping a sleeve across his mouth. "Watch it with the food, I'll want my share of that too."

The beens were full of sawlt and little peppirs that burned his mouth. Asel didn't complain. He wolfed them down without shame, wiped the tin plate with one of the peculiar rounds of bred.

He tried not to look at Sylvan, and Sylvan did the same. Eating like a commoner was, in itself, a gross humiliation. Poking about with your very own *hands* was something else again. They each turned away and wiped greasy fingers on the wall. It didn't seem to help, but it gave them something to do.

"What do you suppose we'll get for supper?" Asel asked, after the pair had sat in silence for a while. "I don't guess it would do much good to ask."

"Wouldn't think so, no."

"I had beens once. But it was not like these beens at all."

Sylvan didn't answer. He had gripped the high sill of the window and pulled himself up for a look. Sylvan's arms bulged. Asel wondered if there might be labor genes in this fellow's line somewhere.

"Get down from there. You'll strain some part, you keep doing that."

"I don't like the looks of this, Ace."

"What? What do you see out there?"

"A rabble, a mob, a whole bunch of shaggy, unwashed brigands and scamps of every sort."

"Wearing those peculiar straw hats."

"That's the ones. Cheap, Polly Hester shirts like they sell you at NERF. Got your pyneappul pattern. Got your classic jungle byrd."

"My God. People have no color sense at all. You would think—"

Sylvan stopped him with a hand that said *halt*. "They're up to something. Something I don't like at all."

"You said that. Just tell me, all right?"

"Building something."

"Building what?"

"Something's got steps. Something's got a platform on the top."

"Local architecture is not our concern. We need to speak to someone who'll let us out of here."

"Shit, Ace . . ."

"Now what? Do I have to climb up there and—"

The heavy door flew open, slammed against the wall. Asel jumped back. Two men faced them with greasy firearms from the past. For the first time since their capture, Asel had a chance to view these louts up close. He was shocked to see one had a clumsy metal arm, while the other had two, rather battered legs, screwed together like a plumber's nightmare.

Before Asel could get himself together, a short, broader fellow pushed the men aside.

He looked at Asel, grinned at Sylvan, hanging by his fingers from the sill.

"If you genul'men will follow me, we'll git this over with fast," the man said. "Won't be no big thang a'tall."

The broad man spat on the ground and turned away. The men with guns poked Sylvan and Asel out the door.

"I don't like this," Asel said, squinting against the afternoon light.

"I believe that's what I said."

"Did you note these fellows have a number of metal parts? The big one, I feel he's wearing a bucket on his head."

"Don't care 'bout *his* head, Ace," Sylvan said, with a certain note of dread. "What I care about's that thing they're building over there. Do *not* like the looks of that. . . ."

~ SIXTEEN ~

Sylvan's words were lost on Asel. Coming upon this place in the dark, he had seen very little besides the great wall. Now, in the incandescent glare of the sun, a vast, sprawling heap of rubbish lay before him on the dry and dismal plain. Trash, garbage, a seemingly endless dump, rubble rising two, three, four stories high. Clearly, the scrap, the crap, the waste of the world had been left here in perpetual decay . . .

. . . yet, in a blink, his eyes found dismal order in hopeless disarray. This heap, this clutter, stacked against the high stone wall, was home to this mean and crippled horde. This was a town of mutilated men who creaked, hobbled, humped, and squeaked about. Hollow men, husks, who lived in a city of clutter and rust. And, they were everywhere, stumbling, fumbling, this way and that. Some of them rattled and some of them clanked. All of them were wild-eyed, shaggy, and clearly out of sorts. Worse still, Asel noted, now and then they dropped their parts.

"I have never imagined such squalor," Asel said, "or such a sorry lot. I feel we should be done with these fellows at once. They've treated us crudely, Sylvan, but I think we'd best try and overlook that."

Sylvan stared. "Are you totally inert? You hear what I said? They teach you history shit up East?"

"We didn't do *school*, Sylvan. I think I told you that. We had discussions sometimes. With sandwiches and ti. Uncle Hal talked about business, finance, bribery, and such."

"Cut the talking," said the man with the tin bucket head. "Keep them bastards moving, Ed."

"You see what I mean? This won't do at all. Do what they say, Sylvan. I'll step up there and speak to the fellows, and have us out of here."

"You listening to me?"

Asel picked up his stride, made his way to the newly built platform and climbed up the steps. The wood was old and rotten in spots, and rife with rusty nails.

"You, git down from there!" Bucket-Head shouted, and let fly a string of curses in an ugly, foreign tongue.

Asel ducked beneath a beam that was raised overhead, stepped around a hole, which clearly had no purpose at all.

"Shoddy work," he said to himself. "Wouldn't put up with it at Iacola Keep."

He stepped to the railing and raised his hands to the crowd. "A moment, if you will, people. There's been a mistake. My friend and I have been unjustly detained. Unless there has been some damage to our truck, I'm willing to drop the issue right now. No hard feelings, all right? I'm sure you have no idea who you're dealing with here."

A cheer rose up from the crowd, a happy roar, followed by near manic applause. Men stomped the ground with artificial feet. One fellow had a clever pair of wheels. Another waved a stump fashioned from an axe.

He wondered, sadly, how these fellows would feel, if they could see the great coils of copper, nickel, and gold, the silvery wire, thin as gnat hair, the tiny jeweled motors that made it all go, the shiny plastic tubes that hummed and thrummed as they pumped in oatmeal, kocayne, and ti, sucked it all out again from Father's lovely chrome encapsulated chair.

It wasn't so bad if a fellow was totally impaired, not if he owned America East, and had the best goodies one could buy. And, of course, a horde of Swizz doctor flunks dashing all about. . . .

Wandering free in hapless regions of the past, Asel scarcely saw the fist that sent him falling, sprawling to the floor. Shaking cobwebs aside, he gathered his wits in time to dodge a blow from Bucket-Head's imitation foot.

"Up on yer feet, fella, or I'll damage you severely, leave you numb an' helpless, crying, beggin' for mercy, writhing about in 'scruciating misery an' pain. Agony an' suffering's one of life's blessings, an' I'm not greedy, I'm willing to share!"

"I'd do as he says," Sylvan said. "You clearly don't understand that we're doomed, finished—no use making it worse than it is."

"Nonsense. I spoke to these fellows. They seemed to respond quite well." He came to his feet, facing Bucket-Head. "You, sir, are an exception. If you attempt to strike me again, I shall have to knock you down."

Bucket-Head laughed. "Ed, give me that weapon of yours. I intend to shoot this insolent bastard in the knees."

Ed, who had one good arm, and another made from an ancient floor lamp, drew a pistol from his belt.

Bucket-Head grabbed it, blew down the barrel, then aimed it at Asel's right knee.

"Wait, you don't want to do that," Asel said.

"I believe he does," Sylvan said.

"Shut up, the both of you. I am Lieutenant-Major Brill, and I've had enough out of uppity strangers comin' in here and—aw, damn it all, what's *he* want?"

As he turned away from Asel, his voice took on a dark and somber tone, no longer reflecting the fun of homicide, the joy of a bloody afternoon. Now, the sound from under the bucket was clearly one of anger, displeasure, and disgust.

Asel chanced a glance at Sylvan, then looked past his captors at the sight down below. The shabby crowd cheered once more, and, for an instant, Asel's spirits lifted, as his own, familiar stolen truck pulled up to a stop not far from the platform itself.

"You see, Sylvan, what did I say? Everything's working out fine."

Sylvan didn't answer. The defrocked scion of Dixie-Datadog was stunned, stupefied, immobilized with a sense of imminent disaster, a fright he couldn't name. The source of these dire emotions was the man who had stepped out of the truck, and was nearly to the platform itself.

At the fellow's sight, all cheers ceased from the grim and shabby crowd—no stumpy gestures, no shouts, no huzzahs of any sort. Nothing but a quiet moan of wonder, awe, and fearsome respect, a collective drawing of sour breath, then silence most complete.

And, Sylvan thought, if the rest of these fellows were filthy, mean, and likely obscene, this one, clearly, was king of them all. A boiler was his belly, and a gutted engine was his chest. Half an ancient mower sat atop his head. Worst of all were the eyes, for they were vile, coppery green, and they peered out of a face born of trouble and pain across the agonizing years.

"I am Colonel Mac Macadam," said a voice like a shriek, like the stripping of a gear, "commander of the 39th Irregular Brigade of the TechsMechs Rangers. *You* poor fellas have made a serious mistake, and you *will* be goddamn sorry that you did. Sergeant-Minor Grate, read the charges if you will."

The Colonel reached in a sack that hung by his waist and drew out a rusty tin box. The box said,

"*Charge Number One, Sir. Intrusion. Security Area Are-Em-Seven-Niner-Two. Disorder. Dishonor. Suspicion of Discord, Sir. Charge Number Two—*"

"One's plenty, Sarge, that'll do." The Colonel dropped the box back in his sack.

"—*Number Two,*" said the box, somewhat muffled now, "*Probable Disturbance, Possible Dissent—*"

Colonel Macadam slapped the box hard, and it spoke no more at all.

"Colonel," said Lieutenant-Major Brill, "with all respect, sir, I'm takin' care of this."

If the Colonel heard, he made no sign of any sort. He peered at Asel with some disinterest, then turned his curious, multi-colored eyes on Sylvan McCree.

"By God, I don't think I've seen a person of the darky persuasion in a good long while. What you doing up here?"

"I must resent your manner, sir," Sylvan said. "I don't know what century you people think you're in, but time has clearly passed you by. I cannot imagine why you live in primitive, odorous conditions in this miserable place, but it is no fault of mine. And, ah, furthermore, I feel you have no right to, to . . ."

Sylvan paused, suddenly aware that he had lost himself in a tangle of chatter, said things he likely shouldn't say, things that popped out of their own accord. Asel, he noted, was staring at him with confusion and dismay.

Following Asel's gaze, he was also aware that Bucket-Head had tossed a coil of rope, then another after that, across the beam overhead, ropes that ended in nooses made of fine, import hemp. Possibly, it occurred to Sylvan, the only items that were clean, new, and in perfect condition, in this shoddy encampment beneath the high wall.

"Now you've gone too far," Asel said. "I am forced to tell you I am Asel Iacola, Prince of Christler-Coke, unjustly shorn of my titles and my lands. And this, a man you have insulted, demeaned, and said horrid things about, is Sylvan Lee McCree, a most honorable and—*grrrrrk!*"

The noose cut Asel's protest short. He was getting to the part about justice, fair play, the duty of louts of the lower persuasion to respect their betters, and do them no wrong. Now, he forgot exactly what came next.

". . . and, by the power festered in me," read Colonel Macadam, "I do defirm and reclare this execution was carried out in a just and harmful manner. That the hangees have the right to protest this action within sixty days of their demice, that they shall—"

"Stop this," Sylvan shouted, in the throes of strangulation, his toes rising off the ground, "*I am—gentle—born—you—pale—ass—pink—neck—bastard—!*"

Asel said nothing. He could see pretty lights, now, wonderful colors he'd never seen before. And, though it didn't seem the time for such a thing, he suddenly recalled a golden moment from the past, a scene from an ancient, crackly holo in Father's quaint museum. A scene, a sound, a line that brought chills to a pampered child of nine:

"*. . . we was flat surrounded, boy, then by God, I heard a bugle sound, an' shots rang out across the plains. . . !*"

And, as the world went dark, Asel imagined he heard those very words again. . . .

~ SEVENTEEN ~

A boom, a blare, a harsh resonation, a painful cry, as lead struck the hangman's tinny features, struck him with a *whang!* with a *spang!* sounds in the best tradition of the long forgotten past.

Bucket-Head wobbled, jerked, staggered, and lurched, dropped the deadly ropes. Took a drunken step and crashed through the railing, tumbled to the ground.

Everything—as it does at such times—seemed to happen at once. Asel yanked the noose from his neck, drew a precious breath. Looked at Sylvan, certain he was dead, flesh a sooty gray, eyes rolled back in his head. Still, Asel loosed his friend's rope. It seemed the thing to do. Sylvan came alive, gagged, heaved, threw up something bad.

"Now that is disgusting," Asel said, "stop doing that at once."

"Can't—help it, Ace . . ."

"Well, try. What if you got it on me? I—God, Sylvan, *I'm shot!*"

At that very moment, as if the world had stopped, turned itself off then back on again, Asel was suddenly aware of the clamor, the clangor, the din, the thunder of guns and the cries of angry men. Through the choke of burning powder, he caught a sudden glimpse of Colonel Mac, as he blazed away with antique pistols through a choking cloud of dust. Someone didn't like the Colonel, or the Colonel's shoddy crew.

What do I care? Asel thought, from some distant region of his mind, *I've taken a bullet in the heart. Nothing really matters anymore. . . .*

"You've got a little scratch," Sylvan said, "looks like a splinter might've nicked you on the ear. Take a little spit, kinda dab at it some."

"I will not. And don't try to make me feel good, it's much more serious than—Sylvan, what are you doing down there?"

Sylvan knew why there was a hole in the platform floor. Bodies were supposed to drop in, after a neck went *crick!* went *snap!* Still, he was glad to see it now. Slipping quickly through, he motioned for Asel to come down as well.

For once, Asel didn't argue. There might be bugs down there, but there were bullets up above, and the choice was quite clear.

"I don't know who those fellows are," he told Sylvan, peering through a crack, "but they're playing hell with the Colonel's bunch. They don't have a lot of weapons, but they're mostly not impaired. I believe that helps."

"I should think it would," Sylvan said. He came up next to Asel. "Our best move is to get to the truck. Even if these new louts win, I doubt they'll care about us. We don't make a good impression on the poor."

"Great idea. I don't see how we can reach the truck unscathed, and there's no use going if we don't."

"There's no sense staying here. If Colonel Mac wins, they'll hang us for sure. I hated that. Don't think I could handle it again. If the other brutes succeed, who's to say they won't do the same?"

"We could wait until dark."

"Dark is maybe four, five hours, man. No way I'm waiting 'round till then."

"And I'm not dashing about in the light. You don't understand, Sylvan. I've been wounded once. I could be maimed, or possibly killed next time."

"You got a scratch. It doesn't even show."

"I never had a scratch before. I don't want to start."

Sylvan gave Asel a thoughtful look. "If I make it to the truck, I'll try and come back."

"Wait. You'll—you'll what?"

Sylvan didn't answer. He slipped past Asel, pushed a loose plank aside, ducked out of sight.

Asel was stunned by such behavior. One does not walk off and leave one's companion simply crouching somewhere. A common person might, but not a man of gentle birth.

He thought about his flunk, his perky little Britt. He thought about tohd paté and a lovely weasil stew. He thought about Father, Mother, and Uncle Hal, everyone else who'd vanished from his life and left him in dire and lonely straits, angry and afraid, on the Oklahomer flats.

Then he pulled the loose plank aside, dashed into a horde of sweaty louts, into a hail of deadly fire, into pointy objects of every shape and size, into desperation and danger undefined. . . .

Asel had never imagined such chaos, horror, such awful disorder. Everything was wrecked, wracked, nothing and no one was totally intact. He stumbled over whole people, half people, leftover parts. The groaning, the moaning, the dying, and the dead.

Someone shouted, cursed at him and roared. It sounded like the gravelly croak of Colonel Mac. Asel kept going, didn't look back. A bullet whined overhead—hit solid flesh with a sound like *thwack!*

A lummox with tiny eyes came at him from the right. Another lumbered at him from the left. The lummox from the right caught a gut full of lead. The giant on the left growled at Asel, and swung an iron beam above his head, The fellow was a bumpkin, a lackwit who drooled as he walked. Still, a fool could kill you the same as an earl.

Asel backed off, stooped and grabbed a weapon, stood and faced the great lout. Weapons weren't a problem. There were weapons everywhere. Spikes, pikes, bludgeons, and clubs. Knives, pistols, augers, and drills.

Asel found something that was long, something that was bent. He saw, at once, it was one of the Rangers' legs. He dropped the thing at once. Rubbed his hands on his trousers, grossly offended, wondered what he might catch. While he wondered, the lackwit swung his weapon. Asel caught the hint of lubrication as it hummed above his head.

Someone shouted, called out his name. The giant swung again. Asel ducked, caught a bit of spit instead. Ran, stumbled through a veil of dust. Saw a Ranger with no legs at all, slashing at a fellow with a very little head.

"Over here, damn it! Come *on*, Ace!"

Asel nearly shouted aloud as he saw the truck bumping, humping over the injured and deceased, over the crippled and the maimed. The engine howled as Sylvan stripped a gear, struck a poor fellow, sent him flying through the air.

Asel leaped in, gripped the dash, held on for dear life. Sylvan turned left, roared across the plain, jerked the truck right, left—right and left again.

"We're going around in circles," Asel said. "We're not going anywhere at all."

"If you know a way out, please share it with me," Sylvan shouted over the din.

"The driver is the one who's supposed to point the truck. I'd suggest you find the way in. That will surely take us out."

Sylvan muttered under his breath, and jerked the truck savagely to the right. Madmen scattered, ran for their lives. The truck hit a pile of rubble. Nuts, bolts, and something horrid hit the windowshield.

"All I can see is that enormous wall," Sylvan said. "Damn thing doesn't seem to end."

"Of course it has to end. Everything ends, no matter how long it is."

"It was dark, Ace. You were driving, not me. I was—shit!"

Lead peppered the side of the truck, pinged on the hood. Sylvan made a violent right, back left again.

"We cannot keep this up. One of those wretches will get lucky for sure."

"We can't stop, either. We're dead if we don't stay with the truck."

"We're also dead if we do."

"Fine. I'll get dead inside. You can get—"

"I'd be suggestin' you both shut up, you want to get out in one piece. Turn left, fella, up here. Past that shack then give 'er all you got."

A dirty hand gripped Asel's shoulder from the back. Sylvan nearly wrecked the truck.

"We'll get inter'duced later," said the stranger who popped into sight. "Right now, you morons oughter do as you're told, you want to live to see tonight. . . ."

~ EIGHTEEN ~

Sylvan didn't retch, didn't panic, didn't pee. Did as he was told. Didn't even look to see who'd popped up behind the seat, who was smelling up the cab with his vile and evil breath.

The shack in question appeared, vanished in a blur. Asel gripped the dash, slammed his feet against the floor. The way ahead narrowed, leaving an inch on either side. Rubber burned, sparks flew.

"You're awfully close," Asel said. "I'd watch my steering if I were you."

Sylvan's answer was lost as a fender ripped itself free, tore past the hood and disappeared.

"Doin' fine, lad," said the voice behind the seat, "coupla seconds then left . . . left . . . better hit it hard, better hit it fast . . . *Damn it, boy, now!*"

Sylvan had scarcely a blink to jerk the wheel, pump the brakes, do it just right. Do it right the first time or slam into the unforgiving wall.

The truck shuddered, nearly spun itself around, moved at an agonizing pace toward pain, oblivion, injury, and death. And, at the very last moment, straightened, without a gnaht to spare, choked, nearly died, then roared into the western sun, sending Rangers diving for their lives.

Gunfire pursued them, puffing up dust. One struck the door on Asel's side, then it was over, over and done. Asel leaned out the window, surprised to see the wall already far behind, a dark, ominous wedge against the burned-out sky.

"Not real bad driving," said the stranger. "Wouldn't care to try it again, once is 'bout all my ailing heart could stand."

"I don't know who you are, or what you're doing in our truck," Asel said, "but I guess we owe you our thanks. It's possible you saved us from disaster back there. I fear we were in some trouble at the time."

"Think so, do you?" The stranger gave Asel a crooked grin and a load of horrid breath. "I'd say you're right. I'd say you're a couple of goddamn fools is what you are, running around in the middle of an outright war. Don't suppose you knew what you was doing, I'll have to give you that."

For the first time, Asel had a chance to get a good look at the stranger, and one look was really quite enough. His cratered nose, rheumy eyes, black and broken teeth clearly told the fellow's tale. His skin was florid, crimson, and flushed, the veins thereupon a road map of wealth, poverty, and every weary stop in between, a chart of dissipation, a celebration of days in agony, and nights ill spent, a lifetime of pleasure, pain, intemperance, more than a little carnal bliss. Here, Asel saw, was a fellow who had squandered every moment without a second of regret.

"I'm Robert Lee-Meade the Fifth," the man said, offering Asel a callused hand. "Most people call me Goodtime Bob. You guessed right off what I'm doing here, boy, and that's saving your miserable lives. I ask no thanks or no reward. I devote myself to helping out folks in distress. Bringing joy and hope unto others is what the Lord put me here for. What *you* two are doing in this dry and empty land is for you to tell me. That's if you care to. I surely won't intrude if you don't want to say. Don't feel any obligation just because I brought you safely out of doom and despair."

Asel exchanged a look with Sylvan, an act that didn't go unnoticed by Goodtime Bob.

"We're grateful, sir, for what you've done," Asel said, "and we have no reason to keep any secrets from you. We're visitors here, and know little of your land. I, myself, am from Switzerland, across the sea, and my friend is from Frants. We were on our way to enjoy the sights of the West, when we were captured and held by those fellows back there. If you would give us directions to the nearest village or town, we would happily treat you to a beverage and then be on our way. I fear we've taken up a great deal of your time."

"Yes," Sylvan added, keeping his eyes on the road, "that's what we'd like to do."

Goodtime Bob nodded slowly, and wiped a filthy cloth across his face. "That's a kindly offer, lads. I appreciate your friendship and your trust."

"It's the least we can do," Asel said.

"Absolutely," Sylvan said.

"By damn, I don't believe I ever come across a finer couple of lads from overseas in my life," said Goodtime Bob. "And honest, too. That's a quality I dearly admire. What I was 'fraid I'd hear was some cocked-up tale 'bout uppity snots from America East, and the Greater New South. How they stole 'em a truck, broke out of NERF, and took off west with *no* fuckin' idea where they was headin' at all.

"That about it, you think? I leave anything out, some little item you recall?"

"That is clearly the most ridiculous story I have ever heard," Asel said, forcing a laugh, getting no help from Sylvan at all. "This is no way to treat strangers to your shores, Mr. Bob. We are tourists overcome by brigands, and we've already thanked you for your help. I see no reason to—"

"They wasn't brigands, boy. An' neither was the folks they were fighting back there. Colonel Mac's bunch is just what he said: The 39th Irregulars, guarding the Oklahomer Wall. Not a bad bunch, if you got sense enough to keep out of their way."

"Why?" Sylvan asked, checking the dusty mirror again to check for pursuers behind. "What are they guarding the wall *from?* I fear I can't imagine who'd wish to carry it away."

His words brought a smile from Asel, but not from Goodtime Bob.

"Like I said, you don't know nothing at all. An' it's a i-rony or somethin' that you don't, for it's the rich, overfed lords of the East and the South what sent those poor devils out there a hundred and somethin' years ago."

Bob saw confusion, puzzlement, and doubt, two mouths agape, and no words coming out.

"Uh-huh, got your attention now, do I? No lies, no shams, no cunning whoppers this time? Well, that's a start, as I see it. It's true, is what it is, even you coddle-brats can see that.

"The land o' plenty's east of the Oklahomer Wall. Past it, there's poor folks thicker than flyes. Your great-granddads made sure them persons of the starvin' persuasion didn't start pissin' on their lawns, wanting what your fancy lords and ladies got. That's what the Irregulars are for. Keep 'em hungry, keep 'em out.

"Mostly they don't have the heart to fight back. You seen some that did today. One day, here or somewhere along the line, there'll be enough of 'em, and they'll break down the wall."

Bob showed Sylvan and Asel a fearsome smile. "Now won't that be a surprise for you lads in sissy underpants?"

Asel shook his head. "I cannot wholly credit such a tale. No offense, but I see no reason why generations of these—these Irregulars would stay in this horrid place losing legs, arms, most of their parts—even, even heads. I doubt you could pay some lout enough to do that."

"Even if their cause is possibly just," Sylvan added. "Which I suppose, they imagine it is."

"Right. I meant to say that."

Goodtime Bob ran a hand across his scruffy chin.

"Food's your answer, lads. Only kind of *pay* worth fighting for on the Wall. Trucks haul it in from the East ever' day. Kowleg, pigg head, chikun feet, liver-ripple pye. Mudfysh, brokalie, buzzerd ice cream. Anything the lads want, that's what they get on the Oklahomer Wall."

Bob laughed so hard, his veins nearly popped. "Why you think you got Colonel Mac so riled? Wasn't just your uppity airs, boys. Man's expecting poodul parts, gets a load of them fuckin' statuettes. If that's not a hangin' offense, don't know what is. . . ."

~ NINETEEN ~

"I didn't look back there," Asel said, "I had no idea. Thought you checked when we stopped to fix the truck."

"Why would I be looking, Ace? What you've got in back doesn't matter to the front."

"Oh, excuse me, Mr. Motor Person. You'd know all about that."

"Was me that fixed it, friend."

"You accidentally pushed a knob."

"Made it go. Didn't see you doing that."

"You fellas want to hold it down some? I'm not getting a lot of sleep back here."

Asel made a face. Sylvan pressed his thumb and forefinger to his nose. Goodtime Bob was curled up on the floor behind the seats. On top of the snoring, a constant odor arose from Bob himself, a horrid mix of smells from his inner and outer parts. It didn't seem right to force him out. Besides, neither Asel nor Sylvan were certain they could handle the task. Goodtime Bob was ugly, but he seemed to be in fairly good health.

And, he *had* done them quite a good turn, saving their lives back there. Moreover, he hinted now and then he could lead them to reasonable quarters for the night, and set them on a path far from the Oklahomer Wall. True or not, it seemed the best bet at the time.

"I think we should empty the back, next time we stop," Asel said, when Bob began to snore in a steady rhythm again. "Taking a truck from a penal place is bad enough. Stealing souvenirs is likely a serious offense."

"I expect you're right about that. I suppose he's really asleep."

"I'm not sure you could fake a sound like that."

"We must watch this fellow carefully, Asel. I'm sure you know that."

"I've learned more about common persons than I ever hoped to, friend. Though it pains me to say it, some of these people could teach your corporate noble a thing or two about vile, cunning, shameless behavior."

"I'm afraid you're right, Ace. That asshole with the bucket head? Reminds me of Redeye Spiggin, used to run Cayenne-Coal & Ryce over to Memfish and Gnashville 'fore Lefty Plumm took him down. Lefty, he reminds me of Colonel Mac. Cold-eyed son of a bitch. Just as soon gut a man as buy him out—"

"All right, I give up," said Goodtime Bob, bouncing up so quickly Sylvan nearly ran off the road. "Decent man of the big sky country can't close his eyes without some pantywaist mama's boy yakkin' in his ear. Sliver, Silver, whatever it is, stop this thing 'fore I let loose right here in the truck. I don't think you want to witness that...."

Asel took the wheel and Sylvan slept. Now and then Goodtime Bob woke long enough to stretch, fart, and mutter directions: "Little to the left, little to the right, keep 'er straight ahead..." Then, at once, he would drop back into a coma, a stupor, a trance of a most disturbing sort. Somehow, Bob had learned to doze and decompose, without the benefit of death. It was all Asel could do to keep from leaping from the truck, fleeing across the flats.

So weary, dizzy from holding his breath, Asel failed, for some time, to notice the change in scenery outside. It was still quite barren and dry, devoid of any life, but something different had appeared. At first, he thought it a natural deviation of the land—ditches, gullies, and slopes, a countless array of furrows spread across the flats like the beds of rivers long arid and dead.

And, as the truck drew closer to the scene, he could clearly see these gullies were peppered with holes along their banks—big holes, little holes, holes that delved so deeply into the earth, they defied the bleaching sun, and left shadows on the land.

"Most peculiar," he said aloud, "a feature I've never seen before. Of course, nearly *everything* I see I have never seen before."

In the ordered, refined world of Iacola Keep, geography past the front lawn was a major event for those overcome by the spirit of adventure on a Sunday afternoon. Until recent times, Asel had felt there were indoor diversions aplenty to keep him occupied. Breakfast: served by a perky little flunk with Jipsee eyes; playful encounters: Touchie You-Touchie Me, and assorted other games with assorted cutie-pies; Nap: rest up for lunch—

"My gawd what the hell you thinkin' 'bout boy!"

With that ear-splitting exclamation, Goodtime Bob threw himself bodily over the seat, crushing Asel against the dash. Bob grabbed the wheel in both hands, jerked it violently to the left, then to the right, nearly tossing Sylvan through the door.

"Get off me," Asel shouted, flailing this way and that, "have you lost your bloody mind!"

"Grab the wheel, hold 'er tight, or you'll lose your *life*, sissy lad," Bob said, the words hard between his teeth. "Slam it to the floor, don't stop no matter what. Somethin' gets in your way, run it down. Goddamn, do *exactly* as I say!"

Bob gripped Asel's shoulders to the bone. His foul breath came in heavy, rapid beats. It was hard to miss the cold edge of fear in his voice, something Asel had never heard from this fierce, mean-eyed thug.

"Asel, we're going too fast," Sylvan shouted, his fingers clutching the dash. "This device was built for haulage. It does not require excessive speed."

"You." Bob stabbed a finger at Sylvan's chest. "Shut up an' sit still. All right, lad, keep 'er left—left, I say. Hell's fire—*left!*"

Asel wrenched the truck as far as it would go. Tires squealed, two wheels off the ground. For a sickening moment, he was certain they would go all the way, roll, tumble, and kill them all. Finally, all four wheels hit hard, driving Asel's head into his shoulders, bouncing him off the roof.

Sylvan moaned. Bob wiped blood off his cheek, cursed to himself. The truck stalled. Asel punched every button, pulled every knob, turned on the lights. Nothing worked at all.

"Not that one, man," Sylvan said, "*that* one. Don't you ever learn anything at all?"

"Shit," said Bob, "*aw, shit—shit—shit, oh mother, dear mum—*"

Asel stared. All the florid coloration had drained from Bob's face, leaving him pale as death. Asel followed his glance, and that's when he saw them. . . .

There was nothing, only a shiver, only a blur of motion that rippled across the arid land. Then, in a wink, in a horrid blink, they spilled out of every ditch, every hollow, every hole, spewed like a vile corruption, like a foul elimination from their burrows in the earth.

There were hundreds, thousands, a countless multitude of gaunt and naked creatures, gray and bony things held together by gristle, filth, blemishes, and sores, blisters, vile suppurations, warts, welts of every sort. And, in an instant, they covered the truck like beetuls, like beas, pounded on the hood, on the roof, on the doors. With jaundiced faces, toothless mouths, great enormous eyes, they pressed against the windows, staring in wonder, in agony and pain, foul and scabby fingers clawing at the glass.

Asel could hear their shrill and angry cries—again, like insects swarming about a hive.

"Get—this—goddamn—thing—*moving*, boy, get it moving now if you want to see another day!"

Asel could hear Bob clearly, but his body wouldn't work, wouldn't move. He was stunned, struck motionless with fright. Sylvan was muttering to himself, searching for the magic button on the dash, the one that meant *go*. One of the creatures found a stone, pounded, pounded with all his might. The windshield starred, like splintering ice.

Asel came alive again at once, pushed Sylvan roughly aside, punched the proper button with his fist, slammed his foot to the floor.

The truck roared, jerked into motion, slamming Asel flat against the seat. Wasted, feeble creatures began to slip off the hood, slide down the cracked windowshield, clawing for a hold, eyes agape with fear. Asel felt the bile rise up in his throat as the truck gave a lurch, then another, and another after that. Faint, horrid cries rose up from below, sounds Asel knew would forever haunt his nights.

"That's it, boy," Bob said, gripping his shoulder, his voice so distant Asel could hardly hear him speak. "You must keep going, it's what you have to do."

And, though it seemed an eternity to Asel, scarcely a moment passed before the sounds were gone, the lost and pitiful creatures far behind.

"Don't need to be asking, boys, I'll save you the trouble of that," said Goodtime Bob. "It's Hammerillo Flats, is what it is. Nobody knows how many poor bastards there is, might be a million or so, maybe more'n that.

"You seen the ones got strength enough to fight. Those back there's the ones that don't. It's what the Oklahomer Wall is all about. Keep 'em over here, keep 'em out.

"Lord God help us if they ever broke through. Be like locusts, it would. They'd eat ever' bug, ever' blade of dead grass, strip the land bare."

"They thought we had food," Sylvan said, as if no one else was there. "That's what they wanted. They thought we had food back there."

Bob exhaled a breath of foul air. "Don't matter if they did. Knew there was eats up *here*. . . ."

~ TWENTY ~

After their fearsome encounter, Goodtime Bob insisted on driving. It was clearly Bob's fault that Asel, at the wheel while Bob took a nap, had blundered into Hammerillo Flats. Asel couldn't see any use in reminding him of that. Bob was clearly shaken, tense, wound up tight, ready to blow his ugly stack. As anyone could see, the man had severe personality disorders to start. This was not the time for advice on mental health.

Now and then, Asel spotted dark, scarecrow figures on the distant, wavy horizon. Silent, unmoving shadows, watching the truck pass by. If he hadn't known better, Asel would have named them dead and brittle trees.

Bob never spoke, never glanced from the road. Sylvan sat beside him, Asel in the cramped, comfortless space behind the seats. Goodtime Bob had left his mark, a near visible array of horrid smells. Asel was almost too tired to notice, but not tired enough.

Even when the familiar, arid flats gave way to sparse desert growth, gray clumps of brush and stunted, olyve-colored trees, Asel found little relief. Ahead, the sun was sinking in a veil of amber clouds. Sinking, but not fast enough—for behind them the night swept in bringing fright-dreams on the wing, hollow-eyed things, eager to swallow up rogues and the noble-born alike within their hungry maws.

What if the truck stops, what if they smell us, what if they find us out here . . .

"Not far now, lads," Goodtime Bob said. "Be there 'fore you know it. Good eats and ahle to drink, an' maybe some pretties as well."

Even in the growing dark, Asel caught Bob's sly and bawdy wink. He wondered what a "pretty" might be in this foul villain's head. The image that appeared was Goodtime Bob himself, with tangled curls, vivid red lips, and warts on her nose. Asel shuddered, and couldn't drive this vision away.

He longed for a chance to talk to Sylvan. He was certain his friend was as shaken as he by the shocking events of the last few days. In the orderly world of corporate lords, there were answers for every question one might ask. Though, indeed, there was seldom any need. Why take the time to disturb a pleasant day?

In Iacola Keep, in all of America East, there were common folk, and those of gentle birth. Nobles had their stations and ranks, and commoners did as well. The thing was, everybody *knew* where they belonged, there was simply no question of that.

The lower castes labored for those who did nothing at all. That was the way the world worked, the way it was meant to be.

Still, in the world he'd left behind, even those who toiled wore clothes, had places to sleep and food to eat—clothing, shelter, and food that fit their lesser needs. *None of them were naked, diseased, absolutely bonkers, totally mad. None of them starved, none of them lived in holes in the ground . . .*

Something was not working here, but Asel was sure it had nothing to do with Iacolas of the past. If Father had known about Hammerillo Flats or the Oklahomer Wall, he surely would have said. Since he hadn't, it was all in Goodtime Bob's head. All kinds of nonsense was there, one more crazy notion would take up scarcely any room at all.

The town looked as if a herd of drunks had carved it out of mud. Every structure was squat, sturdy and square, one squeezed tight against the next, with little room to spare. A roach might pass, Asel thought, if he didn't meet another on the way.

Most of the buildings were single-story with lopsided windows and crooked, cockeyed doors. A few, though, were two-, three-stories high, and one was even four. This latter, Bob said proudly, was the "Hotel de Guano, best damn place in town, or Goodtime Bob wouldn't stay there, lads, you can bet your sissy ass on that."

"It's—quite impressive," Sylvan said. "Nothing like this in New Whoreleens or Buttonrooge." He rolled his eyes at Asel, who pretended not to see.

"Well, I wouldn't expect persons of the darky persuasion to match accommodations like this—no offense, of course."

"Certainly not," said the former lord of Dixie-Datadog. "Wouldn't know how to act in a place like this."

In truth, neither Asel nor Sylvan had ever seen a *hotel* or anything like it before, except for the wretched dormitories at NERF. When a noble absolutely had to leave home, he stayed at another noble's estate. Or, had accommodations built if he intended to be there awhile.

"We'll get us some rooms and a tub," Bob said, as he parked the truck on the sandy, rutted street. "Get cleaned up, get our guts full an' have a drink or two. In the morning, I'll show you lads the sights."

"Ah, what sights would that be?" Asel asked.

Goodtime Bob showed Asel an easy grin. "Don't you worry 'bout that. This is Two-kum-curry, ol' Bob's town. I'll take care of the eye-tinerary, don't concern yourself about that."

"Tocum what?"

"Two-kum-curry, Newer Mechsyko, son." Bob looked at the pair with the pity one shows the demented and uninformed.

"Named after a native dish, I understand. The food here'll set your mouth afire, I'll warn you now about that."

Bob paused, squinted at the invisible north, and breathed the night air. "Up thata way is Old Colden'ratty, past that's the Sue Nation. Couple days from here is Almaquirky an' Towse, part of the Papul Shire. Keep going, an' I wouldn't if I was you, are the Franchise States—Aridsoda, Mormoset, Youtaw, Vaguest and the like. All of which belongs to Califoggy West." Bob showed them another meaningful wink. "Don't expect you two got any desire to go there?"

Asel and Sylvan didn't care for the way Bob's comments often ended in a question. The cunning old thug already knew more than he needed to know about the pair, and was always sniffing around for more.

And, as if he sensed their unease, he motioned them to the back of the truck, and gestured inside.

"Didn't see no reason for you *gentle*men to crap in your pants back there, so didn't mention it at the time. Those poor bastards from the Flats was swarming in back, while we was fighting 'em off up front. Cleaned all your souvenirs out. Likely ate the paper boxes, licked off the paint. You get up in the bed, you can see where they tried to gnaw through, get in to *us*."

Bob grinned. "Terrifyin' fucking thought, ain't it, boy?" He slapped Asel roughly on the back, and led the way to the Hotel de Guano front door. "Makes my throat go dry is what it does. Makes me want to find a semi-cold glass of bir and bare-naked gal. . . ."

There weren't any bare-naked gals that Asel could see. Bob spoke to a man behind a shabby desk, then guided Asel and Sylvan up a flight of stairs, and down a dark hall.

"You can bunk in together," he said. "Wash up down the hall. Don't take all night." With that, he was gone.

Asel glanced about the small room. There was one bed, two broken chairs, a peg on the wall. In the corner was a pot with a lid. Asel lifted the lid, dropped it quickly and gave a startled cry.

"My God, Sylvan, this is worse than NERF. You won't believe what that's for!"

"Yes, I think I do. I also think they expect us to, you know—do that."

"I can scarcely say it either. Sleep in the same bed."

"You don't have to say it, Ace. You could keep it in your head."

"I could, yes. But I believe we must face the unpleasant, and speak of things we would not imagine speaking of before. We have been together some time, in circumstances not of our choosing. We have, through no intent, invaded one another's privacy a number of times. I would say we have handled this as well as one possibly could."

"I'd say you're right. I don't feel we need to apologize. Incursions we have borne are no fault of ours."

Asel walked across the wooden floor, and peered out the narrow window. There was no glass, only a paper shade, held together by a few feeble threads. A man threw up in a doorway down the street. A shadow passed before a pale yellow window. A woman laughed, somewhere nearby. Lightning flashed, and thunder rolled in the north. As if in answer, a man stepped into the street just below, and fired a pistol in the air three times.

Asel stepped quickly back from the window.

"I did not mean to ramble, Sylvan. I only meant to say these people are savages, and the further west we go, the worse it gets. I will never forget the TechsMechs Rangers, or the horror of Hammerillo Flats. Goodtime Bob saved our lives, but I doubt his breeding is any better than theirs."

"Likely some worse," Sylvan said. "Colonel Mac's boys made no pretense about manners and such. Bob, he's all smiley in the face, got eyes like a snayke."

With great hesitation, Asel sat down on one of the wooden chairs. Three legs were alike, but the fourth was a rough, barky section of a desiccated tree.

"Nothing in this bleak land seems to have all its parts. I think perhaps that's the key."

"Uh-huh. Key to what?"

"I would like to talk with you, Sylvan. About what we saw back there. It brought some disturbing thoughts to mind. I think we must talk about it, simply because we *don't* know what to say."

"Well, I don't. I haven't the slightest idea what you're talking about."

"Sometimes I think you avoid the issues, in hopes they might go away."

Sylvan stared. "Damn, I take offense at that. Perhaps we of the Newer South are more courteous, better mannered than the nobles of the East."

"You jest, of course."

"Isn't any jest to it. You milk-bellied fellows don't know what decent behavior's all about. Isn't all just power, corruption, and wealth. There's pride, tradition, honor, and—"

Sylvan's words were lost as the door swept open and Goodtime Bob stalked into the room. His face was the usual swollen, fiery red, so dark and florid, Asel feared his head might explode.

Other than that, and his familiar, unsightly features, Asel scarcely recognized the man. His trousers were black, patched, shiny with wear, and ended somewhere just below the knees. His shirt was a flock of malerd ducks, crazed, yellow-billed honkers on a field of noxious green. His tie was a blue stone hanging on a string. Suspenders, picturing various lizirds of the west, completed Bob's costume of the day.

"Just as I figured," said Goodtime Bob. "Sittin' here yakking, haven't washed up, haven't done shit. One thing I can't tolerate, it's a man don't keep himself clean.

"Here, get yourself decent, put these on." Bob tossed a paper sack on the bed. "Isn't the sissy finery you boys is used to, but it won't get you shot in the Guano Grill. You got ten minutes. Haul your sorry asses downstairs, or you're eatin' with the dawgs. . . ."

~ TWENTY-ONE ~

Both Asel and Sylvan washed as best they could. Neither of the two would get near the tub, a rusty device, ringed with bands depicting its sordid past.

The clothes, they agreed, were a notch above the middle-class wear they'd been given at NERF—simple cotton trousers and tasteless tropical shirts. Sylvan's depicted the evening prymrose. Asel's was devoted to freshwater eels. Nothing fit, but they were better, and a great deal cleaner, than what they'd worn through the war at the Oklahomer Wall.

"Well, you lads look fine," Bob said, meeting them on the stairs. "You clean up good, I got to say that."

"We appreciate the clothes," Asel said, for it seemed the thing to do.

"Nothin' at all. Couldn't have you seen in my company lookin' like migratory piggs. I got friends in Two-kum-curry. Got a reputation to uphold."

Wisdom comes from experience, and Asel knew better than to comment on that.

The Guano Grill brought new and bewildering insight into the lives of the lower classes out west. There were gaunt, ruddy-featured men dressed a lot like Bob. Women, as gaunt as their men, dressed in shapeless gowns caught at the neck and reaching to the floor. Wherever Bob's horde of 'naked gals' might be, they were not present here.

As Asel and Sylvan followed Bob into the room, two old fiddlers struck up a tune. Everybody got up, everybody danced. Asel was familiar with dancing as such, but not the way it was practiced here. At Iacola Keep, one danced with pretty flunks, as a prelude to horizontal acts. Here, men and women merely walked around one another, and seldom ever touched. No one smiled. Clearly, dancing was not taken lightly in Newer Mechsyko.

"Isn't one of your uppity resto-rants of the titled and the rich," said Goodtime Bob, "but the food's damn good, and the people'll treat you right."

"It's very nice," said Sylvan.

"It is, indeed," Asel said.

This didn't seem the time to mention that the titled and the rich didn't *have* either restaurants or hotels. They had stately homes, often three or four. Ballrooms, dining rooms, servants, and chefs. There were sunny rooms for breakfast, candle-lit rooms for dinner, late night suppers of curloo soup and ottir chops, flownder a la mode, shrue-eye pye.

Bob got up, came back with drinks. Bir, he said, though Asel had his doubts about that. If the Royal Brewer had served such a mug, Father would have had him shot on the spot.

Bob seemed to love the stuff, smacked his lips every time he took a drink, and wiped his hand across his shirt. More bir arrived, and Bob told Asel and Sylvan the wonders of Two-kum-curry, its history, trade, famous sights, and, with a wink now and then, more about bare-naked girls.

A lot of information, a great many sights, Asel thought, for a town with one street and houses made of mud.

"Trade is the lifeblood of a nation," Bob went on, "even one fucked up as what we got now. I'm not talkin' your merchant kings an' your fat tycoons—no offense, boys—I'm talkin' *manly* trade, where a fellow sweats for what he's got, brings his goods to market, spits and cusses, makes a deal fair and square for all."

"Exactly what kind of goods do you trade?" Sylvan asked, to be polite. "I don't believe you mentioned your business with the TechsMechs, sir, and it's not my place to ask."

For an instant, Bob's eyes went cold. "No, it's not. But since you was rude enough to ask—all kinds of goods, you name it. Dry goods, wet goods, goods of every shape an' size. The market's changing all the time. Keeps you on your toes, I'll tell you that."

"Lucky for us you were there at the time," Asel said.

Bob grinned. "You boys are curious lads, ain't you? Sit tight, now, I'll get us somethin' to eat. Don't talk to no one 'less they're talking to you. We got manners here."

"Asel," Sylvan said, quickly dumping his mug on the floor, "I'll tell you what. I don't believe Goodtime Bob or any of these villains know the first thing about trade. They're thieves, brigands, small-time filchers is what they are."

Sylvan nodded across the room. The fiddlers had stopped, and the couples were milling about.

"Look at those shirts. Look at *your* shirt and mine. Every man in here is wearing a duck shirt, a prymrose, or an eel. They're all new, they're all just alike. And the women's dresses are all the same, too. And everybody's got on green athletic shoes."

"God, you're right." Asel puffed his cheeks and blew out a breath. "I expect they loot trucks. Or pay off the drivers when they come through."

"You can bet it doesn't stop at duck shirts, man. I'm thinking small arms, prosthetic parts, no telling what."

"I'm sure they sell to both sides, too. And I doubt there are any naked girls. That's a come-on, is what it is. Bob's using that to keep us in this lousy town."

Sylvan shook his head. "What for? You and I have nothing he'd want."

Asel didn't answer. Goodtime Bob was making his way through the dancers, both hands full of plates, piled heavily with food.

"All right, young gents, don't never say that Goodtime Bob don't treat his friends right. I had somethin' cooked up special. You haven't never had a dish like this before."

Asel felt something lurch in his belly, and it wasn't from the bir.

There were parts of some byrd, fried in a batter, with onyuns and ryce. Hunger had blunted Asel's taste. After the first few bites, he decided it wasn't bad at all. There were small, charred creatures, with the legs, heads, and tails still attached. Asel recognized gofer and vole, but he'd never had either prepared this way before. Each was stuffed with extremely hot peppers, which scorched the tongue and burned all the way down.

"Billy Guano, runs this place, traps these little fellows himself," Bob said. "Isn't anyone makes 'em any better than Billy does."

"They're real good," Sylvan said. "We make something like it in New Whoreleens. 'Bout as hot as this."

"Yeah?" Bob raised a brow. "I kind of doubt it, boy." He picked up one of the creatures by the tail, dropped the scrawny carcass in his mouth and sucked off all the meet. He looked at Asel and rubbed his sleeve across his mouth.

"You're not finished are you, lad? Miss your Eastern sissy food, do you?"

Asel pushed his plate aside. "I wish you'd stop saying that, Bob. I don't think you know a great deal about our culture, social ways, or culinary habits back East. You are prone to disparage anything that's not the norm in your own neighborhood."

Bob seemed taken aback, but somewhat short of offense.

"I know what I know, boy. More'n you might *think* I do. Goodtime Bob isn't some dumb, unlettered lout from west of the Oklahomer Wall. You'd do well to keep that in mind."

"Asel had no intention of putting you down," Sylvan said, picking at his vole. "He merely asked that you have some respect. Yes, we come from wealth and power, but we have feelings, and pride, the same as anyone else. And we're not sissies of any sort."

"Shoot, this conversation's got to a overly serious tone." Bob shook his head, and donned his familiar imitation smile. "We come through a lot together. We're supposed to be havin' fun, 'stead of finding fault with one another, right? If that's fair enough to you fellows, it's fair enough for me."

Bob stuck out his hand and gave Asel a hearty grip, then offered a shake to Sylvan too. Asel had no napkin, and wiped a considerable amount of grease on the bottom of his chair. He had to admit the peppery gofer was really quite good, but his stomach was growing queasy, and he vowed not to eat any more.

Sylvan, however, seemed unable to stop, and Asel imagined darkies were used to curry in their food. History said they'd come from Frants in centuries past. Uncle Hal had been there, and said the Frents ate quite unusual food, including live dawg.

There seemed to be no set schedule for the dance. Fiddlers played, people danced. Fiddlers stopped, people sat down. Drank bad bir, ate whatever the Guano Grill had to offer, which, at the time, was gofer and vole.

"You think you boys is finished," Bob said, leaning back and patting his tummy, "you got another think coming."

"Thank you, but I've had plenty," Asel said quickly.

"Couldn't eat another bite," Sylvan said.

"Uh-huh." Bob poked a spot of meet off his duck shirt, licked his finger and sucked the morsel off. "That's because neither one of you ever had chikun gizzerd flambé the way Billy's wife cooks it up."

"Maybe later," Asel said, certain, now, his belly had had enough of this, that everything else was coming up.

"Couldn't eat another bite," Sylvan said again. "Maybe later, not now."

A dark cloud seemed to veil Bob's eyes. "*Later* don't cut it out West here, son. We're dealin' with your space-time continyum. Eye-ons, adams, kosmic batter, an' matter that ain't even there. *Now* is where it's at."

With that, Goodtime Bob left and wandered off toward the back. Asel watched him go, somewhat bewildered by this sudden leap into science that Asel scarcely understood.

"I think what we ought to do, is get up, walk outside real slow, get in the truck, get out of here before he comes back."

"And do what? I'm for getting out, no mistaking that. Just don't know where, especially in the dark."

"Your point's well taken," Asel agreed. "But with Bob watching every move we make, surprise may be our only way out."

"You think he'd try and stop us?"

"Sylvan, we don't have time to think about this. Do we stay or do we go? We—"

Asel stopped, gripped the edge of his chair, shocked, stupefied, dazzled by the sight that appeared before his eyes. His heart was a'flutter, and pleasant sensations occurred below that.

Sylvan said something, but Asel didn't hear. The two tall and stunning beauties wore black, broad-brimmed hats, black overalls and no shoes at all. The overalls were cut delightfully low, and barely concealed the tan and luscious breasts that made Asel want to cry.

Bob made no effort to hide his knowing smile.

"Boys, I'd like you to meet some good friends of mine, who'd very much like to meet you. Asel, Sylvan, this is Sister Beth Mary and Sister Mary Beth."

Bob showed them his everyday grin. "Don't say nothing lewd or out of sorts, lads. These here ladies don't care for crude talk, they're the Good Lord's certified Nones. . . ."

~ TWENTY-TWO ~

"Nones?"

"Nones," Bob said, "you want to hear it twice? Holy persons who have taken their vows not to seek out worldly ways."

"We don't condemn anyone for sin," said Mary Beth, or the other way around. "Sin's the way of Man, the way of the world. We deal with it as best we can."

"We have, through grace, found the strength and dedication to restrain from wanton ways, joy and carnal delight, corruption of the all-too-willing flesh."

"Very—pleased to meet you," Asel said, hardly conscious of speaking at all, for, at that very moment, the taller of the two breathed in and breathed out, revealing a pale and lovely sphere, an awesome orb only partially contained. For a blink or maybe less, a taut, pink circularity, a rosy aureole of bliss was bared for all the world to see. It was gone, as quickly as it came, but the vision remained, etched in Asel's mind, etched in a way that had little to do with dedication and restraint, and everything to do with corruption of the flesh.

When he came to his senses, he looked up and saw she knew exactly what he'd seen, that her calm, sea-blue eyes had witnessed such weakness before, that she understood lust had him firmly in its grip, that he would, gladly, revel in her ruination, now, on this very spot, sweeping mugs and the bones of gofers and tiny voles aside, as he took her on the table, here in the Guano Grill.

"I hope you'll excuse me," Asel said, "I didn't mean to stare. Actually, I thought for a moment we'd met somewhere before."

"I don't suppose we did," said Beth Mary.

"I certainly don't recall," said Mary Beth.

"He don't either," said Bob, glaring at Asel with black agate eyes. "You ladies have a seat, I'll find a couple clean glasses and some of Billy's good wyne."

"Wyne," said Sister Mary Beth, who had a lovely mole near her full, and succulent lips, "is a most acceptable drink, if taken in moderation. Saints and believers in olden times drank wyne with every meal."

"In moderation," Beth Mary added.

"I believe I mentioned that, Sister."

"Yes, I believe you did. I don't suppose one can say it too often, in a sinful world such as this."

"You are so right, dear. Amen to that."

Mary Beth paused, and gazed thoughtfully at Sylvan and Asel, a look of such intensity and depth, it made the pair quite uneasy, made them want to squirm, swallow, think of something pure, something good, think about anything but pointy and pink.

"May I ask," said Mary Beth, smiling graciously as Goodtime Bob appeared with two glasses of dark red wyne, "may I ask if you gentlemen are of the spiritual persuasion? Have you confessed your grievous sins?"

"Have you chastised yourself for the wicked, shameful life you've led?" asked Sister Beth Mary.

"Have you sought some painful, torturous penance that might bring peace to your dark and tainted soul?"

"Have you thought about Hell?"

"The cries of the damned . . ."

"Writhing, screaming forever . . ."

"Lost, lost . . ."

"Lost in a lake of eternal fire . . ."

"Burned, burned, your eyeballs bursting, your body a'sizzle . . ."

"Charred, innards a'crackle, juices all a'flame . . ."

"Seared, blistered, scorched to the bone, and yet still alive, alive forever in misery and pain . . ."

"That's where you're headed, Brothers, Hades, Hell, the Evil One's Lair . . ."

"In-*sin*-eration waits for he who takes the crooked road, who walks the murky path . . ."

"Cheers," said Beth Mary.

"Cheers," said Mary Beth, and touched her Sister's glass with her own.

"Well, young sirs," she smiled, her face, the swell of her breasts, slick with a pure and virtuous sweat. "Have you, indeed, seen the Light, or do you rush blindly toward damnation and the pit?"

"I'm for the Light," Sylvan said.

"Me too," Asel said.

"Certainly, we're not there yet," Sylvan added. "Don't guess any of us are."

"No?"

"I'm saying, not a lot of us, right?" Sylvan looked away from those stern and disapproving eyes. "Some, now some *would*. Bound to be one, very likely two."

"Absolutely," Asel said. He managed to look at the fiddlers, the solemn dancers on the floor.

"The righteous path is the only path we seek out here in the west, lads," said Goodtime Bob. "You'd do yourself a favor an' keep that in mind."

Asel had a sudden vision of the portly bishop of Iacola Keep, as he sang the family rites in a dull and dreary monotone . . .

"*. . . And Anheuser-Tusch
begat Canon-Cadillac,
begat Kodak-Smack,
begat Pfizer-Kaiser-Nizer,
begat Motorolacola,
begat AT&Me,
begat Hershey-GE . . .*"

There were thirty more verses, but none, that Asel could recall, spoke of hell or pits or pain, and nothing at all about juices all a'flame. Nones, in spite of their appearance, didn't seem to have a lot of fun.

". . . saddens me greatly, truly breaks my heart," Mary Beth was saying, as Asel returned to reality again, "to know there are so many, many souls gone astray, so many who have never seen the Light."

"It brings us sorrow to know they are out there, fumbling, braying in the dark," Beth Mary said.

"Oh, it does, it leaves us with dread."

"You got to understand, Sisters," Bob said, "these boys are from the East. Abomination's a way of life up there."

Asel frowned. "Now I wouldn't say that, I wouldn't say that at all. We have a full religious life back home. It might not be exactly like yours."

"Same here," Sylvan said. "The Lees and McCrees don't hold with your internal fires, I'll tell you that."

"I've been down South," Bob said, "I know what kinda sin you all up to down there."

"I will have to resent that, Bob."

"You do what you like. I know where I been, I know what I seen."

"Please . . ." Beth Mary leaned across the table, grasping Asel in one hand, and Sylvan in the other.

Asel was startled, stunned, electrified at her touch. His body tingled, shivered, shook, as if sweet lightning coursed through his veins, filled him with a strange and dazzling joy, embraced him in a warm and honeyed rapture of impossible delight.

And, as he drifted deeper, deeper-deeper still, in this syrupy dream, Mary Beth and Beth Mary suddenly appeared, twined all about him like slick and lusty eels, whispered in his ears, promised him sins he'd scarcely imagined, even with sly and willing flunks from overseas, pleasures denied to ordinary men . . . touched him, kissed him, caressed him with warm and varied parts, snared him in long and lubricious limbs . . .

Asel gasped, surrendered, gave himself up to this lovely pair, drew hot and holy skin to his own damned flesh, moaned, groaned, cried aloud in crazed and manic bliss. . . .

~ TWENTY-THREE ~

"*Off* of me, you lout! Some might do it in the East, I know some do it in the South, and there's nothing *wrong* with that—but *I* don't do it, you hear, and don't you forget!"

"My God, Sylvan, I am desperately sorry," Asel said, blinking at his friend's hazy image in the dark. "I assure you I have never had the slightest feeling of bodily desire for your person—not that there's anything wrong with that—I have manly regard for you as friend, I—I don't know what came over me—what happened to the lights? Where *are* we, Sylvan?"

"Don't have any idea, man. Only thing I figure is those Nones did us in. I'm guessing some kinda pointy device. Maybe some chemical shit, had it on their hands, something didn't have an effect on them.

"I can guess where we are. This shaky motion is quite familiar. We're in the back of our truck. Try and find your feet. I expect you'll find they're chained, Ace. We've been kidnapped, is what. Seized, grabbed, snatched, abducted against our will—"

"But whatever for?" Asel felt his legs. They were, indeed, chained, the chain bolted to the bed of the truck. He was greatly annoyed, and embarrassed as well. Those phony, pious Sisters had taken them prisoner, shackled them like common, ordinary folk. Even the people at NERF had respected their princely rights. Bad food and tacky clothing, yes. But they had never stooped to something like this.

"Why?" he asked Sylvan again. "Surely they don't imagine they could hold us for ransom, or something as vile as that. We've already been deprived of our rightful places in life. No one's going to pay to get us back."

"NERF might."

"I suppose we have to think of that. Though they haven't shown much interest so far. Whatever the reason, you can bet that Goodtime fellow's behind all this. He set us up, Sylvan. He's a thief, that's his business. Everyone in Two-kum-curry's engaged in criminal enterprise. He *sold* us, like common goods, merchandise. Like—like *livestock!* What I don't know, though, is what for."

"Might not be, you know, somethin' too bad."

Asel couldn't see Sylvan, but he knew if a man was grinning or not.

"What do you mean by that? I do hope it's not what I'm thinking."

"Might be it is. I had me some real fine dreams of an intimate nature whilst I was out . . ."

"So did I. And that's what they were, too. Dreams."

"Seemed awful real to me."

"You're joking, of course. You don't truly think those duplicitous females have abducted us so we may pleasure them with our noble parts."

"*Nothin'* that's happened to me lately is something I was planning on, man. If I got to guess, I'll guess at something good."

"Guess the worst. You'll come a lot closer." A sudden thought appeared from nowhere at all. "How do we know it's them, Sylvan? I mean, it could be someone else up there."

"Huh-unh. We been taken by vicious vessels of the Lord, Ace. Isn't any question of that. . . ."

Sylvan was silent for a while, and, in a moment, Asel realized his friend had simply slipped away, dropped off into restful sleep. He envied Sylvan, for he knew that he, himself, would never be able to put his cares aside as easily as that.

Instead, he fingered the chains that bound his legs, counted the links in the dark, listened to the steady hum of the engine, felt the truck sway, bounce in a steady rhythm as it took the bumps in the road. And, before long, the sounds, the motion, the dark of the night, all came together as one, and, in spite of all the anger, fear, and dread that filled his head, Asel sank down into a deep, and, thankfully, dreamless sleep. . . .

This time, he woke before Sylvan, who was curled into a painful knot against the wall. Asel's feet were quite numb, but he managed to drag himself as far as the chain would allow, to the rear of the truck. Cracks in the truck's wooden side told him the first light of dawn was appearing directly behind their path. They were heading west, then.

He was pleased at how quickly this knowledge had arrived. So much had changed since he'd left Iacola Keep. He had never had to think about directions. Now, he knew all four, didn't have to hesitate at all. He could get into his clothes by himself, get his jacket and his trousers on right. Eat by himself. And it had happened practically overnight. He had changed, and he had learned. Much of the knowledge he'd gained was nothing he wanted to know. But he *had*, and somehow he'd survived. It was most unlikely he would ever be Prince of Christler-Coke, but he was still Asel Iacola of America East.

"I'm me," he said aloud, peering into the dusty road behind, "and, if you think about it, there's much to be said about that."

"Talking to yourself, that's not a good sign, Ace. I had a cousin did that an' Uncle Mal had to send him away."

"Well I don't have to worry, do I? I've already been sent away."

"There's that. What's it look like, what do you see?"

"A few trees and hills. That's something, I suppose. A great deal of sand and peculiar spindly plants. Very little you haven't seen before. The sun will be up in a minute and we'll likely roast in here. Not that anyone cares. I wouldn't count on breakfast if I were you. What I wouldn't give for the smell of lampree sizzling on the grill. Eegul aigs. Poached. Nettul bred, a little flownder jam. I wouldn't be awake, of course, not at this ungodly hour, but —*holy shit, Sylvan!*"

Asel backed away, startled, then pressed his face against the crack again.

"What?"

Asel waved him away. He could see them clearly now, as lavender began to fill the sky—*choppers!* Five of them. Six. Maybe another after that. A chill touched his spine, left his stomach in a knot. Dark, ugly things, their bent and crooked snouts etched forever in his mind. For he would recall that moment as long as he lived, watch, as they descended on Iacola Keep, thrashing Mother's roses into pink and white confetti, spilling out red-clad troopers as they squatted on the lawn.

"There's no reason to think they're after us," Sylvan said, gazing through a crack of his own. "I saw the choppers at NERF. They're sort of puce, and they only have two."

"They're not from NERF," Asel said. "They belong to the Lord of SEC, and you can bet your ass they're looking for me." He glanced at Sylvan. "Ducky Du Pontiac-Heinz is behind all this. Now that he's stolen America East, he's got the SEC in his pocket. He wants to be sure I'm dead. That's the way the Duck is."

"They could be after me. I got 'bout as many assholes in high places as you."

Asel doubted that, but he didn't say a thing.

"Whatever. They'll get us both, for sure. I really can't think of any practical way to tear these shackles loose and make a getaway.

"Have you ever seen a trooper from the SEC, Sylvan? Their uniforms are rather well cut, I have to say that. But they carry these hideous weapons with little warty bumps. They're not designed to kill, I understand, but they leave you with contusions, and a great sense of sorrow and regret."

"I don't care to hear 'bout it. Something's got to do with bumps and sorrow, I'd stay away from that."

"Good. When you figure how to make them go away, do let me know."

How did they find us? Asel wondered. *Goodtime Bob, or some lout at the Oklahomer Wall?*

Sylvan might be a lord on his own, but he simply didn't understand the power Ducky had gained when he'd taken Father down. Iacola Keep was more than Father's business empire, more than a hundred domains like Christler-Coke. The House of Iacola *was* America East: New Yuk, Vermint, Humpshore, Pencilvain, Myne, the three fat Virgentles and a couple Asel always forgot. Plus all that stuff overseas; Father had had his share of that.

Or did, Asel reminded himself, *until they took him down, Ducky, and the ruthless Jackie Cee.*

The ear-splitting sound broke through his thoughts, and he threw himself down as the choppers, one by one, dipped so low the awesome force of their rotors set the truck a'tremble, picked it up and shook it, slung it all about like a kat who's found a raht, rattled every bolt, nearly turned the thing over, set it right again.

The black creatures circled, doubled back, came in low, nearly level with the road. The first one drew within inches of the truck. Asel could see the dark-clad pilot, the trooper huddled at his side. The ugly, mottled head of the chopper bristled with weapons, each ready stinger topped with a flare, a spout, a sizable lump, a swollen snout. And Asel, seeing them close, grasped the mockery behind these deadly, rigid protrusions, and found them in extremely bad taste.

Then, of a sudden, as quickly as they'd come, the choppers pulled away, turned with a shriek and vanished in the glare of morning sky.

"They're leaving," Sylvan said, one eye fast against a crack. "They're going away."

"Sure they are. They know we're in here. You watch, they'll be squatting in the road up ahead. They'll line us up and shoot us or they'll take us back to NERF. If I had a choice, I'm not at all certain which it would be . . ."

Sylvan kept his eye on the road. "Bad outlook like that, it'll come back at you, happens every time. Think someone's goin' to shoot you, that's exactly what you're going to get. Called your Carmack output's what it is. Bad goes in, bad comes out."

"Is that part of the darky persuasion, is that what it is?"

"You go easy with such talk, all right? All the thinking in the world doesn't come from America East. That's an overseas religion's what it is, comes from the—*oh, man!*"

Asel moved up quickly to peer through the crack. The truck had passed beneath a high, stone wall, a barrier built with much more precision and care than the massive, but clumsy, Oklahomer Wall. A pair of robed figures appeared, and began to swing together two halves of a large, intricately crafted iron gate. The gate clanged shut—a clang with a solemn finality about it, Asel thought at the time.

"Got something written in that scrolly iron stuff," Sylvan said. "Backward, can't make it out."

"I can," Asel said, for he had learned, quite young, the sometimes useful habit of reading things backward or upside down. Now, with a shudder that lifted the hairs on the back of his neck, he read, switching the script from right to left:

*** OUR LADY OF ***
RELUCTANT DESIRE

~ TWENTY-FOUR ~

"You know what we got here, Asel? We are in the hands of female zealots, bigots, loonies, women in awful hats and out-of-fashion clothes, women who have substituted excess devotion for normal desire, women who—"

"I agree," Asel said, "we're in very deep shit, Sylvan. And I have to say we can partially fault ourselves, for we allowed our baser needs to take hold, we were lulled by physical attraction, by fleshly delights that were partially revealed. Transparent devices, to be sure, but it has been my experience they work nearly every time on manly sorts like ourselves."

"They are fine-looking women."

"Yes, they are. Treacherous, but women with slender forms and swelling breasts. Women who beguile one with fiery glances that often mask outright lies. We should have known, when Goodtime Bob introduced them as Nones of the religious persuasion. We should have known something was wrong right there."

"Likely we did."

"We went right ahead."

"No use denying that."

"We didn't even try."

"That one—Mary Beth or Beth Mary, I don't know which—had boomers like I've never seen outside of New Whoreleens."

"I think that was Beth Mary, though Mary Beth was quite well-endowed."

"Yeah, well, like you say, a manly fellow's blind to reason, he comes up against temptation like that."

"I don't see how we can blame ourselves at all," Asel said.

"They're the ones fightin' natural desire, not us."

"Absolutely. Anyone raised in the proper manner would do the same."

"You got that right."

"We were taught to meet the needs of our groinal parts. I will stand by that."

"We got to. You're brought up right, that's what you're going to do. . . ."

Asel didn't care to admit it, but he was more than a little disappointed when neither of the lovely Nones had stayed to release their chains. That job, instead, was left to hooded lackeys, who treated both he and Sylvan roughly as they were guided to their quarters in the dark of the night.

This is becoming quite weary, Asel thought, as he tossed about on the lumpy mattress of his bed. *If we are continually captured by strangers, we will never get where we're going at all. And where, exactly, might that be?*

Sylvan slept soundly. Worse still, he snored. That was another of the many revelations that were coming Asel's way: Both noble and lowborn folk shared many faults alike. Apparently, there was nothing you could do about that.

Morning took forever to appear. It found Asel dull and bleary-eyed, bone-aching weary and extremely out of sorts. Sylvan felt rested, but saw, at once, it was best to keep that to himself.

A big key rattled in the door. A black-robed figure warned them with a gesture to step back in the room, then set two plates and a jug of water on the floor. The plates contained some kind of anymal, unfamiliar joints charred black. Bred, and maybe a taytoe, though Asel wouldn't bet on that.

Neither of the two had very much to say, and no time to say it. They had scarcely wolfed down breakfast when another robed figure appeared, and signaled them to follow down the hall.

"Not a real wordy bunch, are they?" Sylvan said.

"What difference does it make? What would you like them to say?"

"Get off it, Ace. You got complaints, tell it to them, not me. . . ."

The day was fierce and bright, the sun was well up into a raw and colorless sky. Asel and Sylvan were stunned, startled by the scene laid out before them. A lawn, so vivid and green it hurt the eyes, stretched from where they stood to the high, forbidding wall. The color was an unfamiliar sight in this parched and dreary land, and, to Asel, it brought back memories of the vast, verdant grounds of Iacola Keep. Sylvan's image was much the same, the lush estates that had once belonged to the powerful McCrees.

In the midst of this splendor was a carved, marble fountain, with a great spray of water misting in the early morning breeze. Clearly, water was no problem here. Ringing the fountain and brightening the lawn were neat, well-tended beds of multi-colored flowers. Beyond, were clusters of sand-colored buildings, built with such thoughtful design, they might have been part of the land itself.

"Nice," Sylvan said, "except for that wall, and that great, enormous gate."

"And *that*," Asel said, in a tone that caught Sylvan's attention at once. "There's a sight I don't care for at all."

Sylvan followed Asel's glance. At once, the hairs crawled up the base of his neck. Coming toward them, out of a structure much like the one they'd left behind, were a crew of men, marching in perfect time. Each was clad in pale green overalls and floppy, green hats. Each bore a rake, a hoe, a shovel, or some other tool upon his shoulders, as if he was going to a war upon weeds, bugs, and varmints of every sort.

And, most ominous of all, each wore the large, orange initials on the front and back of his clothes: **O.L.O.R.D.** Both Asel and Sylvan were quick of wit, and perceived the meaning of this at once.

"They got a bunch of *men* in here," Sylvan said, as if Asel had suddenly lost his sight. "They're doing manual labor—mowing and hoeing and fooling with flowers and stuff. They're fucking *gardeners*, Ace."

"I know what they are. As a child, I watched labor persons at Iacola Keep. I believe it's where I first encountered sweat. I was terrified. I asked Mother if the fellows were melting. She took me in the house."

"Something similar happened to me. First time I saw a white guy, I figured he was dead. No offense, man."

"I know you're from the South. I overlook that."

Before Sylvan could answer, two familiar figures approached across the grass.

"Damn, I hate to say it. They look just as good in the light. Can't believe anyone with honkers like that have got such hateful attitudes."

"Well don't forget. And don't let them touch you. I doubt if they keep that hideous drug on their hands all the time, but you never can tell."

Indeed, Asel thought, it was hard to deny the allure of Sister Beth Mary and Sister Mary Beth. Even in their black overalls and wide-brimmed hats, they radiated lust and unsatisfied desire. Each step that brought them closer enhanced his growing—and somewhat obvious—longing for heat, passion, immediate release of any kind.

He felt little shame, for he clearly understood there were very few fellows of the manly persuasion who could face such creatures unaffected by intense and rigid desire. There was simply nothing one could do.

"Aw, man," Sylvan muttered beside him, expressing Asel's misery as well as he could himself.

"I hope you had a pleasant rest," said Mary Beth, or the other way around. "Let us welcome you to Our Lady of Reluctant Desire. We pray you will find both physical and spiritual awakening here in this lovely garden of our Lord."

"God's will has sent you here," said the other luscious, slightly more fully endowed of the two. "Here you will find comfort and peace as you nurture the land, as you mow, hoe, weed, seed, and tend the flowers, bushes, and grasses of every sort."

"Praise be, Sister."

"Praise be, my dear."

"As you work, as your plants thrive and grow, so shall your spirits thrive and grow, and you—"

"Thank you," Asel said, "but I think I speak for us both when I say we politely decline. We were taken against our will, thanks to the perfidy and greed of one Goodtime Bob. We are being held unjustly, Sisters, and I am certain those other poor fellows are as well. That's not my concern, of course, but I assure you we will not join your corps of—of *yardmen*. That is not our calling, and we would truly be of little use to you here."

"Yeah, that's right," Sylvan said.

Asel waited, his look both expectant and annoyed. Clearly, he expected his wordy friend to take it on from there. Sylvan, though, looked away at the toiling workers, now spread across the lawn, under the watchful eyes of their guards. The cowled figures stood like unmoving posts, not far away from their charges, but just far enough.

Catching his glance, guessing his thoughts, the Nones smiled, as if to show understanding in their hearts.

"Many of our workers for God feel at odds with their state at the start," said one. "You will learn to be happy here. Joy will come to you in time."

"It will. You wait and see. The Lord knows your needs."

"Indeed he does. He sees."

"Praise His name."

"Praise Him, Sister."

Time? In *time?* The words gave Asel a chill. "What—what exactly kind of *time* are we talking about here?"

"Not that we care," Sylvan added. "We won't be here, you understand."

The None Asel felt was likely Mary Beth, gave a sigh that nearly set her full and wholesome bosom free.

"Time has meaning only in this sinful world, dear sirs. Know that if you do well here, there will be moments of joy, as well as labor."

"I like to pick my own joy," Sylvan said. "Works out better that way."

"Oh dear." The Sister looked pained. "We don't like for you to show anger in our Lady's garden."

"No, we don't like that at all . . ."

It was a nearly imperceptible glance, more like a whispered thought, a hint, a mere suggestion of a nod, but Asel saw it, and, from the corner of his eye, caught the blur of motion to his left and to his right, motion all about, as a dozen robed figures swept their garments aside, brought wicked, snouty weapons to bear, and fired them in the air.

The deafening explosions sent a wave of pressure, a fierce concussion of heated air across the lawn. Asel, and Sylvan as well, nearly jumped out of their skins. The workers, though, poor fellows sweating in their green workwear, reacted in a totally different way. When the weapons fired, they all went still, stunned, frozen, like garden statuary. Not very good statuary, but clearly well trained.

"Vile and hateful manners pain our Lord so," said Mary Beth with the hint of a tear in her haunting blue eyes. "I hope we don't have to go through this again. . . ."

~ TWENTY-FIVE ~

"I am not going to do it, Ace. If I want to wear something tacky and cheap, I'd like the son of a bitch to fit."

Sylvan looked extremely absurd, holding the shirt up to his chest, but Asel couldn't bring himself to laugh. He had a shirt and green trousers too, folded on his cot, the same dreary shade, with the lurid O.L.O.R.D. initials on the back. A look at the other poor bastards mingling about told him the clothing only came in one size.

"It looks bad," Asel agreed, "it looks quite common, and no, it surely doesn't fit."

"Doesn't matter if you're fat, skinny, somewhere in between. I've got pride in my appearance. I was brought up that way. Fashion isn't all there is to life, but it doesn't hurt to look nice."

"I quite agree. But think about it this way, Sylvan . . ." He glanced around to see if anyone was close. The barracks were plain, no pictures, no attempt at décor. Cots in two rows, and a narrow walkway in between. There were half a dozen workers present, milling about the far end. They all looked weary, drained, and out of sorts. None of them were stout, Asel noticed. Most of them were stooped, bowed in the back, clearly a natural posture in the gardening trade.

So far, none of them had even come near. Sylvan and Asel were new, outsiders, men they didn't know. Strangers, who had caused the guards to fire their weapons in the air. Better to leave them be, just watch them for a while.

". . . I'm trying to look on the good side of this," Asel went on. "I think—sit down, let me finish this. I don't wish to wear these outfits either, but there's something we tend to forget, something we ought to remember from the harrowing moments we've shared since we met.

"We were, as you have pointed out, raised to wear proper attire, to express our noble bearing and taste through color, fabric, and style. What we have learned, to our dismay, is a great many people don't live that way. Dull and tawdry is the fashion in the world we've come to know. We no longer stand out. We haven't since we left NERF. We certainly don't stand out now."

Sylvan waited. "You going somewhere with this?"

"I am, yes. I'm saying these ugly, ill-fitting garments are the only advantage we have. We look like everyone else, friend. It is hard to comprehend, but we have become simply faces in a crowd."

"Maybe you didn't notice. My face is some different from anybody here."

"I know. And I regret that, too. It might pose a problem in our getaway plan. We will have to keep it in mind."

"What getaway plan is that? I guess I don't recall."

"We haven't discussed it, but we will. We cannot survive in this place, and those Nones will never let us go. I propose we wear these garments, and appear to fit in. We can easily learn the names of various tools—how to hold them, what they do—by watching the others work. It shouldn't be long before we aren't noticed at all."

"Oh, God." Sylvan raised a hand to cover his face. "Of all the shit that's happened to me, this is worst of all. Even when they shipped me off to NERF, I felt like I was *somebody* still. Now I'm just a dumb cropper with a hoe and a rook."

"I believe that's rake."

"Whatever."

Asel and Sylvan tried not to look at one another in their gardener suits. When it couldn't be helped, the looker politely glanced away. Both agreed to skip the noon meal. They had been through this at NERF. It was agony to think about standing in line, eating with people you didn't know.

One of the ominous, robed, well-armed figures appeared, and told them they didn't have to eat.

"You may do without if you like, but you will work the afternoon shift. I expect you will wish you had consumed a nutritious meal, for it looks to me as if you've never worked a day in your life."

"Hey, you're right," Sylvan said, flattered by the remark, "we appreciate that."

"Those fellows give me the creeps," Asel said, when the guard had walked on. "Talk like they swallowed a stone. Like they've got a chikun bone in their throat. Like they come from a very cold clime. Like they—"

"They talk real funny 'cause they're mean. Your mean, vile sort of person, they're all going to talk like that."

"We're going to have to eat, Sylvan, but I'd rather put it off as long as we can."

"Which I think'll be tonight."

"Yes. The noble and the bumpkin have similar organs inside. I fear it will have to be tonight."

The men filled the barracks after the noonday meal. Some sprawled on their cots, others gathered in tight little knots. It was clear the newcomers were the topic of the day. Finally, one fellow left the others and came toward the pair. He walked in a hesitant, shuffling manner, bowed and listless like the rest.

No wonder they don't make any trouble. Those lovely Sisters have broken their spirits. They don't know how to fight anymore. . . .

"That's us," Sylvan said, guessing Asel's thoughts, "if we don't get out of here."

As the man grew near, Asel could see he was right in judging the prisoners a dull and passive lot. His features betrayed scarcely any emotion at all. A scarecrow, a bundle of sticks, a man who'd been worked to the bone.

"Hello," the fellow said. "You haven't been here before."

"No," Asel said, "we haven't."

"Uhuh. Where you been, then?"

"Why, lots of places, actually. Where have you been?"

"I been here."

"Where before that?"

The man looked puzzled, then his face split into a foolish grin. "I'm Henry."

"I'm Asel and this is Sylvan."

"Somethin' happen to you? You look awful dark."

"You look awful white, man."

"Sylvan—Henry, how long have you been here? Do you remember that?"

"You missed lunch."

"Yes, we know."

"It was good. We had meet."

"That's fine, I'm sure it was quite a treat."

"And bred."

"Bred's good. Henry—"

Henry's eyes began to glaze. He stared at Asel and Sylvan as if he'd never seen them before. Then he turned and walked away, in the manner Asel came to know as Our Lady's Shuffle— or, as Sylvan put it, the Fucking Gardener's Hop . . .

The thought struck them both at once. Each felt the same chill, the same sudden dread.

"Gods help us, Sylvan, it's the damn *food*. That's the way they do it, same way they got us here, putting something on their hands. We knew it, just didn't put it together at the time."

Sylvan let out a breath. "Fogheads, lackwits, that's what we got here, man. Those crafty Nones have sucked their minds clean."

"They are definitely on something, all right. I've heard of Woozies, Kickers, Red High. The servants used to drink import ti."

Asel sat up wearily on his cot. "We ate breakfast. It's already in us. It's too late, Sylvan. We're just like them."

"Huh-uh. No, we're not, Ace. We said we wouldn't eat with those louts because they're not our kind. Well, we're sticking to that."

"Till when? Tonight?"

"I get hungry, I'm going to think about Henry in my head. Sylvan Lee McCree, with his mouth hanging open, drooling on his shirt. I'm going to see a de-fective white man without a lot of sense."

"There is still something lacking in our friendship, Sylvan. We are different, somehow."

"Difference is good. Gives you something to strive for, man. . . ."

Gardening was worse than Asel had even imagined. Learning which end of the complex tools went where was easy enough, but the work was too horrid, too appalling to believe. Less than an hour under the broiling sun, Asel was appalled to find he couldn't stand up. His back was bowed in knots of agonizing pain. If he tried to stand, the fiery spasms gripped him and drew him down again.

There was water, all you could drink. The Nones knew their workers would die without that. But labor called for food as well, and Asel knew he was quickly running out of fuel.

The sweat stung his eyes, dulling his vision, but he soon learned you didn't have to *see* the work, or even think about it. The body took over for the mind, and shuffled about with no direction at all.

Step . . . shuffle . . .chop-chop-chop. Step, shuffle . . . chop-chop-chop . . .

It was killing, stupefying work. Asel could see how numbing drugs were the key to this sort of career. The other workmen seemed to do fine in a stupor, in a trance.

Asel chopped groggily through a patch of lovely blossoms, slicing off their tender heads. A robed figure caught him, shifted him off another way.

At suppertime, the others dropped their tools and staggered to the mess. Asel caught Sylvan's glance. Sylvan mouthed *no*. Asel sighed and nodded back. Bent, haggard, close to comatose, they headed for the nearest building and a bit of blessed shade.

A figure appeared and blotted out the sun.

"You two don't have to eat Our Lady's generous bounty," Beth Mary said, or maybe Mary Beth. "But you don't get to sit and waste Her time, either. On your feet—I don't mean later, gentlemen, I mean *now. . . !*"

~ TWENTY-SIX ~

"This is not going to work. I suppose we knew it from the start. We may be noble in heart, but our bodies will betray us, there's little doubt about that."
  Sylvan didn't answer. He lay on his cot and stared at the darkened ceiling. A fly buzzed and circled about, landed on his brow, tasted salty sweat. Now and then a muscle twitched in Sylvan's back. Clearly, bodily parts complained unless you showed them proper care.
  "Call me coward if you will," Asel went on, "but I can't go without food another day. I will cease to move, or possibly die."
  "We give in, we're going to be droolers too."
  "You don't have to tell me that, I know what I'll be. I'm not looking forward to being a moron with a hoe."
  "We don't have to decide right now. Get us some sleep. We'll take a vote on it before breakfast time."
  "A vote?"
  "That's the way to do it. Each of us get to have a say."
  "There are only two of us here. What if we don't vote the same way?"
  "That's going to happen sometimes."
  "No offense, but that makes no sense at all. If there were three of us, say, or fifteen, a vote would be fine. I've watched folk of the laboring persuasion do it all the time, playing at their games at Iacola Keep."
  "But I never saw them do it with *two*. Two just isn't enough, I'm afraid. I—Sylvan? Are you listening to me? It's rude to ignore a person when he talks. You just—*Sylvan*. . . ?"

✼   ✼   ✼

Asel sat up straight, his heart beating wildly against his chest. The bone-chilling howl swept any dregs of sleep away. At first, it seemed to be only one man. In a moment, though, his cry was taken up by another, then another after that. Soon, the entire barracks were awail, screaming, moaning in the night.

Harsh beams of light cut through the dark, found a pallid face, moved on to the next. Finally, a pair of robed figures converged on one man, subdued him with ease, quickly dragged him away.

The room went quiet. Not a breath, not a sound. Now what was that all about? Asel looked at Sylvan. Sylvan hadn't budged, hadn't heard a thing.

Asel lay back again. He was drained, hungry, aching for sleep, certain he would lie there red-eyed, awake through the night.

Just before he dropped off, he saw the face of the man they'd hauled away, the lout who'd come out of his stupor long enough to flip, long enough to lose the small hold on sanity he had.

Henry. The only man he'd officially met at Our Lady of Reluctant Desire.

Asel broke first.

An hour after he and Sylvan skipped breakfast, he fell on his face in a bed of flowers with variegated blooms. Efficient robed minions carried him in, threw cold water in his face, made him eat the breakfast he'd missed: Phlegmy tode soup. Kabige and beens. Thornberry pudding with lumps inside.

Asel threw it all up. Mary Beth/Beth Mary were both on hand to watch. They ordered the guards to stuff him again. That was too much. Everything came up, Asel went down.

He woke on his cot in the late afternoon. His mouth was a sewer. He dozed for a while, woke when they brought Sylvan in. Sylvan passed out, retched in his sleep. A horde of lackeys turned him on his belly, pounded on his back.

The light from the high, narrow windows cast golden squares upon the floor. The day died quickly in this dry, benighted land. Almost at once, night would sweep in and catch prey and predator alike, waiting in the dark.

Asel felt empty, hollow, and weak. Throwing up had been the proper thing to do, but the food he'd rejected came back to haunt him, made him sick again.

Sylvan moaned, turned over once, opened rheumy eyes, stared at Asel, went to sleep again.

Just before dark, six robed figures walked into the barracks. Two stood guard with their stubby shotguns. Four swept down the narrow aisle. Studied the off-duty workers, stopped, picked out three. Asel was puzzled. The chosen didn't cry, didn't moan, didn't seem bothered at all. Instead, their slack faces spread in loutish grins. Asel pictured three demented rubes, going to the Fair.

The other men laughed, clapped their hands as the trio crossed the room. And, as the guards led their charges away, two of the robed figures paused, hesitated at the door. It was hard to tell about people in robes, but Asel was sure they'd looked directly at him.

The incident left him with a chill. Wherever they were taking those fellows, he didn't want to go. He hadn't been drugged long enough to walk out with a smile.

When Sylvan awoke, Asel filled him in on the odd event he'd missed. He didn't mention the guards who'd looked back. It was likely he'd imagined all that, and saw no reason to burden his companion as well.

Sylvan showed little interest in the smiling louts, or anything else. Asel understood. He was sick, beaten, shorn of any feelings himself. Shaky, dizzy, starved, and out of synch.

"Sylvan, my head's not working, I can't think straight anymore. I'm having some trouble recalling where I am."

Sylvan looked partially aware. For a moment, Asel wasn't sure there was anyone there.

"What I'm thinking," Sylvan said, "is how soon breakfast is going to be."

"That's what I was thinking too."

"I'm guessing we'll make a little sense for a day or maybe two. We'll maybe recall easy words like shoe, head, water, and sky. I hope I remember night and day. I hope I don't remember the name of that shit we got to eat. I don't want to know its name."

"What?" Asel said. "What were we—what were we talking about. . . ?"

~ TWENTY-SEVEN ~

Breakfast was bad.

Lunch was horrid, then dinnertime came and darkness fell again. Asel awoke in a terrible fright. He was covered in foul-smelling sweat, shaking, quaking with an uncontrollable chill.

He decided he was dying. *Maybe I'll go before morning. No soggy breakfast, no fucking flowers, no tacky clothes . . .*

He wondered if he ought to wake Sylvan, tell him goodbye. That would be the proper thing to do. If Mother was alive, she'd be proud of that.

Worse than the quiver, the shiver, the bone-jarring chill, was the sudden, frightening knowledge that he didn't know his name.

Take it easy. Panic is the worst thing you can do . . .

"Sylvan? Wake up, please. I'm sorry, I must speak to you at once."

Sylvan groaned, went back to sleep again.

"No. You simply have to listen. This means a great deal to me. What's my name, Sylvan? That's all I want to know."

"You wake me again, asshole, I'll beat you with a hoe."

Asel give this serious thought. "You're close. I do believe it begins with an 'A.'"

Asel remembered the whole conversation in the morning, and repeated it to Sylvan as they made their way to breakfast.

"It's not just the chills and forgetting everything. I can scarcely remember *anything* that happened yesterday. It all runs together in my head. Those despicable drugs are destroying our minds, faster than we feared. So far, it wears off a little overnight. That won't last for long."

"I don't recall you waking me up. Not any of that. Damn, we'll be getting another dose at breakfast, man."

"We don't have to go. We can try that again."

"Bet that's what every one of these halfwits said. About the second day in."

Asel tried not to look at the others, at the crooked, awkward file of semi-conscious gardeners as they stumbled and shuffled their way toward the mess.

"We have to get out of here, Sylvan, no matter what the cost. Even if we don't make it, it's worth the risk to try. I will not be defective in the head. I couldn't handle that."

"You wouldn't know it. Wouldn't bother you at all."

Asel was appalled. "My God, what kind of talk is that?"

"I hope they don't have frawg again," Sylvan said.

As ever, hooded figures stood behind the orderly array of pots, kettles, and crocks, ladling squishy blobs and runny plops into each man's tin plate. And—as ever—Mary Beth, Beth Mary, and a covey of other lovely Nones hovered near, watchful as Furies, keeping an eye on the blank and somber faces of their happy garden crew.

"Looks worse than ever," Asel said, staring in disgust as a blob trickled into a plop, mixing brown and ruddy red. "Looks like something died."

"I'm thinking that's a good idea. Thinking that's what we better do."

"Better do what?"

"Die, Ace."

"You mean now? Right here?"

"Now would be good. Before we have to eat this shit."

"I don't think they'd let us. I think they've got a rule."

"I am not drugged senseless yet. Until I am, can't any damn None tell me what I got to do. I want to, then I'll—"

The man in front of Sylvan tripped, stumbled, slammed into Sylvan with a force that sent him reeling. Sylvan shouted in surprise. His plate went flying. He flailed at empty air, turned full circle and struck Asel squarely in the head.

Asel fell back, struck the man behind, passing chaos and disorder down the line. Stringy fried myce, jellied snayke, and sticky ryce flew from greasy plates. The noise raised a clatter, a terrible din. Scared, bewildered numbwits stuttered, muttered, knocked one another about.

Nones of Our Lady of Reluctant Desire went into action at once. Small silver whistles, cunningly concealed between fulsome breasts, filled the room with signals of alarm.

Dark-robed sycophants, trained for obedience and instant response, moved like wraiths to quell the riotous scene.

They seemed to work in fours. One squad appeared with mops, buckets, brushes, and brooms. Another, and another after that, converged on the rag-tag line—which, by now, had scattered into no line at all. Working with speed and extraordinary skill, order was soon restored.

Ordinarily, gardeners ate their meals at rough-hewn tables. Now, the stupefied crew were ordered to squat, legs folded, on the floor, while the cloaked ones brought them plates of food.

Even partially dazed, Asel saw through this strategy at once. Alarm and bedlam or not, the workers had to be fed, doped to the gills. Some might have a shred of a wit about them still. And, if anyone betrayed a sign of intelligence now . . .

"No thank you, nothing for me," Asel said, as a plate was shoved roughly in his face. "Snayke gives me gas, and we don't want that."

"He's right," Sylvan added, "does the same to me."

The black-robed guard leaned down, coming very close. "You two. Do not give me any trouble, do you hear?" The coarse, gravelly voice was annoying to the ear. "I must tell you, Sister Mary Beth is just waiting for an excuse to remove your nasty parts."

"She—what?"

Asel drew a breath to speak, but the figure was gone.

"We'll eat, all right? We'll throw up as soon as we can, then put our plan into action."

"There's that plan again."

"I'm working on it right now. Whatever we do, we must avoid lunch. Especially you. No offense, friend. I feel your wits are eroding just a bit faster than mine."

"I was going to say the same about you."

"In your state of mind, I can see it might appear that way to you."

"What if I throw up now? That going to fuck up your plan?"

"Yes, I am certain that it would."

"Right. I'll try and hold it down. . . ."

~ TWENTY-EIGHT ~

The Fates intervene to worsen our condition—or, on rare occasion, to make life better for a change. The chaos of breakfast greatly affected those witless fellows subject to hysterics, spasms, and speaking in tongues. Soon, these symptoms spread through the ranks like the pox, and even those not prone to such behavior began to howl, retch, and throw fits.

And, though it had seldom happened before, work was suspended, the gardeners confined to their barracks for the rest of the afternoon. Crocks of ferit soup and chunks of beetul bred were brought in by the guards.

Eat, Sleep, and Work were the only basic drives remaining in the ossified skulls of this wretched crew. Everyone ate. Everyone ate until the last drop of soup was sopped up with mealy bred. Everyone ate except Asel Iacola and Sylvan Lee McCree.

"Fortune has smiled on us, friend. I doubt we will ever get a break like this again. We must move *now*, and quickly. Tonight, they'll have us back at that garbage trough again."

Sylvan started to find some fault with Asel's plan, which was yet to be revealed. Instead, he lay down on his cot and looked at the ceiling overhead.

"I don't much care anymore that you don't know what you're saying, Asel. It scares me to think I'm getting used to it. You want to get out of here? Fine. We'll make a run for the fucking wall."

"Won't get *far* before those ugly weapons rip us into shreds. Doesn't matter much to me. I'll go down in a multi-colored mess, flesh and organs of various kind, thinking of fine filet of foxx, mullit eye surprise, flamingho *au jus*, and dolfen dick pye.

"And, if there's some kind of life after this, frisky little bare-ass flunks will bring me a cool, bold, but not too aggressive, glass of Alybama wyne."

"Foxx. We don't get a lot of that back East."

"You're missing something, friend."

"Ever eat fynch?"

"Never heard of fynch."

"Marvelous. Father used to have them sautéed in a mylkweed sauce. The thing is, though, you have to eat a great many fynches to really make a meal.

"I believe, when I'm running for glory across those foul flowerbeds, I shall think of Sally Mander pye. Uncle Hal's favorite was Sally Mander pye. When he came to Iacola Keep, Mother would always say, 'Uncle Hal's coming, Asel. I expect he'll want Mander tonight.'

"Are you ready, Sylvan? I am, if you are. I see no reason for delay."

"Broad daylight might throw 'em off. Who'd expect anyone'd do something dumb as that?"

"I guess your mind's not rotted out yet," Asel said. "You've seen right through my plan. . . ."

The easy part of a stupid plan is you don't waste time working everything out. Pesky details don't get in the way. Still, even a fool hesitates, if only for an instant, before he leaps into the abyss.

Asel, his thoughts still intent on fynch, hesitated at the door.

"Wait a minute. Let's talk about this."

"No. Let's not."

"I'm not saying we shouldn't, I definitely think we should. I feel we should consider what we'll face out there."

"This is your plan, Asel. 'Death is a far, far better thing than life without liberty,' you said. 'Though my soul is free, my body is fettered in the chains of servitude. This is a life I will not endure.'"

"I never said any such thing."

"Seems to me you did."

"Well, I didn't."

"We're going to do this, right?"

"Right. Of course."

Sylvan gripped the knob, turned it very carefully, slowly to the right.

"Not locked. That's a good sign."

"No. That's a very bad sign. It means those hooded persons don't care if some halfwit wanders out or not."

"True. But we'll turn that complacency against them. These

folks are rigid in their thinking. Do the unexpected, it'll cloud their little minds. I doubt they'll see us at all."

Asel drew in a breath as Sylvan opened the door a crack, letting in the day. After the grim, near cavernous gloom inside, that narrow slice of afternoon was bright as a fiery torch.

"I was wrong," Asel said. "We'll have to wait until it's dark."

"Dark means dinner. Dinner means drugs and frawg soup."

"There's that."

Sylvan squeezed Asel's arm in a firm, but not unseemly grip. "Just run, Ace, and don't look back. I was a climbin' fool when I was a kid. I figure I can make it over that fancy gate."

"I didn't climb a lot."

"You ready?"

"Ready, friend."

"Good luck, whatever happens, man."

"You too. And I have to say, Sylvan, though I was reluctant to accept your pigmentation, I have come to learn you are truly of noble mien, that you had no voice in choosing your shade of skin."

"I've come to overlook your complexion too. You don't hardly look dead anymore."

"I appreciate that. More than you can know."

Asel, beside himself with new, untried emotions, gave Sylvan a manly hug.

Sylvan threw the door wide. The air smelled fresh, and the pressing heat of the sun swelled their bodies with strength. The two companions ran, wild and free, and, as they ran, they grinned at one another and laughed out loud, for no one—if anyone were there—could ever doubt their courage now.

They ran, ran with all the highborn vigor they could muster, ran a good five yards, six, deftly turned the corner of the barracks, stopped dead in their tracks.

There were four of them, each robed figure gripping a warty weapon that flared obscenely at the end.

"You two men are quite ridiculous," said the first of the four. "Where exactly did you think you were going?"

"This is an escape," Asel said, seeing no reason to mince words now.

"Yeah," Sylvan added, "that's what it is."

"Well," said the second hooded guard, "at least you got that part right. Here." The figure glanced warily over one shoulder, then passed two cloaks to the pair.

"Get these on. Quickly. You are much too tall, but I guess there's nothing we can do about that. . . ."

~ TWENTY-NINE ~

"Don't think I'm fool enough to be taken in by this blatant ruse," Sylvan said. "There is nothing you can do to make me eat. Whatever sense I have left, I'm keeping intact—"

"Do what you are told!" The third hooded figure thrust a copper muzzle in Sylvan's belly, thrust it hard enough to make the point clear.

"You will both obey orders," said Number Four. "We are wasting precious time."

With that, Four and the others led the two friends double time past the barracks and onto the clearing beyond. As they passed the mess hall, Sylvan was sure he picked up the distinctive scent of frawg.

"May I ask a question," Asel said, turning to Number Three.

"No."

"It would clarify an issue, I believe. Is your group new here? I wondered, you see, because the other robed persons all sound alike. As if they had a mouthful of mud. Your group sounds as if the maid dropped dishes on the floor, but you're not as harsh as the rest."

"Do not speak *again!* And try to be short. You are not helping matters by being so tall."

Asel had a great deal more to say, but decided this was likely not the time.

Sylvan gave him a look, a glare, sideways at best, from the corner of his eye. The looked warned Asel not to be lulled or taken in. And, not to eat anything that might be offered by these cunning new friends.

Yes. I quite understand, he nodded back. He wished he could speak, for he had noted, with alarm, they were not being herded toward freedom and the gate, but further away, toward a group of buildings beyond the barracks and the mess—flat, colorless structures where gardeners were not allowed to go.

What if Sylvan was right, and these were not, as his glance had implied, truly friends at all? Still, why would they employ this sly subterfuge, simply to make them eat? That seemed unlikely, but what were they up to, then?

No answer came to mind, but another, frightening question instead. As they passed a row of squat structures, another horde of cowled figures appeared—five squads of four, all bearing wicked weapons with blistered barrels and deadly snouts. They loped, at a furious pace, directly toward Asel's group, as if they intended to engage them head on.

Then, as if some signal had passed between them, they fanned out to the left and to the right, each figure bringing a weapon up sharply, slapping the barrel twice.

"Nicely done," Sylvan said, deciding to risk a remark. "I saw the Tennieshoe 887th Swamp Viper Guards go through their paces one time. These folks are no match for your Southern trooper, but I'll say they—"

"*Get down! Now-now-now!*"

Someone slammed Asel in the back. He went down fast, hit the ground hard. Saw deadly flares of light burst from the building just ahead. Heard the *chatta-chatta-chatt!* of the weapons, heard the buzz, heard the angry whine of lead overhead.

Hugging the dirt, digging at the soil with more zeal, zest, than he'd ever shown with a hoe, Asel saw figures erupt from the building, weapons clutched in their hands, heard the screams, heard the cries, saw them sag, saw them crumple to the ground.

He stared, unable to comprehend the horrid sight before his eyes. Trim and tailored habits were reduced to shredded rags, tainted by death's ugly gore. Elegant, ravishing creatures barely moments before, were reduced to a slender limb here, a shattered face there, golden hair now scarlet in final disarray.

Nones. Six in all, perhaps. Who could say in this tangle, this terrible display? Dust and spent powder rose in a veil from these silent, empty husks, neither haughty nor enticing anymore, only shells of bone and flesh.

Surely this can only be nightmare, a grim illusion, this deathly array . . .

"You. Get *up*," someone said. "There is nothing to look at here. . . ."

* * *

Asel was glad he could not read the features beneath those darkened hoods. Clearly, they had rebelled against their Order; he could scarcely blame them for that. And, for a reason he had yet to fathom, they had freed a pair of prisoners, taken them along on their chill and bloody spree. Grateful on the one hand, he found it hard to trust his benefactors now.

The squads of robed soldiers trotted away as quickly as they had appeared. No one paused to look at the dead. Asel's Four led their charges at a run, stopping at a building a hundred yards away.

Two of the figures stood guard. The other pair moved forward, and swung two wide, wooden doors aside.

Asel could only see shadows. Sylvan, though, whom Asel believed could see much better in the dark, shouted aloud with great intent:

"Shit, Ace, will you look at that!"

And, as Asel was allowed to walk closer, he was greeted by a sight that brought joy to his heart.

"It's our truck," he said, laughing aloud, *"it's our own fucking truck!"*

"That's clearly what it is. And a whole lot cleaner and in better shape than we left it, too."

Sylvan turned to face the Four. "So who's the wizard here? Who do we have to thank for this?"

"It was not one of us," said Number Two. "We know nothing of such things."

"One of the Sisters," added Three. "She had some knowledge of mechanical arts before she took her vows."

"Yeah, well." After what he'd witnessed outside, Sylvan didn't care to talk of Nones. He walked around the truck, kicking gently at the tires. "Whoever. She did a fine job, I got to give her that. Dents. Bullet holes. The works."

"Yes. That is so." Number One took a step forward. "Now. You must make it go."

"What's that again?"

"Which of you is the goer? This is what we need to know."

Sylvan looked at Asel. They didn't need to speak. Neither liked the sound, the nuance, the possible implications of this. They knew this crew had a most efficient way of meeting their needs.

"We are both drivers—goers," Asel said.

"Both of us," Sylvan said. "If I understood you correctly, you are not familiar with this device. An intricate piece of machinery does not simply—go without two goers in control at all times."

The hooded ones looked at one another, then back to Sylvan and Asel.

"You are correct, we do not. However, we have examined the device. There is only one set of goer-things. There is one, not two."

Sylvan grinned at that. "You're not a goer, though, right?"

"I have told you none of us have this ability."

"Then it's easy to see you do not know Goer Number One holds onto the round thing," Asel put in, "while Goer Two taps the dials."

"Dials?"

"Round things under glass, with little numbers inside."

"You aren't tapping dials," Sylvan said, with a resignation and a sigh, "you are not about to do a go."

The Four conferred once more. "If this is so, both of you will be required."

Sylvan showed them his finest smile. "Then both of us will be pleased to do all that we can do. . . ."

~ THIRTY ~

Sylvan explained to Asel that he, Asel, had been Goer One before, it was only fair that Asel should now serve as Goer Two. Thus, the hooded ones warily took their places in the truck—one squeezed in front, another in the space behind the seats. Two of the crew took a careful look outside, opened the double door, ran back, and piled in with the rest.

The motor sputtered, coughed, wheezed, and then died, awarding minor strokes to Goers One and Two. Finally, the engine caught hold, thrummed into life. Asel and Sylvan grinned, to show they had never been concerned at all.

The sun was veiled by clouds of varied hues—coral, pink, mauve, and a quite outlandish rose.

"I think I should ask which way I ought to Go," Sylvan said, above the engine's roar. "Those of us who've been unjustly detained are not familiar with the grounds."

"The gate, of course," said Number One, in a somewhat surly tone. "When you pass the last structure, you will see it again. Turn this thing in that direction at once."

"That gate will be closed," Asel said. "I hope you've made allowances for that."

"And who did you imagine *keeps* it closed?"

"We do," said Four. "We do the open, we do the close."

"Exactly," said Three.

"Just do your job, Goers," said One. "Do not waste time on matters that scarcely concern you at all."

Sylvan muttered under his breath, but nothing the others could hear. He said no more, but took great joy in plowing through every neat, well-kept bed of flowers he could find, veering sharply off course to ruin some colorful array.

Asel was alarmed at this bold and vengeful act, but the hooded ones apparently didn't care. They clutched their weapons and stared straight ahead. Maybe, Asel thought, they imagined jerking recklessly about was part of the ritual of Go. Meanwhile, as Goer Number Two, he tapped the row of dials now and then.

As they passed the last structure, Sylvan, as instructed, turned sharply to the left. There, indeed, was the high, foreboding gate, with its curlicues, whorls, menacing spikes, and the legend—backward from a prisoner's point of view—OUR LADY OF RELUCTANT DESIRE.

Asel gave a sigh of relief. Here, indeed, was the final barrier to freedom—escape from drugged oppression, gardening, and really disgusting food. Once they were past, once this dreadful place lay behind—

Shouts, cries, shrieks of alarm thrust Asel's thoughts aside. For a moment, he imagined the horror he'd witnessed had returned to confound his mind.

Instead, he saw to his dismay, this was yet another site of slaughter, misery, and pain. Bent and twisted shapes lay sprawled in disarray among a vibrant field of asphydel, bloobell, nuttercup, and flox. Some, a few, were dark-robed guardians. Ten, a dozen, more than Asel cared to count, were silken-clad Nones. All of them flaxen-haired, all of them beauties, *all of them dead . . .*

And, as if this horrid scene were not enough, before his unbelieving eyes, one of these torn and bloodied figures rose, clutching an ugly weapon in pale and shaking hands.

Asel felt as if the blood had frozen in his veins.

Mary Beth! Beth Mary! Great God, who could say which?

"It is. It is she, for certain," said Three, clearly reading Asel's thoughts.

"Stop. Stop this device at once," said Number One.

Sylvan, who felt this was not a sensible move at all, did as he was told. The truck had scarcely screeched to a halt before Number One raised a heavy weapon, sighted down the barrel, and gave an audible sigh.

"You really—don't have to do that," Asel said. "I doubt she can hit us from there."

"No. I don't think she can," said One.

The weapon slammed twice against a robed shoulder. The harsh explosion rang in Asel's ears. Mary Beth/Beth Mary was yanked off her feet, as if some giant had tugged her on a string. She fell, arms and legs a'sprawl. One hand twitched, and then she was still.

"An excellent shot, if I may say," said Three.

"You may not," One said. "You and Two, see to the gate. Four, stay here with me."

One turned to Sylvan and Asel. "I have watched your every move. Do not think that I have not. I have observed that it does *not* require two goers to keep this machine in motion. We shall discuss this matter quite soon. . . ."

~ THIRTY-ONE ~

The sun had scarcely vanished before the shroud of night swept quickly across the land. Asel guessed the gate was a good half-hour behind before Number One told Sylvan to stop. The two friends were ordered away from the truck, while the Four huddled together to talk.

Asel felt this whispered discussion was ominous at best. Clearly, Number One had seen through the "Two Goer" ruse. The future of one of the friends was very much in doubt.

"If they decide on me," Sylvan said, "which they very well might, since they know I can drive, I shall run off the road and kill the whole bunch. If I should survive, I'll come back and give you a decent burial, Ace. You can count on that."

"No," Asel said, "that's asking too much."

"It's the least I can do. We have been friends for some time."

"It may be they won't choose you. For the very reason that they *have* seen you drive. What I suggest is we don't wait around to find out. We can make a run for it, Sylvan. It's getting quite dark, and I think we would have a good chance."

"That Number One is a real good shot."

"True. But if we run in opposite directions, I doubt we will both be hit."

Sylvan's expression told Asel what he thought about that. Asel, as a fact, wasn't too fond of this proposal himself. He had no love for Beth Mary/Mary Beth, or the other Nones as well. Still, it was dreadful to think of those twisted, lifeless forms. Especially if you were one too.

"All right, it's a plan that has flaws. Still, we are both of noble mien. Our families would feel we had done the proper thing if we went down fighting, instead of—instead of the other way."

"Your family's all dead," Sylvan said. "So is mine."

"True. But if they weren't."

"You got to come up with something better than that."

"Fine. You're welcome to suggest a better idea."

"I'm thinking I've got a fifty-fifty chance of getting blown away. Same as you."

"Some of your family may have survived, Sylvan. It is possible I have an Iacola nephew or two somewhere. It's them I'm thinking about, not us."

"Good. You think about 'em all you like. I'll be thinking—"

Sylvan stopped, raised a curious brow, then squinted at the darkening sky they'd left behind.

"Look at that. Tell me what I'm seeing back there."

Asel followed Sylvan's gaze. A distant, but quite distinct glow appeared on the horizon, a flare of red light that brightened, faded, then brightened again.

"Something's on fire, I believe. And there's nothing back there except the compound. It can't be anything else."

"It isn't. You are quite correct in that...."

They turned as one, startled to see a hooded figure there.

"It's the Nonery," said Number One. "I hope those we missed are inside. If any got away, my people will track them down."

In spite of the hot and muggy air, Asel felt a chill.

"You did that? You—burned them alive in there?"

"Don't be foolish. Of course we didn't. You were with us, you shouldn't have to ask. Everyone has their duties. The incineration—the honor—went to the Little Mothers. No one would deny them that."

"The little what?"

The hooded one sighed. "You are boorish and ignorant at best. Still, I suppose you have been quite helpful in this. The Little Mothers are chosen by the Sister Superior. They are chosen to breed. You saw us remove three gardener persons in the night. Their task was to fertilize next year's crop. Offspring from this are sold to dealers from Califoggy State. The Sisters made a very nice profit out of this."

Asel shared the hooded figure's disgust. "Those—those dimwits had carnal enterprise with Nones? That's monstrous!"

"The Sisters?" Number One laughed, a fairly pleasant sound, for a change, neither deep nor overly coarse. "Certainly not. The

Little Mothers are the unfortunate ones among us chosen for this despicable act."

Asel looked bewildered. He glanced at Sylvan, back to Number One. "Among—among *us?*"

"You couldn't know, of course. I never thought of that. My companions and I are—were, acolytes of Our Lady of Reluctant Desire. We are taken, brought here quite young. We do as we're told or our families suffer."

For a moment, Number One looked thoughtfully back the way they had come. "I have not allowed myself to consider this moment before. Now, it is done. We are no longer bound by our vows. I see no reason we cannot put these hateful, cumbersome garments to rest."

With that, the figure before the pair swept the dark hood aside, loosed the heavy robe. Asel and Sylvan were stunned, struck dumb by what they saw. Even in darkness, with only the light of the stars, they were dazzled by abundant locks of raven hair, by a full and generous mouth, by questioning brows, by dark and penetrating eyes.

"Gods save us," Asel said, "you are, aren't you? You're a person of the opposite persuasion, a—a *woman* is what you are!"

"Any fool can see that I am," said Number One, with more than a hint of impatience in her tone. "And, in your position, I would not be hasty to condemn us for what we are. There is no disgrace in our gender, only the shame the cursed, and double-damned Sisters have put upon us. I pray they are burning in fires much hotter than the ones they suffered here. . . ."

~ THIRTY-TWO ~

"Most girls are taken from their families when they are ten. The Sisters are ruthless, but they are deviously clever as well. A girl is quite vulnerable at that tender age. Old enough to long for her former life, but young enough to be trained. She is frightened, of course, but she understands what can happen to her family if she disobeys.

"She learns very quickly what punishment can mean. You know to do as you are told. If you do not, you will suffer at the hands of the Sisters of Reluctant Desire."

"How long has this terrible injustice been going on?" Asel asked. "Surely this can't be the first time someone has tried to escape those walls?"

Number One showed him a weary smile. With her heavy cloak and hood cast aside, she no longer seemed the uncaring creature who had gunned down her foes only hours before. Now, she appeared to be an attractive young woman, scarcely over twenty or so —a woman able to speak to outsiders for the first time in years.

"I cannot answer your question. I don't *know* how long the Sisters have been getting away with their wicked ways. Who can say? You don't think they'd tell *us*, do you?"

"No," Sylvan said, "I don't suppose they would. But surely some of the older—acolytes would know."

"Older?" For a moment, the woman paled. "There are no *older* acolytes. No one older than those you see here. When you're past breeding age, you're sent—somewhere else."

"You're not sent somewhere else. They sell you, is what they do. To those filthy Rangers, or men in Two-kum-curry."

While Number One had been speaking, the other acolytes had

begun to join her, one by one, reluctant at first, then all three were there.

"That's the truth," said Four. "You see a friend one day, you never hear from her again."

"If we'd stayed around much longer," said Two, "the same thing would've happened to us."

"I know what *acolyte* means," said Number One. "We're not supposed to know how to read, but most of us do. It means you're a novice, training to become something else. Only that doesn't happen at Our Lady. No one gets to be anything more than they are."

There were always twenty-seven Nones, Asel and Sylvan learned. It was a magic number of some kind, part of their secret rites.

If a Sister died, another was brought in from outside, always a younger woman from some wealthy family in Califoggy, or one of the Franchise States. The daughters of the rich were honored to become a part of the Sisterhood. And, each time a Sister was brought into the fold, the Order gained new entry into the world of commerce and trade. Their web stretched far and wide, and their riches had made them a power far beyond their iron gates.

It always comes to that, Asel thought, *always the threat, growing from the West*.

Now they were reaching out to swallow the Eastern empires like Iacola Keep. Sylvan had never said Califoggy was behind the ruin of his Southern domains. If this were true, he surely didn't know. But it wasn't hard to imagine Jackie Cee played a part in Sylvan's downfall as well.

And, after they had the whole country under sway? They would reach out to foreign corporations as well. There weren't just pretty flunks overseas, Asel knew, there was business for the taking, too.

"If there was money in it," Number One said, "the haughty bitches had their hands in it somewhere. Those trucks that go by day and night, they're full of those hideous statues for the San Clemente shrine. They must sell millions of the things out there."

"Tourist folk," said Number Two.

"People of the Aisyatic kind," said Three.

"Austrilites. Hindy-doos, too."

"We are familiar with the manufacturing process," Sylvan said. "We were held against our will for a while, the same as you."

"A friend of mine," Asel said, "Hank Jockey-Visa—well, not a friend, really, but I knew him at the time. He fell into a vat. Or, it may be that he jumped. He was awfully depressed. So was everyone else, of course, but Hank was the only one who fell. Or— whatever it was he did . . ."

The women looked quite puzzled. Asel let the matter go at that.

"It's getting quite late," Number One said. "And since we have nothing to eat, I suppose we should all get some rest. My companions and I will sleep in the bed of the truck. I suggest you take a care. There are always rattulsnaykes and scorps about. Other than that, I believe you'll be all right."

"Ah, shouldn't we press on awhile?" Asel suggested. "There might be some pursuit."

Number One looked surprised. "Who? There's no one left back there, I promise you that."

"I guess I forgot."

"Yes. I suppose you did." The dying glow of distant flames flickered across her cheek. She looked at the two companions a moment, then she was gone.

"I wonder," Sylvan said, "if you have any knowledge of the scientific arts. Nothing of the sort was covered in my schooling, or mentioned around the estate. But I have come to see that once you are a'venturing, there's a need for information of every kind."

"I have noticed that as well. Was it anything special you wish to know?"

"One thing in particular comes to mind. When we lie here and look at the stars, they seem to be the very same ones I have noticed at home. As a fact, the same ones that were above us at NERF. I am wondering how far we would have to go before they change."

"Change into what?"

"Into different stars, Ace. I mean, what if we were off in some foreign clime? What would you see up there then?"

Asel slapped at his cheek. He was sure he felt something with a great many legs try to crawl into his ear.

"My Uncle Hal was of a philosophical bent. He knew the names of trees. I'm certain he told me once the stars were far away. I would guess that's true. If it is, one would have to travel quite far before one saw something else."

"Makes sense. Doesn't tell you *how* far, though, does it?"

"I'm telling you what Hal told me. I'm afraid I can't add much to that."

"The one with dark hair. Number One. She's a pretty, she is. All of 'em are, especially the tall one. She's got a nice neck."

"You like necks."

"Lot of things I like. I do like a woman's got a fine neck. You take a woman, head kind of sits there like a pumpkyn on a fence . . . that woman is not attractive to me."

"I would have to know what a pumpkyn is, Sylvan, before I could comment on that."

"You haven't seen one, no use going on with this."

"I'm not too busy right now."

"If I can't eat, I'm goin' to get some sleep. Maybe I'll dream about that tall one with the neck."

"A neck is good, but there are more interesting features than that. I'm thinking of a certain flunk, a little Britt. I was quite fond of her. I hope she's being treated well. Female persons are nice. They are not like us, of course. But I imagine they're not supposed to be."

Asel was pleased with the thought. "I guess I have a philosophical bent myself. Uncle Hal would like that. I mean, if he wasn't quite dead. I don't suppose you bother about such things, after you've gone through that. . . ."

~ THIRTY-THREE ~

Asel wished Sylvan hadn't brought up that business of the stars. Now, he couldn't think of anything else. That, and pumpkyns. Whatever those might be. People shouldn't start conversations if they didn't intend to stay. You shouldn't go to sleep when someone's talking. It's not the thing to do.

"What we ought to be doing," Asel said, to the silent hump next to him, "is making a plan. We ought to be thinking what to do when the sun comes up, which can't be very long now. I do *not* intend to leave my fate in the hands of someone else. These acolyte persons clearly think only of themselves.

"And, frankly, Sylvan, though we've come to know each other well, what I ought to be thinking about is *me*. Reflecting on your actions up to now, I have to say your concern seems to focus on you . . ."

"Do you do that a lot? Sit in the dark and talk to yourself? I find that a strange thing to do."

Asel sat up at once. The girl appeared out of nowhere, a phantom against the dark.

"Have you been sitting, there, listening to me? That's very impolite."

"I haven't been here long. And I didn't hear a great deal. What I did hear was quite fascinating. You must remember, I haven't heard very many males talk. Mostly the poor dimwits at the Order. They didn't have much to say."

"That's not really their fault, is it?"

"No, of course it's not."

She looked rather frail, sitting there, hugging her shoulders. Asel thought it a wonder that a cloak and a hood could call up such a bold and frightening presence, one so quickly tossed aside.

She sounded different, as well. He had caught that difference for a moment, earlier in the night. The way she'd laughed, without that coarse and irritating tone. Now, she sounded very much like a young woman should.

And she damn well looks like one as well . . .

She caught him watching, and quickly glanced away.

"What I was *saying* was I felt your speech was much more than meaningless babble. I thought it was remarkable for a man."

"I guess I'm quite flattered."

"I meant I hadn't heard a lot of men who weren't on drugs. I intended no offense."

"I know about the drugs. I've never felt so helpless in my life. I also think I know why you caused that chaotic scene in the mess."

"Well, we didn't want you both totally senseless. The food is heavily dosed for the evening meal. Keeps the men from roaming about. If you were in *that* condition, I doubt either one of you could operate the mechanical device."

Asel felt her reasoning was sound, but he wished she hadn't put it that way.

The woman studied the ground a moment, then looked up at Asel again.

"You and your friend met the Sisters in Two-kum-curry. With that horrid Goodtime Bob."

Asel nodded. It wasn't a question, it was something she knew.

"I don't have to tell you what they were. They used their wiles upon you, and one of their toxic potions as well. They — I don't know how to say it, I am not used to words like this. They cultivate their base desires. Their insane drive for carnal union with a man. They nurture these feelings, and punish themselves by repressing them every day of their lives. This is how they reach their ecstasy, their joy. This is the madness of the Order. This is the fever that drives them to seek great power, and bring pain and misery to everyone else."

Asel was glad when she was done. The young woman was right: She was not used to speaking on matters of a lustful, erotic nature. And, while it didn't appear to make *her* uneasy, the words had a startling effect upon him.

"I find it hard to imagine a discipline more peculiar, perverse, unusual, to say the least," Asel said.

"No. I doubt you have any idea what it was like."

"I am sure that's true. I could see how you might find matters of the intimate persuasion quite distasteful, after all you've been through."

"Oh, but we don't. We don't feel that way at all."

"Ah—you don't?"

"No. Not now. We did, of course. Acolytes are put on drugs when we reach the age of deviant desire. Not the same as the gardeners get, but it numbs the mating urge quite well. We're addicts, same as the poor creatures back there."

"That's terrible. I'm very sorry about that."

"Don't be. The Sister who handed out the pills got very ill. All right, we *made* her very ill. The new Sister wasn't very smart. We all cut down our doses. Everyone did. That's how we found the will to get free."

The young woman smiled. "Our voices don't sound so awful anymore. Like frawgs, or something. I know you noticed that. I'm sure it won't be long before we're not disgusted with the thought of copulation, and perversions of every sort. I probably shouldn't tell you this at all. Please don't take offense."

"No, that's quite all right," Asel said. "If there's any way I can help—"

"Thank you. I don't believe you can right now." She rose, then, gracefully unfolded and stood above him, against the bright stars. She had fashioned a crude sort of garment out of her robe and cowl. She had no taste for style, and little knowledge of what a woman covered, or what she left revealed. Considering his own shabby wear, Asel felt he had no business offering fashion advice.

"I almost forgot. My name is Cele. I haven't been able to use it since I was ten."

"I'm very pleased to meet you, Cele. Formally, that is."

"And you're Asel. He's Sylvan. I never saw anyone painted brown. We'll talk again in the morning. About who we'll pick to be Goer, I mean. . . ."

~ THIRTY-FOUR ~

Asel woke cold, hungry, eyes full of grit. Woke from a dream in which Nones thrashed him soundly with astyrs and flox. Later, strange leather devices came into play.

There were whirly patterns in the sand where he'd slept. He was certain snaykes had crawled on his person in the night. He turned to wake Sylvan, to warn him serpents were about, but Sylvan wasn't there.

Things began to itch. Asel reached in his trousers to scratch. A chorus of laughter brought him to a stop. He sat up quickly and watched. Former acolytes romped and pranced about in their hastily fashioned wear.

Asel's heart skipped a beat at this most delightful sight. A flock, a pack, a covey of long-legged lovelies was almost as good as breakfast and a bath. Almost, but not quite. Cele, though, and the one with curly hair, he might give up the bath.

Why couldn't I have a dream like that? Why can't you dream what you want to, instead of something else?

Sylvan appeared from behind the truck. The night before, Asel had parked it under a stand of trees, hoping for shade the next day. He noted, now, the trees were devoid of any leaves.

"Truck looks fine, Ace. Got a little sand on the glass, took care of that. Didn't start it up, those ladies were asleep at the time."

"They are certainly not asleep now."

Sylvan grinned. "Isn't that a sight? Who'd of believed what wonders lay hidden, beneath those tacky robes? Here, thought you might like a swallow of this."

With an elegant gesture, Sylvan reached behind his back and thrust a weathered bottle under Asel's nose.

"Water?" Asel stared for an instant, then snatched the vessel and drank it down, spilling a great deal along the way.

"Where in hell did this come from? Not in this blasted place." He turned the bottle over, in case he'd missed a drop. "I hope there's more. I believe I drank it all."

"Nice of you to think about others. I didn't find it. Arlene did, the one with dippy eyes? Out doing her business, found a kinda spring. Says that's why we got trees. Says we got water down below."

"It tastes like snayke, but I will gladly overlook that. I don't suppose she found a suitable inn. Somewhere we can get a decent meal."

"Ought to be grateful for what you got."

"I wasn't brought up to be grateful, and neither were you. We have sunk beneath our station, but I don't have to like it, friend. Since we lost our rightful due, we have seen a lot of people who have nothing at all. I am sorry they don't, but there is nothing I can do about that. What I'd like to do now is get another drink, and discuss our plan to get out of this dry and dismal land."

"Good idea. I'm listening, man."

"I didn't say I *had* a plan. I said we need to discuss the matter."

Asel glanced at the four beauties again. They were sitting in a circle, now, in the shadow of the truck, beneath the desert trees. In a moment or so, the sun would swallow the dawn and begin another blazing arc across the sky.

"I talked with one of the women last night. You were asleep. She told me some fascinating facts about her life back there."

"I know. 'Fascinating' falls short, you ask me."

"You were awake? Why didn't you say something?"

"You were doing fine. Didn't want to stop the flow."

Asel gave Sylvan a curious glance. "You were awake. I went to sleep after the girl left. Why do I think you didn't go to sleep too?"

"I was fascinated, couldn't drop off at all."

"Right. And you did what then?"

"Who said I did something? Didn't say that. Okay, I took a little walk. Ran into that tall girl, the one with the neck."

"The one who found water."

"Huh-uh. That was Arlene. This is Linette. The one with the neck."

"You and Linette, you mention who'd be the best driver today —as a Goer for the truck? How you can handle a mechanical device, with no help from your friend?"

Sylvan looked appalled. "What are you saying? I am hurt, Asel.

This, from a fellow noble, a person whose pasty skin I have come to overlook, because he is my friend."

"All right, you didn't. So I apologize."

"I don't know if I accept."

"You see how it might look to me. I'm talking to this attractive person who is barely clad at all, she is telling me erotic behavior is fine, now, she might want to start. Then she tells me she doesn't *know*, just yet, who'll be the Goer today. And you're out working on votes in the dark."

"Wasn't votes I was working on. Had something else in mind."

"The one I talked to, Cele. Thinks you're painted brown."

"Linette thinks I look just fine."

"I never said you didn't."

"You never said, 'Sylvan, I admire the dark intensity of your skin.'"

"You think I'd say something like that?"

"Wasn't thinking you saying it *that* way, just that you nev—"

Sylvan didn't finish. His mouth moved properly but nothing came out. He stared past Asel, over Asel's shoulder at the fast approaching dawn. His eyes went wide, his jaw went slack. Asel heard it, before he could turn around—the snarl, the whine, the angry buzz of beas, of hornets pissed to some degree.

Sylvan shouted something, jerked him to the ground. The sound, the shriek, grew louder still. Asel heard a noise like *snicka-snicka-snack!* Dirt rose in geysers, stitching an even line across the sand. Asel clutched the ground as something roared by, only inches overhead.

One roar followed the first, then another and another after that, slamming waves of wind to the earth, leaving the stink of kerosene.

Asel pulled himself up, spat out sand, saw the women scatter, saw one trip, saw she wasn't hurt, turned and squinted at the sky.

There were three of them, boxy craft in shades of yellow-green. One by one they veered sharply to the left, circling low, nearly out of sight.

"Shit," Sylvan said, "damn Nones aren't all dead yet!"

"It isn't Nones," Asel said, for he had spotted the leaping vole painted on the craft, a black, furry creature with blood-red eyes, the symbol of Disney-Dow, an emblem that filled him with a rage he could scarcely contain.

"They're Sony-Chanels. Two-seater, double-wing. K-Sevens or Eights. Hard to tell from here."

"Come on, you got no more mechanical bent than me."

"I doubt I have any at all. Father got the company when he bought out the Sweeds. By rights those are *my* devices that are trying to kill us, Sylvan. This is intolerable, it's simply not fair— Damn those fellows, they're coming back again!"

No one had to tell Sylvan. He hit the dirt fast. Asel came to his feet, raised his fists at the screaming craft, firmly stood his ground.

The rattle, the chatter, the *snicka-snicka-snack!* of gunfire filled the morning air. Fountains of sand peppered the earth at Asel's feet, but Asel didn't move, for he was overcome with fury, rancor, bile, and dark offense, so filled with wrath that fear had no chance at all to gain hold.

Sylvan tried to pull him down. Asel shook him off. A sudden clatter of weapons, a *ticka-ticka-tick* instead of a *snick*, told him the women were returning the attackers' fire. Sprinting for the truck, Sylvan grabbed a spare repeater and tracked the last craft as it howled overhead. Too late, he recalled he had little knowledge of weapons, didn't know what to pull. Still, in the furor of combat, no one seemed to care, no one noticed at all. . . .

~ THIRTY-FIVE ~

The sudden silence held the morning in unnatural suspense. Lead had pruned the scrawny trees, scattered dry branches about. The raiders had hit the truck twice—once in the bed, once in a fender up front. There were craters in the sand. A herd of aunts was angry. A rattulsnayke was dead.

None of the acolytes had been injured in the fight, except for Linette. Linette had skinned her knee. Sylvan was giving his full attention to the scratch, and assured everyone she'd be fine.

"Those fellows were terrible shots," Asel told Cele, as they walked around the truck. "They'd never make it at Iacola Keep. Mother had her flunks raise turnips. I never learned why. Marksman Clydde could snap the head off a hayre from fifty yards away. They never got a turnip, not while Clydde was around."

"We were very lucky," Cele said.

"Yes, we certainly were. I wouldn't count on luck if they come back again."

"Oh, they will. I'd say two, three hours at best."

"You would?"

She smiled at his sudden apprehension. "Of course, you wouldn't know that. We've seen flyers come over now and then. They pester that Ranger bunch, over to the east. I think their field is south. Past Karl's Bed, maybe El Pasta, down there. They'll have to refuel, arm their weapons again."

Asel frowned. "Flyers like those? Like the ones we saw today?"

"Not exactly. Skinny blue ones, I think. Blue and white, with only one wing."

"Baccarat-Porsche, I'll wager. Mono J-Fours. Hershey-GE sold them to Ole Mechsyko. Watched their stock go to hell on Father's ticker, last day at the Keep."

He bit his lip and looked at Cele, tried very hard to center his attention on her face. Though her features were endearing, his eyes kept straying to other parts as well.

It was hard to look at Cele and even think about matters like breakfast, shade, death from the air. All of the women from the compound were somewhat attractive—all of them, now, scantily attired.

Cele, though, was special, a young and slender miss with incredible legs, and whoopers that were, in Asel's eyes, just the right size. That, and a belly button that made him want to cry. It wasn't an innie, as he usually preferred, but precious all the same.

"I was afraid of this. I have to say I think you're likely right. Those louts will be back for sure."

Cele raised a brow. "You know something I don't know. Maybe you'd better tell me what it is."

Indeed, a thought had been scurrying about in Asel's head, a thought that was fraught with anger and dread.

"I don't think they're after your people. I think they're after me."

"Why, though? And if they are, how would they know you're here?"

"I've tangled with Califoggy State before. Your former enslavers are tight with those people, you told me so yourself."

Cele chewed her lip. "I think I need to talk to the others. If what you say is true, we have less time than I thought."

"Rest assured, my companion and I will do all we can to help. You got us out of that horrid place, and we're not ungrateful, Cele."

"That's very kind. Truly, it is." She held him with a somewhat heated gaze, held him, suspended, for what seemed to Asel a wondrous, agonizing moment in time. When she finally looked away, turned and disappeared beyond the truck, Asel was aware he'd been holding his breath, that he might have exploded if she hadn't gone away.

Reason and logic said this was no time to be struck by a pretty girl's charms. But, as Asel knew, reason had no place in matters of love, fascination of the moment, or simple carnal desire. That sort of thing was simply *there*, at convenient or totally awkward times.

And, truth of the matter, none of them had much chance of

getting out alive. There was no place to hide. A man in an areo-machine would have to be blind not to spot them in this flat and featureless land.

And, even if a fellow couldn't shoot worth a damn, he could come back later and watch them all starve.

Still, we have a little time, Asel thought. *She has said that drugs no longer cloud her mind. If I can make her see we have no right to deny ourselves, before we leave this mortal plane. . . .*

He woke in a sweat. The sun had reached its noonday height, eaten up the shade, left him on the wrong side of the truck.

He couldn't believe he'd dozed off. Worse still, though his throat was parched, the pangs of hunger had simply disappeared. That was likely a very bad sign.

He drew himself up to his knees. Paused, and tried again. A welcome shadow blocked the sun from his eyes.

"Bad idea, sleeping in the heat out here. Take a drink, Ace. Not too much at one time."

Asel grabbed the bottle and drank it down. "I didn't intend to nap, I'm not as dense as that. You should have gotten me up. We must get out of here, Sylvan, there's very little time."

"Yeah, we need to do that."

Even in his fuzzy state of mind, Asel detected something in Sylvan's tone, something that wasn't right.

"What? Let me in on it too."

"In on what, man?"

"You tell me."

Sylvan looked away. "I guess we need to talk. Let's get out of the sun."

"Let's not. I'm used to the heat. I'll die a lot slower in the shade."

"No one's going to die, Asel."

"Don't tell me what to do. What's going on? Let's get to it right now."

"The women. They had a kind of meeting."

"Okay."

"They are not content with the situation here."

"I'll go along with that."

"They feel they need to take alternate steps. To think in a different perspective, as they say."

"I'd welcome a different perspective. If you'll give me a hand, we can join the discussion now."

"No, we can't do that."
"Why not?"
"Because this perspective we're talking about—shit, man, they're not here. They're gone."
"Gone?" Asel sat up. The motion sent the sky circling dizzily overhead. "What is this, Sylvan? Gone where? There's no fucking place to go!"
"Yeah, there is," Sylvan said. He was clearly miserable, wishing all this would go away. "They're going north. One of 'em, Ettie Dee? She's got family. There's supposed to be a river a day from here, a settlement where they can rest, maybe get food, go on and find Ettie's folks."

Asel was bewildered, too much was rushing into his head.
"All right. Fine. Can't stay here, no question of that. I suppose you're going to tell me why they went ahead without the truck. Walking out in the heat, that doesn't make sense. We go pick them up. They could've ridden from the start. We—What, Sylvan? I know that look, I don't think I'll like what I'm going to hear."

Sylvan peered over the flats. "They don't want to *go* in the truck, don't want to be anywhere near it, those flyin' things come back. What happened is, you went and told Cele those fellows are looking for *you*. That's kinda what it's about."

Asel pounded a fist against his head. "Yes, right, that's what I said. I didn't think she'd—use my words against me. My God, Sylvan, who can you trust in this world? I've been deceived, betrayed at every turn. Every time I think about Father, Mother, Uncle Hal. *Everybody's* dead but me.

"So now what do we do? Those ladies have an answer to that? We just leave the truck here, walk up to—to Addie, Eddie, whats-her-name's place? Will this Arlene of yours find us a spring? A nice place to eat? Sylvan, if we follow these goofy women we're going to perish out here."

"It isn't just the truck."
"What's not the truck?"
"It isn't just the truck. They said they're sorry, they hope you understand. They feel if you go along, that might put them in severe straits too."

"Oh, well shit. Thank you very much."
"No, now, it's going to be okay, you'll see."
"I can see it is."
"Here's what I'm thinking, what we ought to do. I kinda told Linette, and 'course the others too, I'd see 'em safe till dark, get

them on their way, settled for the night. They can rest up, take a couple days before they head on.

"What I'm suggesting is, you go east with the truck. Keep south of Two-kum-curry, TechsMechs, all that shit. I catch up where we crossed that river, you know the one I mean? Wasn't any deeper'n spit, we ought to—"

"*You traitor, you miserable fuck!*"

Asel swung on Sylvan, hit him with a right, struck him with a left that sent him sprawling, knocked him hard against the truck. Spent all he had with two blows, fell back on the sand.

"Damn, Ace, what's got into you?" Sylvan shook his head and rubbed his jaw. "Something I said?"

Asel leaned his arms against the truck. "After all we've been through, nobles on the run, comrades in arms, you turn on me like this. Everybody else, I'm getting used to that. You, I expected something better. I never imagined you'd run like a dawg."

"Hey, that's about enough." Sylvan picked himself up. "You got no right to say that. This is a wrenching decision for me. Those ladies were scared, Asel, frightened half to death. That's why I said I'd help. And you ought to know I'm coming back."

"Don't give me that." Asel laughed, more a hack, more a croak than anything else. "Those *frightened* ladies slaughtered a couple dozen people yesterday, you don't recall that? What this is about is that very tall girl, the one with the neck. The one that has sexual congress with—with persons from the South."

Sylvan went rigid. Asel saw the look in his eyes. Saw there was no longer anger there, only pain and despair.

"You know I didn't mean anything by that."

"Yeah, you never did."

"Well I didn't."

"Try and take care. Remember that right wheel wobbles, you try and turn fast."

Asel drew a parched breath to speak, but Sylvan had turned away, walked around the truck. Asel wanted to tell him again he didn't mean what he said. Or didn't think he did.

The other thing he thought was he wished he'd asked Sylvan the way to the spring. Now he had to find it by himself, and pretty fucking quick. . . .

~ THIRTY-SIX ~

He wanted to stop, wanted to quit, wanted, with dull desperation, to give up, let the sun have him, lie down and sleep, forget the whole thing. Instead, he stumbled about, half blind, dazzled with the heat until he fell, at last, and tripped over the spring. It wasn't like the spring he'd imagined. Nothing but a trickle under cracked and weathered stone. Still, it was the finest trickle he'd ever seen.

Someone, Sylvan or the deceitful acolytes, had, in the throes of kindness, left a bottle and an empty can in the truck. Asel filled both vessels, drank all he could hold, and staggered back.

He tried to eat the dead snayke. Threw it up at once. He guessed it was three, four in the afternoon. If the raiders came back, they'd likely do it soon. And when they did . . .

He took a precious swallow of his water, climbed in the driver's seat, started up the truck. Breathed a sigh of relief, let the engine idle, took another drink.

He wondered how far he could get before they came. Using all the logic he could muster, he knew how far didn't matter at all. They were up there, he was down *here*. The desert was flat, there was no place to hide. They could see for miles. Maybe this time the gunners could shoot. He didn't have a weapon, couldn't shoot back. The women hadn't been as generous as that.

He tried to keep Cele out of his head. She kept coming back. She could have said goodbye. Was that too much to ask? He'd felt they were right on the edge of romance. Now she was gone, before they'd given lust a chance.

It was five or maybe six. He lay in the shallow pit beneath a stand of desert brush. Some kind of creature had dug a hole, made some kind of nest. The dirt was loose, and easier to dig. He jerked up other bushes, piled them atop his hole. Tearing off a piece of his shabby trousers, he soaked the cloth in water from the spring, and laid it over his face.

The hole was cooler than the sun-baked surface, it wasn't too bad. Now and then, he took small sips from his bottle, never as much as he wanted, never enough to make the thirst go away.

He dozed now and then. Woke up each time, crying out, thrashing about to get free. Dreamed every time he was lying in a grave. Started laughing and couldn't stop. The dream was no fancy, it was very likely real.

He thought it was close to seven. The shadows were long, the sun had vanished behind a bank of clouds. He was drifting off a lot. There were sudden bursts of sound. Bright lights flashed. Round things darted before his eyes. He didn't know if the lights or sounds were in his head. Once, when he was twelve, he'd swiped a bottle of chedyr wyne from Mother, gotten awful dizzy, but this worse than that.

He knew the aero-machines were real. Nothing in his dreams had snarled or whined, nothing made that sputter-fart sound when the engines missed and caught again. He listened awhile, raised up and risked a look. There were two this time, barely visible, tiny dots against the clouds. They made a wide circle, came around twice, then veered off toward the fast-approaching night.

Asel waited until he was sure they were gone, then threw the brush aside, filled up his bottle at the spring, staggered back to the truck. Califoggy snaykes, assholes. They'd never come close. They hadn't seen the truck at all.

The moon was full and the sky was full of stars. He waited as long as he could to use the lights. For the most part, the country was flat, but there were stands of brush and prickle plants about. Washed-out gullies where he had to slow down.

He was tired, parched, worn to the bone, but he knew he couldn't stop, knew he had to get as far as he could before dawn. The fliers might not come again, but he couldn't count on that. He had to find cover before the sun came up. The only trouble was, there wasn't a shred of cover anywhere around.

He found it. Just as the first dim glow of false dawn smeared the morning sky. *Trees.* Not spindly dried-up, twisty fucking trees, real trees, trees that grew close. Trees that had trunks, trees that had leaves.

He knew, if he hadn't been half-asleep, he might have expected trees. The land had been rising, and even in the night you could see the desert giving way to greener, thicker brush.

He wished he had listened when Uncle Hal talked about trees. He recalled the names of three: Mapul was one, asch was another. And helm. There had been a lot of helms around Iacola Keep.

None of those trees were here. He thought one might be a pyne. The other kind was smaller, with ghostly, sheer white bark you could see even before the light.

Asel didn't care about names. What he cared about was cover from the sky. He squeezed the truck as far as it would go between the white trees, turned off the engine and doused the lights.

"What I'll do," he said, after he drank as much of his water as he dared, "is get out and stretch, have a look around, get a little sleep. Then, in the morning, look for some water, find a decent place to eat."

He thought about deep-fried krow. Gofer tail, nettul soup, chipmonkee pye. He thought about water, cold, pure, and crystal clear. Parsnyp ahle. Sennypead bir.

Before he could think of anything else, his body drew him down into deep and syrupy sleep. When he woke, a thousand tiny suns were flashing through the branches overhead. Byrds he'd never heard before were chirping, cheeping, clucking in the trees. Asel wondered how he could catch one to eat. Byrds could fly, one had to consider that. What you needed for byrds was something like a net.

He drank the last of his water, saving a drop to wet his eyes, set the empty bottle down, wondered if he'd left anything in the can. Leaned down to look. Froze, knew something was wrong, something that should be wasn't anymore.

Byrds. The byrds had gone silent. Not a tweet, not a peep. He heard the other sound then, and knew why.

People. The happy laughter of women, the hearty chortle of men. People were having fun. People close by. It sounded to Asel like a whole fucking town was headed for the truck. . . .

~ THIRTY-SEVEN ~

Asel had done enough hallucinating in the desert to know it wasn't a vision, a whimsy, a figment of any kind. It was simply there, there was no denying that. Past the grove of trees was a broad strip of lawn, a garish, unnatural green, so bright it hurt his eyes—even brighter than a pack of Nones could conceive. The grass stretched out to the left and the right as far as he could see.

High, stilted towers followed the grass, one every fifty yards or so. There were fat, wooden tanks atop the towers, and the towers were full of water. Hundreds, thousands of gallons of the stuff. Asel knew this was so, for a crew of men were watering the grass with hoses, all along the line. So much water, making that bilious green greener, while Asel's bottle, Asel's can, didn't hold a drop . . .

There were men with hoses, men with clippers, men pushing clacky mowers. And, to Asel's dismay, there were sullen, thick-bodied men, walking about with weapons cradled in their arms.

His heart nearly failed when he saw the brightly colored tents. The tents held white, tailored cloths, tables sagging with meets, froots, breds, kakes, and creemy tartes. There were silver pitchers on the tables, and bottles on ice. Asel's mouth watered, loosing more liquid than he'd had all day.

Most maddening of all were the men and the women thrashing, swinging, this way and that, tearing up the grass with their drivers, putters, cutters, and irons. These shiny sticks were carried in bags by gaunt and weary youths, lads who weighed no more than the burdens that hung across their backs.

Asel knew about gahlf. He had never played, for he saw little sense in sweating in the heat, when one could drop the little ball in a hole with no effort at all.

Prince of Christler-Coke

Mother had tried it—had a twenty-holer built behind the house. Played about a minute and half. Had the thing plowed up, planted turnips there instead.

Asel saw gender played no favorites here. Men and women alike wore white, cleated shoes with tacky white flaps, baggy knickers, and variegated socks. The knickers were plaid, no two patterns alike. Some of the socks bore a pattern of clocks. Some showed a flock of ducks. Everyone wore short-sleeved shirts. Everybody had a cap. Some of the women looked good in their shirts. Most of the men were older, with bottoms and paunches to match.

And, it was at that moment, when he noticed the paunches, when he took a closer look, that his knees nearly failed him on the spot. Everyone wore patches on their shirts. Even the mowers, the clippers, and the hosers, the boys who carried the heavy bags. The patches bore the symbol he'd seen on the aero-machines as they peppered him with lead—the mark of Disney-Dow, the leaping vole with bloody eyes.

Asel knew, at once, he had lost his way in the dark. That he hadn't traveled south or east. That he'd circled around somehow and headed farther west.

He ran, staggered to the truck, backed out of the grove. Prayed no one could hear the engine. Knew he couldn't wait for dark, knew he had to get away fast.

First, though, he went belly down through the trees, into the tent where the great spread of food and drink lay, took off his shirt and filled it like a sack, as close to bursting as he dared.

If they caught him, fuck it. He wouldn't die hungry, he wouldn't dry parched, desiccated, dried up to the bone. . . .

~ THIRTY-EIGHT ~

The day seemed dreary at best. Sorely indistinct. The land ahead was just as he'd left it, before his escape from the aero-machines, before his encounter with gahlf.

The desert hadn't changed. It was, he decided, a natural effect. Whatever the reason, empty was the norm. No people, no anymals but aunts, scorpos, and snaykes. Desolation was the key. Flat was the decorator scheme. Altogether, a dismal place to be.

On the good side, he was free. No TechsMechs Rangers, no gahlfers, no crazed Sisters of Our Lady of Reluctant Desire. Except for lack of sleep, a bath and proper clothes, dire lacerations, bruises of the flesh, he was doing rather well. He even had half a sack of food, water, and two quarts of Idahoo bir.

On the bad side, he had made a serious blunder, driving in the dark. Now, east was out of the question for a while. Until he got his bearings, it would have to be north. Take it slow, stay alert, hope for a route that would let him circle around everywhere he didn't want to be.

Asel tried not to think about Sylvan. Sylvan and Cele. They had headed north too, but somewhere back along the way. Even if he dared turn around, he could never find them now. Maybe they'd never reached the river, never found a settlement. Maybe the aero-machines tracked them down. Maybe they stumbled into another gahlfer horde.

He didn't want to think about that. Sylvan and Cele had betrayed him, yet he cared for them a lot. It struck him that he'd always had family and flunks—but never truly a friend, or a woman who wouldn't do anything he asked.

What hurt more than anything, were Sylvan's words before he left. *"I'll be back, you can count on me, friend . . ."*

"I do wish you hadn't said it," Asel told the empty road ahead. "I wish you hadn't told me that."

He saw it by the side of the road, slowed down to look, nearly lost his lunch. Stepped on the pedal, but not soon enough. Though he quickly turned away, the image of this horror caught him and held him and wouldn't let him go.

Carnage, chaos, deathly disarray. Lumps, chunks, pieces and parts strewn every which way. Heads lopped, bodies chopped, innards, outards stacked in ghoulish display.

And, on a cracked and weathered rock above it all, scrawled in a crude and bloody hand:

BiG BUGG WERE HERE

Long after this dreadful sight was far behind, the stench of this nightmare scene filled the cab with its fester, with its rot, with its stench of the dead.

What hellish thing happened there, he wondered. *Who were the killers, who were the slain?*

Answers came to mind, with no effort at all. An image of the hungry hordes descending on the TechsMechs Brigade. Perhaps, if he weeded through the tangle of dead back there, he would find a Colonel Mac, a Lieutenant-Major Brill.

Maybe that ravenous mob has already seen the truck. Maybe they're waiting just ahead.

Asel drank half a jug of water. Threw it up at once, grabbed another bottle, threw it up again. . . .

The engine coughed, wheezed, gave a final sigh. The truck rolled forward a moment, gave up, clattered to a stop.

Asel felt panic and alarm. There were dials of every sort on the dash. He had never imagined what any of them meant. Colored lights flashed, then winked and disappeared. Even on the move, the desert was oppressively hot. Standing still, it sucked the marrow dry.

He was angry, afraid. He had come to depend upon the truck. It almost seemed like a friend. Or had, until it betrayed him, left him here for whatever loonies came along.

The list of those who'd turned against seemed to grow by leaps and bounds. Ducky. Goodtime Bob. Maniac Nones. Cele. Sylvan Lee McCree.

Oh, Sylvan . . .

"Who can a fellow trust," he said aloud. "If honor's flag be sullied, are we no better than the base, the poor, persons from overseas?"

The thought of such a vile and ugly world left him with a great sense of pity for himself, compassion well deserved, for he had endured what he had never imagined, safe behind the walls of Iacola Keep . . .

He noticed, then, the road was melting, sticking to his shoes.

It was not much better on the shady side of the truck. Still, if he could keep the water down, it might be possible to reason things out. The truck contained a complex device, somewhere in the front. Sylvan had felt it played a part in compelling the truck to move.

If this was true, perhaps the device had simply died. Many things did. Even things that weren't alive. Maybe creatures of the mechanical persuasion simply had to rest. If they did, how long a rest might that be?

Heat and mental toil quickly sapped his strength. Asel tried to sit. The road seared his hands and sent him quickly to his feet. His head struck a portion of the truck. The pain nearly brought him to his knees. He stepped back in the cab, found his jacket, brought it to the shade, rolled it up and sat.

His skin felt hot and cold. At least he had water, he'd be dead without that. As the sweat stung his eyes, he gazed across the dull and arid flats. There was nothing of interest to see. The sun played tricks upon his eyes. The line between the sky and the land was indistinct, blurred by waves of silver heat. A mountain range appeared. Upside down. Asel knew they didn't do that. For a moment, there seemed to be trees. Possibly sickamoors or okes.

Two figures came into view, walking on a lake. Asel sat and watched, having nothing else to do. The figures vanished on occasion, abruptly reappeared. The illusion was artfully conceived. One of the figures, the smaller of the two, appeared to sing. The other, a large imposing fellow, wore a heavy fur coat. This attire seemed out of place, considering the heat. Asel looked again. Good God, it wasn't a man at all—it was a *bair!* He recognized the creature at once. They frequently appeared on *Anymals of Our Past*.

Asel blinked and rubbed his eyes. The vision refused to leave. Clearly the heat had damaged some organ in his head.

The illusions halted several yards away.

"Afternoon, friend," said the bair. "You headed thataway? We could sure use a lift."

Asel wondered how to handle this. He hadn't supposed that bairs could talk, but clearly this one did. Certainly, it wouldn't hurt to be nice.

"I'm afraid I can't help," Asel said. "The truck doesn't work. It simply won't go."

"I'll have a look," said the bair.

With that, he lumbered around to the front. A lid popped up at once. Asel was impressed. Illusion or not, the bair had mechanical skills.

Asel turned to the anymal's friend. "Well, it is really quite a hot day." It seemed polite to speak. "It might get cooler later on. Or maybe not. It doesn't look like rain. But then, of course you never know."

The man didn't answer. He seemed detached, completely out of synch. His face was dark as wood, dry as withered froot. He appeared to be frail and in his prime. Sapped and strong as iron. Gray hair hung to his shoulders, braided with a dirty yellow cloth. A broken feather topped an ancient derby the shade of dust. Donald Duck shirt. Formal tails and boxer shorts. Athletic shoes with nice beadwork on the toes. He hummed to himself, teetered as he swayed. "Hai, hai, ya-yo," he said. Found a bottle in his coat and took a drink.

"Everything under the hood's okay," said the bair. He slammed down the lid. "I'll take a look on top."

"On top?"

The bair didn't answer. Asel watched as he climbed the cab and stomped about. The creature was immense, exceptionally broad. Yet, he certainly seemed an amiable sort.

"Well, there's your trouble." The bair walked to the edge and peered down at Asel. "Your solar cells is stopped up. Engine isn't gettin' no power. Where'd you park this bugger last night?"

"I'm not sure. I don't have a chart of any kind."

"I'd say under a tree."

"Why yes, I suppose that's true. How did you know that?"

"Byrds," the bair said. "Byrds eat in the day an' doo-doo all night. That's what's wrong with those cells. Calcinated crud. Optical restraint. Byrd shit is what you got."

"Really. Imagine that."

The bair gave Asel a curious look. "I'm goin' to make a wild guess. You got no idea how this thing works. Haven't got a clue. Energy conversion hasn't ever crossed your mind."

"I don't have a philosophy bent, if that's what you mean. I imagined we had an ample fuel supply."

"Uh-huh. You're not from around these parts, are you?"

"No. Most decidedly not."

The bair muttered to himself. From somewhere within his heavy pelt he found a blue handkerchief and a battered canteen. He went to his knees and crawled across the roof. Moments later, he was back on the road.

"Give her a minute, then try an' start it up." The bair took a long swallow, wiped his muzzle clean, and offered the canteen to Asel. "Better have a swig or two. You're lookin' kinda bad around the eyes."

Asel was appalled at the prospect of drinking after a bair.

"Thanks. I, ah, have water in the truck. Plenty, if you need to fill your vessel."

"Fellow's all right," said the bair. "Not from around here, though."

"Hai, ya-yo," the friend said.

Asel was surprised how quickly he was getting used to the talking bair. Hardship teaches us to get along with creatures we might meet. . . .

~ THIRTY-NINE ~

The motor started up at once. Whatever the bair had done, it seemed to work quite well. Zolasels, or something of the sort. The bair was rude, but quite right. Asel had scarcely thought about how things worked. He had thought even less about how they would not.

"I have learned a great deal in a very short time," he muttered to himself, "mostly things I didn't care to know at all."

The road looked much as it had before. Desolate and flat. Nothing to delight and please the eye. Quite soon, Asel began to feel rigidly confined. The driving art was trying at best; addition of the bair and his friend gave him little room to steer. Moreover, there were several new scents in the truck. Rank set the tone. A fugue of olfactory offense. Woodsmoke and sweat. Whyskee and snuff. Malodorous attire. Gastric disorders of every sort. Asel leaned out to suck in the desert air.

The bair's friend continued to sing. A sound between a mutter and a wail. It scraped at Asel's nerves, made him want to scratch.

"I hope you don't mind, but is he ill or what? He might need medical advice."

"That's a dirge is what it is," the bair said. "Al's a Ute. Does it all the time. You get accustomed to it in a while."

Asel doubted that. "What's he dirging *for*?"

"'Cause there isn't any Utes except him. He's got a lot of ethnic sorrow in his heart. Drinks to some excess. I don't guess I got your name. Mine's Phil."

"Asel Iacola," Asel said, thinking at once it might have been wise to give the bair another name.

"I'd guess you're from the East."

"I guess I am."

"Knew an Asel Ottir once. A quarter-bred Kree. Thought he was a stone. Seldom ever spoke. Where exactly in the East?"

"Just East," Asel said, then decided this would prompt further questions from the bear. "Pencilvain. New Yuk. Ohiyo South. The Northern Virgentles sometimes."

"Don't guess I heard of those," said the bair.

Asel brought his attention back to the road. There might be mountains to the right, it was difficult to say. The highway wavered and vanished in the heat. Inversion seemed the rule.

Now and then, Asel checked the mirror, peered up at the sky. He wondered if the stubby craft from Califoggy State could pick up his trail. There were plenty of tracks on the road— big trucks, he guessed, hauling souvenirs out to San Clemente Shrine.

Sylvan had always imagined NERF would run them down. Asel thought his foes were more ominous than that. Sylvan had been in Oklahomer too long. He was prone to the penal attitude.

Phil began to scratch his pelt. Asel pictured earwigs and mites. Shingles and hives. The bair opened a drawer in his chest and examined it with care. Asel nearly ran off the road.

"I don't much care for your habits at the wheel," Phil said. "You have a tendency to veer."

"Never mind that." Asel caught a glimpse of lights and wires. "Just what are you up to over there? I'd like an answer right now."

"Cooling agent's on the blink," Phil said. "Water 'round here's full of minerals and salts."

Asel was appalled. "I don't care for this at all. A person has a right to know who or what he's picking up."

"Don't get in a snit," Phil said. He touched the drawer, and it quickly disappeared.

"Well, it's clear you're not a bair. I suspect you're an electro device."

"Listen, I got feelings too."

"One could argue that."

"Hai, ya-yo," said Al.

"You did fix my truck. I am not ungrateful for that. Under the circumstances, you are welcome to stay. I'm sure there's a town up ahead, I'll be glad to drop you there."

"Huh-uh."

"What's that supposed to mean?"

"No town. There isn't no town."

"There has to be a town. What's a road for, if there isn't any town?"

Phil scratched his ear and gave Asel a thoughtful look. "Correct me if I'm wrong. No offense at all. It's my guess you don't know where the shit you are."

"Well of course I do. Don't be absurd. I am west of the Papel Shire. South of Santy Faye. Almaquirky and Towz. Karl's Bed. Not far from Arkansak. I expect we'll reach Milwookie quite soon."

"Great God A'Mighty," said Phil.

"I am not a seasoned traveler, but I can find my way about."

"Where you are," Phil said, "is Aridsoda East. Fagstaff. Feenigs. Franchise of Califoggy State."

Asel was not surprised, but somewhat shaken, at the mention of Califoggy State.

"I really don't want to go west. I was thinking of turning about."

"I think we oughta get you a map."

"Once, all this land belong to my people," Al said. "The white man's treaty lies. The buphalo are gone. Our women sell their parts. Our young are into rack and roll."

"Right," Phil said, "settle down, friend. . . ."

The structure seemed reluctant to appear; first, from a mile or so away, a blemish in the silver tiers of heat, a dull insinuation on the land. Closer, somewhat more defined, it was still less a building than a natural event, a dull coloration of chikun wire and tin, scrap wood and bald rubber tires, worn mud brick, each part in happy conjunction with the rest.

"Pull right in here," Phil said, and Asel did.

The sign read BUCKSTOP in faded, fancy type. A bleached pair of auntlers was nailed above the door. Asel climbed down and stretched. A broad window spanned the building's front. Asel peered in, but couldn't see past the sand-frosted glass. He noted that a number of foreign objects were mortared in the walls. Totally at random, as far as he could see. An interesting effect. Bits of colored glass. Bottle caps from long ago. The bones of a snayke. A clock that said 8:45. A nifty geological array.

"Come on," Phil said, "I been thinkin' about bir all day. In the bottle. On tap. Frost on the glass."

"Whyskee," Al said.

"We'll see," Phil said.

Asel was grateful to be inside. The sun was still high. He felt dull, mentally oppressed. He was certain the heat had a feebling effect upon the mind.

The interior was pleasantly dim. Plain wooden floors. A counter and stools. An assortment of tables and chairs. Tacky plastic booths. Sun-faded vistas of the West. Asel had the strange, but somehow comforting thought, that he had stepped back into a long forgotten past. Sensible décor was scarcely an issue then. He had read somewhere about that.

He joined Phil and Al in a booth. The bair took up one side, Asel was left with the Ute. A rather spare figure emerged from the back, a man with bad skin, slicked-back hair, and lizird eyes.

"Hey, Tom," Phil waved an arm in greeting. "This here's Asel. Asel give us a ride. Asel, this is Tom Micks. Cold bir for ever'one, Tom. First round's on me."

Micks looked at Asel. "You from the East?"

"I guess I am."

"You better behave."

"I don't care for that remark."

"Phil, you can sit out front if you like. Just don't go and get settled in. I got a load of them Oryintul tourists comin' on the scenic bus ride. One of those boys sees a bair at the bar he'll likely have a shit fit."

"Right," Phil said. "Send your friends out back. That's fine. I'll go an' get bit by an aunt."

Micks seemed to give this some thought. "I think what I'll do is just turn them fellas away. I sure don't want about forty-two big spendin' folks of the Oryint persuasion buying three-inch steaks and those drinks with umbrellas on top. Cleaning me out of every postcard and snayke ashtray in the place. I'd rather sell bir to an artificial bair."

"I appreciate that," Phil said.

Micks turned and stalked away.

"Tom's all right," Phil said.

"I can see that."

"I'm used to bigotry and strife. It's a way of life with me. Nobody cares about nature anymore. Profit is the key."

"Once, the great waters teemed with selmun and trowt," the Ute said. "Beever and dawg filled the streams . . ."

"Damn right," Phil said.

Asel smelled something awfully nice. A hand with nails painted lavender and pink appeared right before his eyes with a bir.

"Hi, there." A pretty face and sizzled yellow hair. A desert tan and white teeth. "Listen, I'd say you were from the East."

"I'd say you're right, I am."
"I'm Betty Louise Ann."
"I'm Asel."
"Phil honey, don't you pay any mind to Tom. He's been an ol' grouch all day. Rattlirs got up in the pump and Tom had to shoo 'em out."
"That'll put a man out of sorts," Phil said.
Betty Louise Ann leaned closer to Phil, a posture that greatly increased Asel's chances for a peek. He prayed for gravity and excess moisture in the air. Saw a fetching collarbone. Glimpsed a swell of fine dimension as it vanished out of sight.
"If I was you," Betty Louise Ann told Phil, "I'd be around when that bus starts to leave. Tom'll be so busy he won't even know. Those boys are picture-taking fiends. Ought to be some good pocket money in that."
"Betty Louise, don't take no affront," the bair said. "I am not a tableau. If I wanted to subject myself to shit like that, I'd have stayed in Mellowstone Park. I've got pride like anyone else. I got certain unalien rights."
"You got to pay for all the birs you put down," said Betty Louise. "You give some thought to that."
Asel followed the girl with his eyes. He was struck by her charms. Dazzled by her tall and bony shape, by her cute and sluttish ways, by her unaffected grace, by the crude and common manner of her speech.
"She's a looker, all right," Phil said, guessing Asel's thoughts with ease.
"She isn't real well groomed."
"She'll flat break your heart is what she'll do. Al, I bet them tourists haven't ever had their picture took with a genuine Ute."
"Whyskee," Al said.
"Bir," said Phil. "Whyskee money's comin' on the bus. . . ."

~ FORTY ~

The tour bus arrived in the late afternoon, disgorging short men attired in business suits and lurid tropic shirts. They descended on the Buckstop with enterprise and zeal, determined, as Tom Micks had said, to consume great quantities of meet, drinks adorned with froot, hot appul pye, takos and bir, chikun and choclit kake. They seemed to delight in excess. They photographed everything in sight. The Buckstop, the auntlers above the door. Dead prickle plants in the yard. Several hundred leg shots of Betty Louise, a slender calf, a shapely knee, a swelling breast. 1/100, *f*-8, sometimes with film.

They bought plaster rattulsnaykes, wally-nut salad bowls, bogus Zoony pots, phony opal rings, silver buckles big as dinner plates—not exactly silver, as it were, but close enough.

"They're soakin' up color's what they're doing," Phil explained. "That's what your vacation shit is all about."

"Appalling," Asel said. "Where does Tom *get* this stuff? I never saw such disgusting items in my life."

"Chiner, Kureuh, Tie-won-on. Send you a big catalog. Can't read the damn thing, but the pictures is mighty good."

And, before all this came about, Betty Louise fixed Asel a surreptitious meal. Asel devoured chikun-fried steak, frents fries, and apercot pye, put it all away among ten-gallon drums of beens, pungent onyun sacks, dusty cases of bir, announcing, after he was through, that he really couldn't pay.

Betty Louise said she wasn't surprised to hear that, and she'd figure something out. Tom Micks always tacked a rider on the Oryintuls' bill, an error up to fifty-two percent, and she could slip Asel's tab into that. If he liked, if he didn't mind the strong scent of onyuns in the air, he was welcome to sleep on the surplus army cot. Asel said he would. Whatever a cot turned out to be, it couldn't be as bad as the truck.

Asel couldn't sleep. The cot was hard as lead. The desert, to atone for its sins of the day, turned frigid in the night. Blankets didn't help. The cold was simply there. Finally, Asel dozed. Woke to a scorpo waltz in a wan square of moonlight on the floor. Watched this graceful and terrible gavotte, watched the couple step to jerky tunes, watched their stingers wave in pale illumination in the night.

Slept, then, and dreamed of better days, dreamed of Iacola Keep, dreamed of sparkling fountains and colonnaded halls. Dreamed of privilege and charm, dreamed of courtesy defined. Dreamed of fine sylken shirts, dreamed of vikuna socks, dreamed of sayble underwear. Dreamed of perky servant flunks from Zanzybar, saucy girls with auburn hair. Dreamed of glazed bunnie toes, dreamed of cormorat soufflé. Dreamed of owyl stroginoph, dreamed of dolfen pye. Woke again to the essence of onyuns, day-old doenuts, and sour bir.

Asel gave up on sleep. He slipped into his clothes and walked out beneath the night. The desert sky was cold with tempered stars. The land seemed endless and dark, a frightening thing to see. Barren and wild, in awesome disarray. There was no clear order here at all. Yet, Asel saw the desert had a certain savage charm.

"I see you couldn't sleep," said Betty Louise. "Same thing with me."

Asel started at her voice. Betty Louise laughed. "Didn't mean to sneak up. I guess I do. Tom's always saying, 'Betty Louise Ann, for God's sake, make a little noise.' I try, but I guess it isn't me."

"You really are very quiet," Asel said.

"Well, what's a girl to do? Some folks are into stomping. Not me. I guess you're what you are."

Betty Louise placed her arm in his, and they walked along together through the night. It seemed a totally foreign thing to Asel, yet the natural thing to do. He felt a slight intoxication. A stirring in his heart. Her closeness had a pleasant, tingling effect. Asel drew in a breath. Lord, this girl was a symphony of smells. Frents fries in her hair. Harsh detergent on her skin. Scents he couldn't name. And, overwhelming all the rest, the dizzying aroma of anymal intent.

It struck him, of a sudden, he hadn't thought of Cele in possibly an hour and a half. He tried to feel a little sadness, guilt, and regret. Remembered *she* had run away from him, and felt a lot better after that. If they could get together some time, maybe they could work things out.

"It's nice to be out here," Asel said, for lack of proper words. "There seem to be a great many stars."

"The desert knows your secret name," Betty Louise told him. "I read that in a book. I reckon it knows mine, 'cause I don't know where else to be. My mother was a dirigible pilot. I suppose I tried to live up to that. The romance of the rigid airship's in my blood, but I guess it didn't take. There isn't much magic in my life."

"There isn't a great deal in mine," Asel said. "There was, but there isn't anymore."

"The hand of Fate has a clobbering effect."

"I'd say it does."

Asel was slightly chilled. The girl wore a thin cotton robe, but didn't seem to mind. The Buckstop seemed far behind. There were various rocks all about. Small clumps of plants that emitted dusty spice. They came to a sudden dip in the land, a depression filled with derelict vintage autokars, wrecks so old and pitted with rust, Asel could see right through them to the stars.

There were small hills of garbage, tin cans, debris of every sort, and, off to one side, a singular, enormous shape that seemed to dominate the rest. It was large and difficult to miss. With sudden recognition and alarm, Asel saw it was his truck.

"Betty Louise—!"

"It's just fine. Isn't anybody going to drive it off."

"But what's it doing *here?*"

"Well, for heaven's sake, Asel, it is a stolen vehicle rife with bullet holes. You can't just leave it out front. Phil drove it in this afternoon. Won't anyone spot it back here."

Asel felt a quick touch of fright. "What—what an outrageous thing to say. Do I look like a thief? How can you even imply . . . What makes you think—"

"Hon, what you *don't* look like is a trucker." She gave him a reassuring pat, a patient sigh. It was clear she was totally unimpressed. "You ever *see* a trucker, Asel? Up close and in the flesh? Well you aren't one, I'm here to tell you that."

Asel was dismayed. He felt he was coming unraveled like a sock. The fears he had carefully put aside rose up to slap him in the face.

"Betty Louise," he blurted out, "I don't know what to do. I can't think. I've lost communication with my legs. I cannot relate to this terrain. Everything's wrong, my world is out of place. Oh, God, you're so attractive in the night. I feel so lonely, I feel a great need for carnal bliss!"

Asel reached out in desperation, grabbed whatever he could find. The girl knocked him silly at once.

Asel's face stung with tears. He felt sick, contrite, partially confused. "I'm terribly sorry. I don't know the local customs at all. I suspect that wasn't right."

"The local custom is you *ask*." Betty Louise gave Asel a long and thoughtful look, apparently more curious than annoyed. "Asel, you're not real heavy on romance. You got an awful poor approach."

"I guess I maybe do."

"It's clear you weren't raised with any tact."

Asel felt a thirst for violation, tenderness, and pain. "I think I'm overcome with desire," he told her. "I can't take much of this. Tell me what to do, what I have to say."

"You just ask a girl, Asel. That's all. She says yes or no."

"I'm asking, Betty Louise."

"Well, now that's a lot better." She showed him a gentle smile and took his hand. "You can be real sweet when you try. . . ."

Asel was still awake when the first hint of slate-colored dawn found the room. He watched her as she slept, as he had throughout the night, afraid if he dozed she would somehow disappear. He marveled at the magic of her dusty, honeyed-skin, at the hollows of delight, at her beauty both common and sublime. He ached for each tasty imperfection, each flaw and sweet defect. She stirred, then, and muttered in her sleep; the blanket slipped away and revealed a bony hip. And, at this very moment, as if by some design, the first flash of sun kissed this precious peak of flesh, lit a stretch mark and a mole, lit a choclit cookie crumb, cast its shadow like a needle down her thigh.

Sometime in the night, he had wanted to ask her where she got her name. He had never known a family named *Ann*. But then, he'd never known a Betty Louise.

Betty Louise awoke, yellow hair tangled over sleepy Western eyes. "You just lookin' over the territory, or what?"

"I find it hard not to look," Asel said. "Betty Louise, I don't know what's happening to me. I'm sure you must think me a fool, but I have never experienced such pleasure, such total fulfillment of my needs."

"You sure are cute when you talk."

"How can I make you understand?" Asel found it difficult to speak. The sight of such wonderment exposed made him giddy in the head.

"I scarcely know where to begin. Yet, after what we have shared, I feel I must. I want you to see what I am. Share my sorrow and discontent. You don't *know* me at all. I'm a person of privilege and class. I am not used to chikun-fried steak. I have never seen a cot before last night. Iacola House owns all of America East.

"All right, we did—we don't anymore. Everything was stolen by corporate scalawags. I was unjustly sentenced to a penal institute. It was absolute hell. Completely middle-class. Double-knit suits. Faulty stereo. I escaped and stole a truck. Myself and a friend. We were taken by Rangers for a time. A person called Goodtime sold us to the Nones. I cannot describe the abuse and discomfort we suffered at their hands. Rebel acolytes finally set us free. Aeromachines from Califoggy State then tried to gun us down. I stumbled on gahlfers before I came here. I encountered something awful on the road, I can't even talk about that...."

Betty Louise looked more than a little confused. "Asel, I'm not sure I'm getting much of this."

"It doesn't matter. The thing is, I'm here now. And I don't have the slightest idea where here *is*. I'm a fugitive from NERF. I have no place to go. That truck was full of statuettes, before we were looted by the poor. That's what you do on hard time. Make stupid souvenirs."

"San Clemente Shrine."

Asel stared. "You know about that?"

"Asel, we get truckers in here all the time. That's what most of 'em do. Carry cheap shit out to Califoggy State."

"You see?" Asel groaned and shook his head. "I have unwittingly done myself in. I *can't* go West. Those people are crazy out there. I don't know which way to run."

"There isn't a whole lot of directions from here."

"Oh, God!" Asel took her in his arms. "You are the only decent thing that has come into my life on this whole sordid trip. You are giving. Assertive in your lust. I have only had congress with imported flunks from overseas. It's not the same at all."

"Shoot," said Betty Louise, "you fornicate with the help, you can't expect pure delight. You're thinking lust, they're thinking 'bout their day off...."

~ FORTY-ONE ~

Phil was having baykun and aigs. Wawfles and hahm. Pankakes and toahst. Kaufee and ti. The Ute was staring sadly at the wall.

Tom Micks gave Asel a menacing stare. "Guess you'd like breakfast now, too. Clean napkins and a silver finger bowl. I can go out and cut a rose."

"I don't want to be any trouble," Asel said.

"You want to tell me why a mechanized bair has got to *eat*? I figure he does it out of spite. I ought to get in the welfare trade. Goddamn it, dawg, get out of here!"

Asel saw a black and white blur making for the open back door, trailing a grisly prize in its wake.

"I never seen a dawg yet wasn't a born garbage hound," Micks said. "They'll attack a paper sack at its weakest point of strength. Eat through a grease spot and suck all the trash through a hole. If you keep a kat around, a dawg'll track it all day long. Wait for that kat to get sick. Next to trash, kat urp's a dawg's great delight.

"Laird Weck out at Hollow Point fell down and died in his house last spring. That poodul of his ate him quickly as he could. I doubt poor Laird was scarcely cold. Loyalty fled and sheer canine greed took hold. Man's best friend, my ass."

Betty Louise Ann came out of the kitchen with a horrified look. "God, that is plain disturbing, Tom."

"Well, I believe that's the point. Asel, this place'll be chock full of truckers 'bout nine. I strongly urge you to keep out of sight."

"Betty Louise told me," Asel said.

"Good. Mutilation's not my cup of ti."

Asel sat down across from Phil. "Thank you for handling the

truck. I feel rather foolish. Evidently, I'm quite transparent to everyone here."

"Safe to say that."

"Doesn't he ever eat?" Asel nodded at the Ute.

"Not to my knowledge. I never caught him at it. Your savage folk aren't the same as us. I expect they get nutrition from the air."

"I can't imagine how."

"You been around Al long as I have, you'd see a lot of things you haven't seen before." Phil set down his kaufee and looked soberly at Asel.

"He wasn't always like this. Shoot, Al was a star. Right at the top. You shoulda seen him at the Georgie Custard show. They'd have a few singin' and dancing acts, Georgie'd tell a coupla jokes. Then here'd come Al, riding down on the troopers with the whole Sue Nation.

"They always made Al a chief. Said he had that real somber constipated look. Them Mechykans and Asyaticks would flat go berserk. Goddamn Waltification Act finished all that. Mechanized the whole thing. 'Course, that meant steady work for me, but real folks were shit out of luck.

"Al got a few Pweblow gigs after that. Took to drinking pretty bad. Did the Apatchy Wells thing awhile, they shut all that down, too. The West ain't the same anymore."

"I guess not."

"Hai, ya-yo," said Al.

Asel stayed in Betty Louise's room atop the Buckstop, sat by the window and watched the seemingly endless desert flats, watched the lakes of heat, listened to the silence, the awesome stillness of the land.

Then, of a sudden, a smudge appeared against the east, a growing trail of dust looming larger, larger still, and with it came a rumble, a tremor that Asel could feel in the ancient boards beneath his feet.

The sound grew, grew until the Buckstop shook. The first truck emerged from the storm of its wheels, then another, and another after that. They descended through the dust like great, mindless beasts. Then, engines howled and blasthorns tore the air. Men laughed and shouted and swung down from their cabs, cursed, spat, and pounded road dust from their boots.

The sight brought a chill, a petrifying fear that Asel had never felt before, even when the TechsMechs had nearly done him in.

The Rangers enjoyed their work, found pleasure in beating, maiming, doing unto others the evil that had been done to them.

These men below, men with dark beards and wulfish eyes, men with studded leather garb, with weapons at their sides, this was a different breed, men of a different kind. Violence, fury, and cruel assault were natural to them, a way of life with neither purpose or intent.

Asel had never imagined such a breed in his still and ordered dreams. Life before had been sheltered from the coarse, unruly ways of the world. From filth, hunger, untamed emotions, horrid smells, and even death.

Now, he was sheltered no more, and, though he had tried to face this dreadful truth—he had also sought to hide it in some safe and comforting corner of his mind.

Now he knew the world had changed, long before he had come along, long before Iacola Keep. All he'd ever known was America East, and the vague, shadowy spectre of Califoggy State. It seemed there was also a South, ruled by lords like Sylvan Lee McCree. And, Phil had told him, the Sue Nation in the north. Whatever that might be.

Most of all, he had learned this was a country without a name in between, a place of horror and dread, of the hungry, the homeless, and the mad—people who believed in death, torture, and gahlf.

Something else had happened, as well. A new, peculiar knowledge that had crept unbidden into his muddled head. He had known about the Lower Classes, since he was a child. It was easy to tell who they were. *Everyone* was low, except family and friends. Now, he saw there were other kinds of people as well—people of clearly ignoble birth, yet decent enough as well. How could that be? What could he say about someone like Betty Louise—the most alluring woman he'd ever met in his life? Common as dirt, unkempt, careless in her manner, and no respect for position at all.

And, the Buckstop itself. Décor had come to a screeching halt a hundred years ago, possibly longer than that. Still, it was a quiet, dismal, comfortable place to be. Here, he had learned to sleep on a cot, eat chissbuggers, takos, and things he couldn't identify.

In a few, harrowing weeks on the road, he had learned about tacky socks, how to drive a truck, learned that water was the finest drink of all.

Some of the things he'd learned, the people he'd met, he'd like to forget. Then there were people like Sylvan. Sylvan and

Cele. Now there was Betty Louise, from the family of Ann. Phil the bair, Al, and Tom Micks.

He wasn't too sure about Micks. Tom was kind of on the fence. He might be a friend, or an absolute pain, it was hard to say which.

Good things seemed to happen, along with the bad. Good was Betty Louise. Bad was the men down below with rowdy laughter and gaudy silver belts. He felt he had gained a little confidence and courage in the hectic weeks past. These new qualities were tested, now, for he feared these men—what they were, what they did. And, more than the men themselves, the oppressive powers they stood for, the corporate masters of Califoggy State.

He waited, then, sitting on the edge of Betty Louise Ann's bed, waited for the bullies, the rowdies down below, to pass out, throw up, get in their trucks, and go away. . . .

~ FORTY-TWO ~

The Buckstop looked as if chaos and combat had occurred. Chairs were broken and overturned, bottles transformed into shards of broken glass. Bad smells were all about. A ceiling fan had fallen to the floor. Asel noted Mechsykan food adhered to several walls. Tom Micks sat among the ruins, looking carefully at nothing at all. The dawg lapped up pools of bir.

Asel searched for Betty Louise, and found her outside. She was sitting on a rock in the sun, face buried in her knees, curled in a painful little ball. Asel was concerned, and went to her at once. At his touch she looked up, and Asel saw tears.

"Good heavens," he said, "are you hurt? What did those maniacs do? I cannot see why Micks allows this sort of thing to go on. Business or not, it simply isn't right."

"Oh, Asel . . ."

Fresh tears began to flow. Asel stood, puzzled and confused. Betty Louise seemed unhurt, yet she was clearly out of sorts. He wondered what to do. Then, he looked past the yard, past the scrubby desert growth and saw the bair, saw that he was carrying the Ute in his arms, walking out across the sands.

Asel waited, standing well aside. It was clear Betty Louise didn't really care to talk. After a while, he walked inside. Tom Micks was making piles of splintered chairs. When Asel walked in, he stopped, looked thoughtfully at Asel, moved over to the bar.

"Those fellas always leave a lotta shit behind," he said. "Hats, socks, perverted magazines. You never know what."

Without looking up, he handed Asel a wrinkled sheet of paper, tako-stained, and limp with bir.

"I expect you'll find this disturbing, but I feel you oughta know."

Asel felt his stomach do a flip. The picture was a very good likeness. They'd spelled his name right. WANTED! he felt, was larger than it needed to be. . . .

Phil had the truck all ready, and Betty Louise had packed more food and drink inside than Asel thought he'd ever use. Still, when one had no idea where one was going, ample provision seemed the proper thing to do.

"I'd head north if I was you," Phil said, leaning on the cab. "Then double back east. Get out of the Franchise States as quick as you can. From what you told me, nothing good'll happen to you here. Don't forget the truckers rule the roads, and don't lose your map. You know how you are about directions. Just stay the hell out of Califoggy State."

"I'll certainly do that," Asel said. "Phil, I wish there was something I could say that would help."

"One day I'll get me a trucker. You wait and see if I don't. Asel, they shamed him to death is what they done. Wasn't nothing more'n that. Just took that hat of his and wouldn't give it back. Thought it was some kinda fun.

"An' I just sat there and watched. If I'd of moved, they'd of burned the place down, and I couldn't do that to Tom. I just sat and looked at Al, and knew he was gone. You kill a Ute's pride, you're going to kill the man too.

"Listen, Asel, you say no if you like, I gotta ask. You mind too much if I was to ride along? I got nowhere to be with him gone, and there's no use you getting lost by yourself."

"That's fine with me," Asel said. "You can keep byrd shit off the roof."

Asel was really quite relieved. Facing the road alone was a prospect he didn't look forward to.

Tom Micks came out and shook his hand. "I wouldn't ask you to leave. I guess you know that."

"I'd only be trouble staying here."

"Watch out for dawgs. Your smaller breeds are the worst. Kockers and Beegles. A Kocker, he'll go for the knees."

Asel was listening to Micks, but his eyes were on the Buckstop's door. He knew she'd say goodbye. She had to do that. Yet, he yearned to put the moment off, hoped for some delay.

His heart leaped when she appeared. At once he felt sorrow and delight. Passion and regret. He held out his arms. Betty Louise stopped, hands on her hips, a curious glint in her eyes.

"I guess I want to come along," she told him. "You got a right to say no if you like. You better not. I've taken a liking to you, Asel. I surely can't say why. I guess I'll have to work that out."

Asel felt elated. Bewildered and surprised. "Betty Louise—I don't know what to say."

"I don't guess you ever do. That's got a certain charm. You're clearly from the East, but I feel you might have a Western heart. My God, is that counterfeit bair going too?"

"I don't take offense," said Phil.

Betty Louise gave Tom a hug, then climbed into the truck, tossing a shabby satchel in back. "I don't guess either one of you has a cheerful destination in mind."

"I got friends in Mellowstone," said Phil.

"I don't have a big need to live with bairs."

"There are quite a few fascinating names on the map," Asel said. "Horrified Forest, Feenigs. Two-Song. Saul's Ache City."

"Oh Lord," said Betty Louise, "just drive and get some air. I'm already getting a rash from this bair. . . ."

~ FORTY-THREE ~

"It is just as easy to have a good outlook on life as it is the other way around," said Betty Louise. "It is also a comfort for those who have to live with the outlookee."
 "I think I have as good an outlook as anyone else," Asel said. He took a deep breath, let it out again. He had read somewhere this helped to clear the head. "I maintain a pleasant attitude, even in the face of adversity, trouble, and—strife—things like that."
 "You're breathing funny."
 "No I'm not."
 "She's right," said Phil. "Sort of a pant an' a halt. You hold it an' let it back out."
 "That's what breathing is all about," Asel said, making no effort to hide his irritation. "In, and then out. Everyone does it. Even imitation bairs."
 "I'm guessing that's a personal insinuation."
 "I'm guessing you'd be absolutely right."
 "That's enough," said Betty Louise. "Both of you. Stop it right now."
 "I didn't start this."
 "No, you didn't, hon. And if I tend to criticize, it's only meant in a helpful and beneficial way. I would never say anything harmful to another person's self."
 With that, she leaned across the seat, stretched in a manner that revealed a belly button Asel was delighted to see. This, plus a hand that gently brushed his thigh, a peck upon the cheek.
 He had only known her four days now, three on the road, and he knew each comment on manners, attitude, and driving skills was followed by a kiss, a caress, a touch on an intimate part. A

pattern well-defined, and not unpleasant at all, if he remembered to breathe in and out each time.

She was partially right, he knew. He had been feeling fine as long as the road took them north. North was the key to turning east again, away from Califoggy State. He had started getting edgy when the road began to veer, somewhat to the left. Phil said that was fine, it would turn right again, it said so on the map.

And, Asel had to admit, the scenery was spectacular to see. "There's a plenitude of natural wonders to behold," Betty Louise had pointed out, and he had to agree.

As the land began to rise, the desert gave way to a vast stretch of color Asel found hard to define. Not gray, not green, but something in between. This most unusual shade, explained Betty Louise, was due to flora like saydge, rabutbush, and squeet. After that there was taller growth—scaboke, joopiner, and pinyun pyne.

She named everything as long as there was daylight to see. Loonyweed, lewpeen, and mary's goal. These plants would bloom in the spring. She wished he could see the country then. Asel prayed he'd be a thousand miles away.

There were mezahs and beauts. High, impossibly delicate spires of weathered stone. Twice, they passed ancient dwellings, ruins built high among the cliffs.

"Pweblows," Phil explained. "Al's people used to pillage and loot 'em in bygone times."

"That wasn't very nice," said Betty Louise.

"Utes didn't have much use for peaceful ways. Kindness to others wouldn't fill your belly, or get you a female back in those days. No offense on the latter statement, Betty Louise."

"I know what things were like, I can read too. And they haven't *changed* that much, you ask me."

Neither Phil nor Asel cared to comment on that.

There were countless varieties of prickle plants, and thickets of yukka that sprang up like clusters of swords. Asel stopped to look at a pile of stone columns scattered by the road. It looked as if some mighty structure had stood there once, then tumbled to the ground.

Phil said they were putrified wood, but Asel didn't fall for that. Bairs, he decided, couldn't handle the truth, or didn't care to try.

Twice, an endless herd of misshapen beasts rumbled by across the road, holding up the truck for some time. They were big, cumbersome anymals with shaggy heads and tiny eyes. Asel felt sorry for the creatures, for they suffered some disease that caused their backs to swell. Phil said he'd seen them before, traveling with Al. He said they weren't sick, they were born that way.

"Yeah, right," Asel said.

At night, they slept beneath the stars. Phil had the courtesy to go off by himself, leave his companions to their personal delight.

And, delightful it was indeed. Asel's heart fairly quivered with joy, and so did everything else. Conflict, discontent, and snappish behavior vanished in the dark. And, when Asel got any sleep at all, he forgot about snaykes, sennypeeds, and mythical creatures like heela monsters that Phil had graphically described.

Just before the night descended, the sun turned the color of embers and dropped below a veil of purple clouds.

"Those aren't clouds," Betty Louise told him. "Those are mountains, hon."

And maybe they were, Asel thought, but they never seemed to be any closer from one night to the next.

Phil heard them first.

He listened, perfectly still except for the motion of his ears. His ears began to twitch, quiver, buzz like curious bees. And, somewhere within this chubby fabrication, deep beneath a layer of simulated fat, auditory circuits clattered and clicked, chattered and ticked, sent an urgent message up to Head, a message that brought Bair Central alert, and sent Phil rumbling quickly down the hill.

Asel nearly jumped out of his skin, instantly awake.

"What? What is it I'm supposed to hear?" he said, huddling in a blanket against the chill. "I don't hear a thing."

"Listen instead of talking. Bairs have keener senses than a man. A bair like me's even better than that."

"I expect you've got a short. Check that drawer you're always pulling out."

"That's a racial remark."

"You're not a race, Phil. You're a pseudo bair."

Asel was annoyed. He liked to sleep. He liked it even better with Betty Louise. Her heat radiation was intense. The night air didn't have a chance.

"I might hear something, okay?" Asel said. "Something like skeeters or nats."

"Something like a whine, something like a hum?"

"Something like that."

"Like *tires*, Asel. Like a horde, like a gathering, an army, a multitude of oversize wheels screamin' against the road."

"Oh, shit," Asel said.

"Damn right," said Phil. . . .

~ FORTY-FOUR ~

They watched, keeping low in the stand of joopiners, or whatever they might be. The massive trucks shrieked as they approached, a shriek that climbed the scale, rumbled down again as they pounded on by—the way things come, and the way they go away. If Uncle Hal wasn't dead, Asel thought, he'd likely know why.

The flash of the lights, the roar of the engines, the scream of the tires, one and then another and another after that, this steady beat was enough to leave you dazzled, leave you in a trance if you didn't watch out. It didn't help that Phil counted out loud . . .

"one-sixty-seven . . . one-sixty-eight . . . no, that'd be sixty-nine . . ."

No one said a thing for a while as the silence creeped in, as the natural world began to stir again.

"Well that's real nice, Phil," said Betty Louise at last, breaking the deathly quiet. "You said *this* road would be fine. 'A trucker, he won't get off the highway, Betty Louise Ann. Doesn't anybody come up here.'"

"There might be repairs," Phil said, scratching something in his artificial hide. "Somethin' like that."

"If there was, don't you think those truckers would've yacked about it while they were drinkin' and tearing up the place? They yacked about everything else."

"It's a little late to worry about that," Asel said. "I'm glad we pulled off the road. I'm grateful this happened at night."

"Me too, Asel." Betty Louise smiled, the way people smile at the mentally deprived. "Because I have never seen a herd of truckers driving in the dark. And neither has Phil, as long as he was loafin' around Buckstop."

Phil didn't answer, and Asel decided not to butt in. Don't go

looking for trouble, Mother had told him more than once. Wait, and trouble will seek you out.
Very little Mother had said made sense, but she was surely right in that.

It was not Asel's favorite day.
Betty Louise frowned out her window at nothing at all. Phil hummed. Hummed in a flat, tuneless monotone that drove Asel insane. Asel sweated. Sweated and drove, fearful every moment he would meet a pack of truckers howling down the road. Stopped every hour, pulled off the side. Said he had to pee. What he did, was throw up in the rabut-bush and saydge.

Before the sun went down, he turned off behind a crumbled building the color of the wasted land itself. Phil said the structure was made of a doby, but Asel paid little heed to that. Anyone could see the stuff was simply dried mud.

He found a weathered sign half buried in the sand. The words read: CUR OS & C LD BEE

He broke it up into pieces and started a fire inside. The food from the Buckstop was getting rather sparse. Betty Louise put everything together and made a nice stew.

After supper, Asel walked out to get away from the smoke that had gathered inside. The sun was down, but he could still see the line of mountains to the west. For the first time since they'd started, he felt they were somewhat close. And, if they were, it was high time they started turning east, leaving Aridsoda behind. The Franchise States were dangerously near, and just beyond was Califoggy itself. Even if they didn't meet another horde of truckers, they were bound to run into someone else—someone who'd seen a poster somewhere.

"If we're not going to talk, I wish you'd tell me why. You can be mad at that bair if you like. I don't see why you have to take it out on me."

"I know I shouldn't, hon, I'm sorry 'bout that." She turned around and faced him, resting on her elbow, letting the blanket reveal her upper parts. As ever, he was struck by her awkward country charms, by her eyes, by her square and stubborn jaw, by her mouth that was clearly too wide, a mouth that could twist out of shape in a moment of passion, or shut like a trap in a fierce and sullen pout.

The longer he knew her, the more he was amazed by this

woman of common birth, by the lusty, captivating beauty peculiar to her kind.

"It's not you, you ought to know that. It's not Phil, either. He didn't know about the trucks, and I never should've left it up to him. He can't help what he is. Underneath that phony fur, he's not real at all.

"What it is, see, is me." She took his hand and held it to her breast. "I never told you this 'cause you never thought to ask. I was born in Trench, that's south of Hammerillo Flats. I had two goals in life. One, to make it out of Trench, the other to follow in Mama's footsteps and learn the dirigible trade.

"That second dream came to naught, and I can live with that. But I found another dream when you came along, Asel. The minute you walked into my life, I knew you were the one. It's true we come from different strata in life, but I feel we can overcome that.

"What happened when those truckers came along last night? I felt such a fear in my heart, I flat lost it on the spot. I thought, 'Betty Louise Ann, you found somebody that's right, and now you'll maybe lose him. Your hopes, your dreams, will be thwarted once again.'"

She broke, then, simply came apart. With a frightened, mournful cry, she fell into his arms. Asel held her as she sobbed, shivered, gave way to her lament. He patted her gently and kissed her hot tears.

He had no idea what he ought to do next. He was touched, moved, somewhat affected by this open display. He wanted to tell her that he cared, possibly loved her, too. It struck him, then, that he might, actually, feel that way. And, strangely enough, if he did, he didn't mind at all. . . .

~ FORTY-FIVE ~

"If I'm not mistook," Phil said, "an' some'll say I likely am, we'll be getting where we want to be soon." He opened the drawer in his chest, and unfolded the dusty map on his knees.

"Al knew these parts right well. Ute country's over northeast—'course there isn't any Utes there now. He came up here a lot. There's a river close by. We can cross over there. After that, we'll head straight east. It'll be high country—you can tell by the little peaks he's drawed here—but the truck'll make it fine.

"Califoggy bastards won't bother you there. Though we might run into the Sue."

"Sue what?"

"He's talking about the Sue Nation," said Betty Louise. "They're not real friendly. But they won't bother us, we don't bother them."

"Good. Then we won't. As long as we get off the truckers' road, anywhere's fine with me."

"I said we would, didn't I? You not hearing good, or what?"

"Phil, just hold it," said Betty Louise.

Asel was relieved to hear they could soon turn east. And, if Phil didn't like the jab about truckers, he could get out and walk. Imitation bair or not, Phil had a bair attitude, and a real bair smell.

Despite his displeasure with Phil, Asel was content. Pert, chipper, glad to be alive. Every few minutes, he winked at Betty Louise, gave her a silly grin. Betty Louise winked back. Blushed a little, wiggled her toes against the dash.

The night had been absolutely grand. After the crying came a time of silence, of holding in the dark, of gentle kisses exchanged like precious gifts. Later, a tangling of limbs going this way and that, knots that neither of them wished to untie. Then, assorted gasps, traditional sighs, all the signs of passion defined, some they simply made up on the spot.

And, even at the height of the day, the tastes, the touches, the wonders of the night were born again in the looks that passed between the two. Even the presence of an odorous, sulky bair failed to diminish their desire to stop somewhere, and do it all again.

This sort of thing would have lasted all day, if Phil hadn't bellowed, shouted, exploded from his seat and bashed his head against the roof.

"Shit, Asel, stop the—fucking—truck—right now!"

Startled out of fantasy nine, Asel slammed his foot to the floor. Tires squealed against the road. The truck pitched, lurched, took a dizzy spin to the right. Jerked to an agonizing stop.

"Damn it, Phil, what's the matter with you? We could've all been killed."

Asel shook, couldn't loose his hands from the wheel. "You want to pee, you ask, like everybody else." He looked at Betty Louise. Her face was the color of ash.

"Let me out," said Phil. "Move. One of you, I don't care which."

"That's the best idea you've had all day." Asel opened the door and stepped out. Phil lumbered past him without a word.

"Take your time. Don't hurry back."

Betty Louise came up beside him. Asel gripped her arm, found she was shaky and out of sorts.

"What's the matter with him? I mean, besides the fact he's a bair."

"I guess that's it, hon. That, and maybe needing spare parts."

Phil hadn't run into the saydge. He was down the road, thirty yards ahead. Rigid, perfectly still. As if he'd had a stroke, as if he'd turned to stone. Maybe Betty Louise was right. Maybe it was due to faulty parts.

"I got sensitive ears," Phil said. "It's not polite to talk to someone behind his back."

"You'd better not be urinating on the road. I've got to drive over that."

"Why don't you come and look?"

"I don't think so, Phil."

Betty Louise shook her head. "Phil's got some bad habits. But I don't think he's doing that."

"No? Then you come too."

"Hurry back, hon."

Asel muttered something to himself, and headed for the bair.

"I hope you're not looking at an aunt," Asel said to Phil's back. "I hope you didn't nearly wreck us to stand and look at the ground. I hope you didn—"

Asel stopped. There wasn't any ground to see. It vanished abruptly, right at Phil's feet, plummeted down, down, into a fearsome void, taking Asel's stomach with it, down into a gaping maw.

"Holy shit," Asel said.

"Damn right," said Phil.

"Something quite significant must have happened to cause a hole the size of that."

"I heard about this. I thought it was somewhere else."

Asel frowned. "You made us stop. Why'd you do that?"

"I had a tuition. Came on me like that. Al used to do it. Maybe I caught it from him."

"We would have gone right in. Straight fucking down. I'm guessing a mile. I suppose I'm sorry for what I said."

"I sorely doubt it, but I'll take what I can get."

"My Lord," said Betty Louise, catching up with the pair. "Will you look at that. I guess I owe you my life, Phil. I regret what I might have said."

"A hug'll do fine."

"I don't intend to hug a bear."

"Doesn't cost a thing to ask."

Asel squinted across the great abyss, let his gaze wander down sheer rock walls, down through layered striations, through a hundred variations of warm and dusty reds, through ochre, rust, copper, and brick, shades he couldn't define.

This fearsome chasm, this awesome bite out of the Earth, stretched out of sight to the left and to the right. At the bottom of this impossible ditch, a river wound its way along a torturous path—a river no more than a pale blue line from this dizzy height.

"That's it, then? This is the river we cross. We cross here, and on through high country to the east. No more problems after that."

Phil scratched under a furry arm. "I was waiting for your response. You've got a natural bent for cruelty and abuse. There's a river on the map. Doesn't say it's in a hole, I can't help that."

"It might get narrow somewhere," said Betty Louise. "You know, the hole? It's got to have an end."

"See there, Asel? This lady's got a positive outlook on life. You'd do well to work on that yourself."

"You'd do well not to stand real close to that edge. I feel a negative output coming on."

"I'll check the truck," Phil said, and hurried off.

"That was overly harsh," said Betty Louise. "I understand how you feel, but you don't have to do that."

Asel peered once more at the chasm's far rim. The other side looked exactly like the side he was standing on now. Only a hopeless distance away.

"You said it had to end. Logically, it does. We didn't go into geographic features at Iacola Keep. I wasn't informed about the states we didn't own. This thing could go on forever. It wouldn't be hard to imagine that it did."

"I'm really sorry, Asel. I said I understand your plight. But Phil's right about your shitty attitude."

"Oh, fine. Maybe you and Phil could form a club. Talk about Asel. Why Asel can't get along. Why he can't be nice like everyone else."

"Asel, hon—"

"Do you understand what this fucking hole means, Betty Louise? We can't possibly get across. I will not drive another mile west. We have to go east and pray this monstrous thing ends. With my luck, it'll turn due south. Right back to Two-kum-curry. Goodtime Bob, or the Oklahomer Wall. Why does everything have to happen to ME!

"me! **ME!**
ME! *ME!*
ME . . . !"

All the rage, all the fury, all the fears that were bottled up inside erupted in a bellow, in a shout, that rang through the awesome gorge and came back at him again.

"Yes, you, you
you *stupid stupid*
stupid SHIT!"

—he shouted back.

Betty Louise Ann was startled, for she had never seen him in such a fever, such a fit. She was glad Phil was back at the truck. She wasn't sure Asel would try to toss him off. She hoped it wouldn't come to that.

* * *

"I'm terribly sorry," Asel said, sure that an artery had burst somewhere, that blood would fountain from his ears. "I believe I lost control. I have never done that before. I might want to do it again."

"Well, don't. I thought you'd had a seizure. I am not trained. I wouldn't know how to handle that."

"I know what you're trying to say. You were worried, concerned. I appreciate that. I—think you know how I feel about you, Betty Louise."

"How, Asel?"

"How what?"

"How do you feel about me? I mean, beyond raw passion and physical desire, as a vessel for your needs? I already know about that."

"Why, I care for you. Of course."

"Care."

"I certainly do."

"Really? Oh, Lord, how blessed am I. Fuck you, Asel. A person *cares* about lunch. I care if I got clean socks. Care doesn't cut it with me. I have given more of myself to you than that."

"Betty Louise Ann . . ."

He watched her stomp away, watched the way she moved with fine, hydraulic ease. Wondered what he'd done. Wondered what he ought to do next—

—wondered at the swift, dark shadow that raced across the sand, wondered, as it thundered through the sky, as it shook the very ground. Looked up. Felt his stomach turn to lead.

Choppers! Six . . . seven . . . ten . . . Black, squat, ugly, and vile. Warty hides and piggy snouts.

"Son of a bitch," Phil said, lumbering up to Asel's side. "What the hell kinda' thing is that?"

"Mikrosoph-Crupps. Modified Nines. That simpering lout, Lord Pierce. SEC. Sided up with Ducky and Califoggy State to bring us down. Shit, Phil. . . !"

Phil didn't answer. Bright plumes of smoke began to blossom along the distant rim. Half a second later, the sound rolled over the earth, one volley after the next.

Asel was perplexed. "I don't know what they're doing, but they're not after us."

"Bombin' those pour souls up in Sue Nation's what they're doing. You still thinking on driving east, I expect you could find out why. . . ."

~ FORTY-SIX ~

Asel had seen one before.

Father had built a dam to dry up a state next door. Everything died, and they sold out quickly after that. At nine or maybe ten, Asel had thought it quite a sight. This one, though, must have been an awesome structure in its time. It was no more than rubble, now, broken and breached, most of it swept downriver by some great disaster in the past. Peering up, though, he could see a fragment left on either side.

"Look real close," Asel pointed, "you can see there was a road up there. You could drive right across from one side to the next."

"I doubt anyone'd want to do that," said Betty Louise. "You'd get sick if you ever looked down."

"Maybe they didn't," Phil said. "What you could do is look straight ahead. That'd be the thing to do."

"If you were up there, you'd *look*. You wouldn't be able to stop. You'd say, 'My, a wondrous vista, I've got to take a look.' Then you'd throw up, so would everybody else."

"Huh-uh. A bair, he gets a square meal, he's not about to toss it somewhere."

"You don't know what a real bair would do. I doubt he'd be up there at all."

"Talk to a human, they got to throw in that ethnic slur."

"A slur's not a slur if it's flat-out true. . . ."

Asel did his best to ignore all this, and think what they ought to do next. Now, the great gorge was off to the north. Crossing was easy enough. Phil found a spot where the water hardly came up to the tires.

Someone in the past had found these shallows, too, he reasoned, someone ambitious enough to cut a rough road below the ruins, up through the cliffs on either side. The truck protested, and scraped the rocky walls, but made it to the top.

Ahead, the land turned abruptly to bleak, near featureless desert again—flat, endless miles of nothing more than prickle plants and scrub.

Still, it's north, by God, and nothing in the way. No river, no great enormous hole.

North. Make sure and miss the chasm. Turn back east. After that . . . After that, he didn't know, and didn't greatly care. He wasn't concerned about the Sue. Those choppers were after them, too. Wouldn't they welcome someone who understood their plight?

"Wouldn't count on it," Phil said, when Asel shared his thoughts. "They're not a friendly bunch."

"I'm not looking for a friend. I'll settle for don't bother me, I won't bother you."

Betty Louise was being cordial again. Not warm, friendly, not yearning for physical bliss. Fine. He had put up with everything else, he could likely manage this.

It was late afternoon when they saw it. From a distance, no more than a patch, a hump, a slight distention of the land. Closer, Asel knew what it was, and braked the truck at once.

His heart beat faster, but the fear he'd felt the first time was guarded caution now, the need to be aware. The stench that marked the other site was clear, but the dead had been long dead here, perhaps a month or more.

There were bones, now, shattered, scattered bits already gnawed and spread about. Stubs of ugly weapons had just begun to sprout. The sand was working on a slow and careless grave.

Betty Louise closed her eyes, shook her head, as if these actions might make the horror go away. Then she was out of there, gone.

Asel looked at Phil. "You're not real surprised, are you? You know what it is." Not a question, not meant to be.

"I could ask you where you seen this before."

"Back there. Before Buckstop. Just like this. Who's BIG BUGG, Phil? Tell me the rest."

"I don't know any rest. You hear about him, is all . . ."

"And what?"

"What do you mean, *and what?*" Phil made no effort to hide

his irritation. "I got to know everything there is? Guess you forgot. I'm just a fucking bair."

Asel watched Phil stomp off, then walked back to the truck.

No one spoke. No one had anything to say. Asel drove. Betty Louise curled up in a ball, pretended she wasn't there.

An hour past the killing ground, Phil began to smell—not just his ordinary, everyday smells, something with a sizzle, something with a zap. A sharp and acrid scent that seared, burned, assaulted the tissues of the nose.

"I think I'm on fire," Phil said. "I think you better stop."

Phil didn't have to ask twice. Asel nearly took the door with him getting out. Phil stumbled past him, rolled on the ground. Smoke poured out of his belly. Phil cursed, moaned, beat at his pelt with both hands.

"I never heard of a combustible bair," said Betty Louise, waving smoke aside. "Never heard of one doin' something like that."

"I don't think the real ones do. It's not a natural effect."

Phil was on his feet. When he opened the drawer in his chest, something crackled, something sparked. Phil poked at it, jerked back fast. Spit on his finger and damped the thing out.

"I believe I got it under control. Some kind of circuit disorder, somethin' shorted out. It isn't me, I don't think. I'm getting interference somewhere."

Asel slapped at a bug. "What's that supposed to mean?"

"Means what I said. Everything of the lectro-mechanical persuasion is tied in together somehow. The parts is the whole and the other way around. Anything that clicks, anything zaps, is one with ever'thing else. Humans is that way too, but you don't know it yet. Pride standeth in your way."

"Can we get moving now?"

"I'm just a soulless device. What you asking me for?"

"We get out of this business, what you going to do, hon? I mean, in the area of personal direction. In a life goal sense."

Hon. Now that's a good indication. Maybe we're back on track again.

"I have tried not to think about that. In a way, it is futile to go back east. That was my home, my heritage, my life, so to speak. But all that's been taken from me now. There is no Iacola Keep. I owned America East for an hour and a half. I'm not a prince of anything, Betty Louise. What I've got is a shirt, and a tacky pair of pants.

"Maybe I'm simply going back because there's nothing else to do. I guess that doesn't make sense. It's not logical at all, but I don't know a thing about the north and the south. I surely don't intend to go west."

Asel waved his hands in a hopeless gesture, tossing the future aside.

"Perhaps that's it. Maybe it's where I *can't* go, not where I can."

Betty Louise was silent for a while. Then she laid a hand gently over his.

"You've got a deep side to your nature, Asel. You don't let it out a whole lot, but you should. It's a quality much to be admired."

Asel was taken aback, pleased at this remark. He had never thought about depth as a trait within himself. He was certain no one, especially Mother, had ever noticed that.

"I—appreciate what you said. I really do."

"I just say what I mean. I think you know that."

"Deep is as deep does," Phil said from the back.

"You keep your thoughts to yourself," said Betty Louise. "You want to think about something, ponder on fire safety for a while."

The shadows were growing long. There weren't that many, for the vertical dimension was rare in this horizontal land. This was why Asel began to notice something different at hand.

At first, it was merely something here and there—a part, a scrap, something he couldn't identify. Then it was a brick, a weathered post, a rusty pipe stuck in the ground.

With every mile, he was further convinced something had been here once, something that wasn't here now. A settlement, a town that was only rubble now. Rubble and ruin, buried in the sand, as far as the eye could see.

"I don't like this," Phil said. "I don't care for this at all."

"You don't care for what? There's nothing here to see. For my part, I am fond of places where nobody lives."

"Like I said. Don't listen to me."

"Good advice. I'll try and remem—"

"—Hon, flick on the lights. My Lord, what's that!"

Asel saw it too, hit the brakes hard. The figure stood in the middle of the road, caught in the harsh beams of light.

It was short, broad. One arm. Two legs. Half a bucket head and a blinking red eye. No shoes, no pants. Gold star pinned on a lumberjack shirt. Its body was a loose connection of rivets, tarnished brass, and corrugated rust. It held its stance, didn't give an inch.

"What did I tell you?" Phil said. "Said I was getting interference somewhere. That dude's made outa static and tin."

The creature suddenly moved. Stalked up to the truck. Jerked, perked, lurched in a spasm, quivered in a fit.

"Eva-ning," it said, in a voice like gravel in a can. "Awe-fisher Fry-day, shir. Ewe be here on bizzzznus or playshur? May I zee you lie-senze pleez. . . ?"

~ FORTY-SEVEN ~

"What is it saying, Phil? You catch any of that?"
"He's a fuckin' recording. He don't have any idea."
"Sir, where does this road go?" Asel asked. "Can I get a turnoff east?"
"Eva-ning. Awe-fisher Fry-day, shir. You be here on bizzzzznus or playshur? May I see your—"
"Thanks. Keep up the good work. You're doing fine."
Asel drove off. Didn't look back. He was sure the fellow was back at his stand, in the middle of the road.
"I hope you don't judge every mechanical person by him," Phil said. "He came out 'bout a hundred years back. I'm not even related to somethin' like that."
"I have nothing but kindly thoughts for the witless creatures of this world," said Betty Louise. "There but for a twisted fate might go you and I."
"Not me," Phil said. "Thought I made that clear."
"I'm pulling off somewhere," Asel said. "I don't want to hit anything at night."
"Try and find a place with no crawlies, hon."
"I can't guarantee that."
"Well try. . . ."

The buildings appeared a mile ahead. Patched, burned out, roofs fallen in. Ten, maybe a dozen sagging structures lined the road on either side. Nothing was over a story tall. Some didn't even reach that. The fact that they were standing at all was a wonder, Asel thought. Nothing was holding them up but rust, rot, and the parched desert air.

He pulled in behind the row on his left. Not that he thought anyone was about, but caution was a habit now.

"I don't see that inside's better than out," said Betty Louise, dusting off her hands as she stepped out of the ruin.

"I wouldn't know how to act," Asel said, "sleeping under a roof, eating real food. Taking a bath. I never imagined life could be as crude as this."

"I wouldn't know, hon. Refinement and ease was never a problem, growing up in Trench. Only entertainment we had was Badjerfest, second day of spring. That, an' looking at the stars. You never looked at the stars, I bet, till you came out here."

"We didn't go outside. There was plenty to do in the house."

"Those girls you were talking about. Flunks from overseas."

Asel cleared his throat. "What I am *talking* about is a way of life. It's different than here."

"I guess those floozies, they'd do anything you said."

"How did we get on that? I just said things are different, that's all."

"Asel, listen up," Phil said. "Somethin' coming this way."

Asel turned, looked where Phil was pointing. There were phantoms standing in shadow, wraiths with missing parts. Things without noses, things without feet. Things with scarcely anything at all. Asel thought at once of the TechsMechs Rangers, but this was something else. Pieces, fragments were missing, but these were Awe-fisher Fry-day's kin, and Phil's as well, though Asel would never tell him that.

One stepped forward from the rest. Formal wear. Frayed black tie. White plastic shirt, hanging in tatters from his skeletal chest. Ponderous legs of pitted steel. No arms. Dented iron head.

"What a pleasure to have you here, sir," it said, in a voice that was alarmingly real. "I am the manager, Mr. LaGorse. I hope you enjoy your stay. If there's anything you need, I doubt if we have it. We don't get many people types here."

"Not many?"

"Not any, that I recall. Not for some time."

"Good. What's up past here?"

"Past here. That is an interesting concept, sir. I shall note this moment and give it some thought. I am truly sorry about the accommodations. It is not like the old days, I assure you of that. Things have rather gone to pot."

"I've noticed. It's occurring all over. Don't apologize. I doubt it's your fault."

"Thank you, sir." Mr. LaGorse gave Asel a shaky bow. Something clanked and fell. "That is kind of you to say. We do what we can, you know. As you can see, I have a full, competent staff on call. Unless you ask for anything, we shall be glad to meet your every need."

"Thank you. I believe that will be all."

The manager bowed again, turned and clattered off. In a moment, he and his staff had vanished in the night. . . .

~ FORTY-EIGHT ~

Asel was exhausted, beat. Dead on his feet from the cares of the day. Clearing the ground, in case of snaykes or aunts. He drew the blanket around him, gave a long sigh, and waited for blessed sleep.

Betty Louise had a tendency to snore. Hadn't missed a beat since that very first night. Mother, a person of gentle birth, had snored loud enough to wake the dead. Had to get a flunk to sit and keep her mouth shut.

The stars blazed overhead in the frosty desert sky. Betty Louise seemed to like the stars a lot. Asel found them awfully bright. Night was for sleeping. Nighttime ought to be dark.

Asel twitched, itched, rolled restlessly about. Finally gave it up, slipped on his jacket, past the sagging structure, back out to the road.

There was nothing there to see, nothing but a pale line stretching north and south—the road, the rubble, the darkened ruins low against the sky. Asel longed for the dawn. Thought for moment, he ought to go back, wake her up, get an early start.

No way. She wouldn't like that. It was best to let Betty Louise get plenty of rest.

Asel stopped, suddenly aware of something odd, something different in the night. A structure up ahead, off to the right, wasn't totally dark. A light glowed through narrow cracks in the wall. Red, then blue. Pink and green and white. Bright, then dim. Dim and bright again.

Asel was concerned, wary of this unexpected sight. Creatures of a mechanical nature didn't need the light. Manager LaGorse had assured him no other humans were around. Hadn't been for unremembered years. Did Mechs ever lie? Certainly they did. For an instant, there, he'd forgotten Phil the bair.

Crossing the road, he approached the building with caution. Wished he had a weapon. A pistol, a blade, a pointy stick of some kind. Closer, now, he could hear peculiar sounds. Rattles, squeaks, whistles, and creaks. Sounds he couldn't define. Harsh, irritating sounds that assaulted the ears, grated on the teeth.

Walking with care, watching where he stepped, Asel followed the glow. And, as it had from a distance, it brightened, dimmed, brightened once again. Now, the sound grew louder as well. Louder, with a most irregular measure, an odd, uncommon beat. It seemed, to Asel, that the light and the sound were one with the eerie cadence, a rhythm, a melody of sorts, turned inside out—

He felt his foot slip, felt the rubble slide, shift, and give way. Tried to stop himself, grabbed empty air, hit the ground hard, struck his head against unforgiving stone. Asel cried out against the fierce, agonizing pain. Everything was red, everything was bright. There were too many lights, too many stars.

He lay there, shaken, fighting for a breath. Waiting for the throbbing to stop, for the hurt to go away. Tried to move his arms. Couldn't feel his legs. Would Betty Louise stick with him? Would any woman want a man crippled, dazzled in the head?

Better get up. Better not ask.

He wasn't sure how long he'd been out. The pain was still there, but he picked himself up, came to his knees. After a moment, he was once again aware of the lights and the sounds. Now, they seemed to blink, clink in synch with the throb and the thrumming in his head.

Cautiously, he came to his feet. Nothing seemed broken, at least not yet. His cousin, Malcomm, from Lesser New Yuk, slipped in a tub. Rode around a year on a hefty flunk's back. Didn't even try to get well. Finally, someone found him out . . .

"Are you all right, sir? May I be of some help?"

Asel looked up into the single amber eye of Manager LaGorse. Wondered how the fellow, still devoid of arms, intended to help.

"I believe I'm all right. Had a little spill."

"They don't keep the grounds in shape anymore. Everything's gone to pot, I fear. Would you like to come in for a moment? I'm certain we can find you a table somewhere."

"Yes, I guess I will. In where?"

"Right this way, sir. Watch your step, now. Don't want to take a tumble again."

With that, Manager LaGorse raised a ponderous foot and smashed in a portion of the wall. Dust, plaster, rot from ancient days, drifted from the ceiling in a veil. When the haze cleared away, Asel faced an astonishing sight.

The room was full of Mechs. A horde, a rabble of artificial wrecks. Bent, broken, malformed devices crushed, cramped, packed so tightly there was scarcely an inch between one and the next. Asel recognized a few, who worked for LaGorse. The rest he had never seen before.

He couldn't spot a one that didn't lack a vital part. One fellow didn't have a head. Another had a head, an arm, and nothing else. He babbled, screeched, dragged himself about.

Each of these devastated Mechs had a clunk, a jangle, a tick, or a click. Together, they raised a horrid clamor, an agonizing din.

"The usual crowd," said Manager LaGorse, as he led Asel through this artificial lot. "There used to be other attractions in town. That was some time ago. Now we all come here."

"It's—very nice," Asel said. "Interesting décor."

"Thank you, sir, I'm sure."

The room, Asel thought, had surely exploded a number of times before. Everything hung, clung, defied gravitation, poised in a state of imminent collapse. The roof drooped and sagged, dangled in tatters and strips. Walls cracked and bulged, spilled dusty innards out.

Hanging from the ceiling was the source of the glow he had seen from the road—tangles, knots, clots of colored lights. Each one blinked, flickered, in a most alarming way. Peering to his right, Asel discovered why. A pair of iron, disembodied legs was welded to pedals that turned a massive wheel. Sparks flew from this device in a dazzling array. Up. Down. Bright. Fade. Do it all again.

"Pleasant greetings, dear. I have not viewed you here before."

Asel turned to find a tall, slender Mech at his side. It was clearly a her, not a him. Her head was rusted chrome. Cobalt eyes. Scarlet mouth, hinged to a boxy jaw. Metal shavings hung past her shoulders, down to a pair of pointy cones.

"No," Asel answered, trying not to stare. "I'm sure I've never been here before."

"I would not know that, babe. I have not *seen* you. That does not imply your presence at all. Would you care to place a bet?"

"Place a what?"

"A bet, sir. Did I not state that correctly? If you wish, I will voice it again, hot guy."

She laid a cold hand on his arm. "Do you object if I touch? I do not register your name."

"Asel. Asel Iacola."

"Asshole eye-a-koda. That is a name of great delight to me. Where do you reside, Asshole?"

"Asel, actually. I'm formerly from America East. I'm not from anywhere now."

"You are most lonely I grasp. Do not feel this lack, sweet pye. I am Debbie Ten. I shall become your footloose, devil-may-matter companion in any way you wish. Would you care to place a bet?"

"You asked me that before."

"I do not do befores. I only do the now. Come, blazing lips. Step this way if you can."

Holding his arm in a not too gentle grip, she led him through the crowd. In the center of the room was a table. On the table was a large, overturned hubcap, clearly a relic from a very big truck. Someone had painted a circle of numbers inside, barely visible now.

A dozen Mechs were crowded about this odd device. They buzzed and whirred in somewhat angry tones, shoving one another about.

"Asshole. What precise amount would you care to wager?"

"I wish you'd work on the name. And I don't know what you're talking about. No offense, but I would like to leave if it's all the same to you."

"It is a simple procedure. A being of normal reasoning power can comprehend the rules." Debbie's blue eyes quivered in a series of rapid blinks. Her hand remained firmly clasped around his wrist.

"I spin this spherical object. You will choose any number you wish, firm buns. You will then anticipate where the object will cease its motion."

"Why would I want to do that?"

"You might win big."

"Win what?"

"What is your bet?"

"Are we back to that again?"

"Would you rather have intra-course with me? Or practice some other perversion?"

"I—guess not, thank you for asking, though."

Debbie's mouth creaked into a grin. "Fine. Then we shall continue this pleasant, but devious game of chance. . . ."

~ FORTY-NINE ~

With a blur of motion, Debbie spun the spherical object. It rattled, clattered, raced around within the rim.

"Damn it all, Debbie, I was here first. That feller, he's gotta get in line."

A massive steel arm came out of the crowd, a hand with tattered, white gloves, snatched up the rolling object and dropped it in Debbie's hand.

Asel looked up. The Mech was a faded shade of blue. Yellow suspenders were painted on its chest. A tin hat sat at a rakish angle on its head.

"No," Debbie said. "Asshole is first. You are second. You will wait on him."

"It's all right," Asel said. "Let him go on ahead."

Debbie's eyes went blank. Her head began to shake. For an instant, Asel feared she was having an imitation fit. Phil had shown that same crazed look when he smoked and shorted out.

"Yes," she said finally. "I shall agree. He can go first. Asshole, sweetie, you will go next. Georgie. You will place your bet."

"I bet three," Georgie said. "Three on number seven. Seven's my, uh, lucky number, ya see?" he told Asel. "Seven's a winner ever' time."

The Mech drew off his gloves. Held out three iron fingers on his left hand, deftly snapped them off with his right. Asel winced. Georgie dropped the digits on the table.

"All bets are properly positioned," said Debbie Ten. She spun the spherical object again. It rattled, hummed around the rim. Red, green, bright fuschia eyes followed its path from the crowd. Finally it paused, rolled down the slope and stopped.

A collective groan arose from the crowd. Without looking up, Debbie Ten raked three fingers into an open drawer.

"The House wins this incident. Georgie, would you care to propose a bet again? Consider the joyous sensations you would entertain if you should win this time."

"Shoot, Debbie, I can't." Georgie held up both hands. Asel counted. One . . . two. "Better, ah, quit while I'm ahead," the big Mech said, and shoved his way through the crowd.

"Next player," Debbie said. "Announce your betting, please."

In the heat of the game, Debbie had clearly forgotten Asel. She no longer gripped his wrist, didn't look his way. Still, Asel stayed and watched. A short, wretched Mech lost an eye and a nose. Another lost a leg. Bet and lost the other one too. Dropped with a clatter, with a rattle to the floor.

Arms. Legs. A handful of wires, jerked from a belly or a chest. And, after each spin, Debbie raked her winnings into the open drawer.

Asel was bewildered. If there was any point to the business, he couldn't discern it at all. There were numbers printed on the rim. The players chose a number and bet. Why? The spherical thing always rolled to the center of the dented hubcap. There was no place else for it to go.

"It doesn't make sense," he muttered to himself. "Gravity is a law, and it cannot be denied. I remember hearing that. Debbie Ten is nothing but a simulated crook."

"Pretty good one, too. And not a bad looker, except for that hair."

"Phil." Asel was surprised to see the bair. "I had no idea you were here. I was out on the road. I saw a light and heard peculiar sounds. I sort of stumbled in."

"Uh-huh. Heard about that. You got a little swellin' up there."

Phil shook his head, in imitation remorse. "It's a shame, friend, a humiliation to the lectro-mechanical kind. These folks has got it half right, and don't recall the rest. They're caught in a loop, is what it is. Don't know what they was made for, can't do nothing else.

"These here are mostly K-fours. Shit, that's near a couple hundred years back. You'd think they'd of bet all their parts. 'Cept they're on a loop, like I said. Ever' now and then, they'll start all over again. Me, I got a self-renewal drive. Don't have to do everything twice."

Asel shook his head. "This concept we're discussing. The thing about a bet. That's the part I don't understand."

Phil rolled his eyes. "You better follow me. I know a good way out. One where you won't be fallin' down."

Except for the dull ache in his head, Asel felt fine. Better, indeed, with a breath of the crisp desert air, away from blinking lights, from the terrible din.

"There's a lot of memories walkin' around back there," said Phil, who hadn't paused a moment since they'd walked back to the road. "I recognize a few, from stuff that Al said. That Ute got around, I told you 'bout that. He was on the circuit with the stars. Shittin' Bull, Silly the Kid. Merrymon Roe an' Barun, the Flying Red.

"Old Georgie Custard. Shoot, who'd of guessed he was still around. Hell, that must've been a time. Listen, Asel, I'm going to put this to you straight. I'm not going on. I got a notion to stick around here."

Asel stopped. "You do? You sure, Phil?"

"As sure as anything there is these days, I guess."

"Well . . . It won't be the same without you."

"You'll get by. You and Betty Louise. Just keep headin' north, then veer off east."

"You've helped a lot. I won't forget."

"Hell, don't know about that."

Before Asel could back away, Phil gripped him in a furry embrace, buried Asel in his odorous pelt. Let him go before Asel passed out.

"Keep the top of the truck clean. Don't let the byrd shit build up, the engine'll choke up if you do."

"I'll remember. Thanks for the advice."

"I'll see you off in the morning. You best get some sleep, make an early start."

"Well. Good night, Phil."

"Night, Asel. For a human person, I think you're all right."

Phil ambled off, vanished in the night. Walking back to the room full of noise and blinding light. Back to his kind, though he was, indeed, a model far above the rest.

Asel decided he would leave out the part about the final embrace. One thing Betty Louise couldn't tolerate was hugging a bear.

He was somewhat surprised to find he was sorry to see Phil go. Relieved, too, glad he wouldn't have to listen to the constant blather, the ridiculous lies. Pleased, to be sure, the truck wouldn't smell like bair. Still, Phil had been a friend, and Asel seemed to be losing friends along the way.

Sylvan Lee McCree. He couldn't forgive the fellow, couldn't bring himself to do that. It wouldn't be the first time lust had come between friends. Asel had cared for Uncle Hal, but couldn't forget he'd stolen Yvette-Marie, a saucy little flunk from Frants. Of course, Hal was dead. Maybe you should go a little easy on someone, after they'd gone through that. . . .

He didn't wake Betty Louise. Fell asleep at once without tossing, squirming all about. Didn't even dream, or nothing he recalled. He woke with the morning sun in his eyes. Sat up, stretched. The pain hit him hard, knocked him down again.

Asel closed his eyes and held his head. If he hadn't gone snooping, lurking about, if he'd stayed in bed . . .

He stood in easy spells. The earth whirled around awhile, then quit. Betty Louise was up. Possibly doing something private in the brush. Maybe getting water from the truck. Water would be a problem soon. There was nothing in town, he'd already asked. Mechs didn't need to drink. Phil did, of course, but that was showing off.

She wasn't in the truck, wasn't in the brush. He walked past the sad collection of buildings, a dull ache pounding in his head.

"What people ought to do," he muttered to himself, "is leave a note, a sign of some sort. It would save a lot of time. Especially if a person was injured, and didn't care to stomp around . . ."

He saw her, then. Stopped. Raised a hand to his eyes to cut the sun.

"Betty Louise? I've been looking for you. Where exactly have you been?"

She didn't answer. Simply sat there, cross-legged, by the road. Not looking at him, looking at the ground. Long hair covered her features, he couldn't see her face.

Asel was puzzled, somewhat annoyed. "I fell last night and hit my head. Didn't want to wake you, worry you with that. Look, if you could just—"

Asel went cold. The man was leaning against a weathered post. Black boots, black pants. Coal-black beard. Arms crossed over his chest. Silver rings in his ears, chains hanging from his vest.

"Hey," the man said, with a lop-sided grin, "it's the poster guy, right? Damn good likeness, too. I'd know you anywhere."

Asel's heart nearly stopped. He looked at the man in utter disbelief, stared at this lout with the arrogant grin, the silly chains, and the tacky black hat. He'd nearly made it, come so very close. Now the bastards had him, Ducky, and the loathsome Jackie Cee. It was over, done, nowhere to run . . .

And, in that very instant, he was overwhelmed by a dark and swelling rage that swept his fear aside. This raw, unaccustomed fury drove daggers through his head, but Asel simply thrust the pain away.

"You," he said, in a voice he scarcely recognized, "get out of here at once. I will not yield to you. I will not toss away my freedom to a rude, uncivil person in a truck."

The fellow looked puzzled, taken aback. There was something here he didn't comprehend.

"What I think," he said, "is you better go over there and sit."

"Don't tell me what to do. I won't put up with that."

"Mister, you're intruding on my space. You stay right where you are."

"I'm sorry, hon," said Betty Louise, as tears formed tiny brooklets on her cheeks. "I thought it was thunder, I came out to look. I ought to of known it doesn't rain a lot here."

Anger had kept Asel's gaze on the trucker. Now, he looked past Betty Louise, saw the great hulks, the behemoths of the road—one and then another, like a monstrous herd. The truckers had made their morning fires, and the tantalizing scent of weedmush, hawkfut, onyuns sizzling in a pan, made Asel more furious still.

"You people are not supposed to be here. I was told by good authority *you never use this road!*"

"Your roads, now, they aren't reliable all the time," the trucker said. "You're in the carrier trade, you got to get your goods through, you take what you can get."

"No." Asel clenched his fists by his side. "I know what you're up to." He took a step forward, another after that. "I know your cunning ways, I have dealt with common folk before."

"Mister, I asked you to stay over there."

"Asel . . ."

"Stay back, Betty Louise. I'll handle this."

"Shit, man, what is it with you?"

Asel couldn't see the man clearly anymore. Hammers were pounding in his head, everything was red.

"Don't—say I didn't warn you, fellow . . . don't say Asel Iacola wasn't . . . fair."

He staggered, saw an image swim before his eyes, swung, missed, and nearly fell. Kept to his feet, flailed out blindly once again.

"You stupid fuck," someone said. "I feel you are overly stressed. . . ."

~ FIFTY ~

Loreli had very nice hooters, but didn't seem bright. Slightly out of synch, vaguely unattached. Ducky kept peeking down her dress. Asel didn't care for that.

"What's he doing here, Mother? I'm the groom in this wedding, not him."

"Manners, Asel dear. Remembah wheah you are from."

"No. Where's that?"

"Two-kum-curry!" said Uncle Hal, looking terribly haggard, looking terribly dead.

"Almaquirky!" said Goodtime Bob.

"Califoggy State!" said a chorus of Nones.

"I'm not! I am not from any of those horrid places! I'm not from anywhere!"

"You got that right," said Sylvan Lee McCree, "you are fucking nowhere, man . . ."

"I'm not!

"I'm NOT!

"I'm—**NOT!**"

"Stop it now, just lie still, hon."

"I'm not, I'm—What? Betty Louise, I urge you not to take part in this dream, this hapless illusion, it isn't any fun."

"I don't guess it is. I'd be grateful if you'd stop. Here, drink some of this."

He snatched the tin cup from her, drank until he choked. His throat was parched, closed up tight. He asked for some more. Betty Louise said he'd had enough.

"Fine way to treat somebody, all they want's a drink. Everything's a blur, would you give me a hand? I need to—sit up."

"I'm glad you haven't lost your sweet disposition."

"Same to you, I'm sure. I—God, the *road's* moving, it's spinning all around. It's that injury's what it is. That lummox hit me in the head!"

"Nobody hit you," said Betty Louise, trying to push him back, calm him down. "You passed out, Asel. And the road isn't moving, you're not on the ground. You're up in a truck."

No, she said something else, she didn't say that...

Asel shook her aside, rubbed a hand across his eyes. No rubble, no ruins, no saydge, no sand. Unfamiliar hills, fences, trees. Kars, trucks, passing swiftly by.

The truth of it hit him, shook him, as it fell into place. He turned, stared past Betty Louise, felt the anger grip him once again.

A small, compact space, window in the side. A bunk, where he was sitting now. A cabinet, drawers. A neat stack of clothes. Higher, even with his gaze, the back of a seat, the top of a head. A head with a hat that had long gone out of style.

"That's—him, that's the son of a bitch who hit me! Betty Louise, you let him take me in."

Asel tried to climb the seat. Betty Louise pulled him back.

"No one's taking you in, Asel. That's Larry Bill, and he didn't hit you, I told you that."

"He's in their hire. He's a denizen of Disney-Dow."

"I don't think he's a denizen, hon."

"Whatever that is, I'm not." Larry Bill turned long enough to raise a sullen brow. "Truckers don't answer to no one. Get that through your head. Ours is a free and independent trade. We haul for pay, that's it. A trucker don't bow to corporate enterprise."

"You had a poster. I remember that."

Larry Bill laughed, and slapped the steering wheel.

"Had one, sure. Can't hardly miss 'em, they're hanging everywhere. I thought I made my position right clear. We're proud, sometimes rowdy, warriors of the road. We don't need no stinkin' re-ward, friend. I'll thank you not to bring that up again."

Asel looked at Betty Louise. Leaned up painfully and faced Larry Bill.

"You don't want me, why did you pick us up? I'd like an answer to that."

"Part of the Code, mister."

"What code is that?"

"Code of the open road. Help one another. As you'd maybe need help yourself one day." Asel was puzzled. Was this the same code that said rip up the Buckstop, break everything in sight? Maybe Larry Bill had been there himself. Maybe he'd laughed at the Ute. Taken Al's hat. Broken his heart.

He looked at Betty Louise, saw her shake her head, knew she was thinking that, too. Right. This was no time to go into that.

She sighed, gave him a deep and thoughtful look, thought a moment more, then scooted up close, leaned her head against his chest.

"I've got to tell you this, Asel. You haven't asked, so maybe you guessed. We're going west. While you were out, we passed into Califoggy State."

"I think I knew that. I know the sun sets in the west. I had to learn directions when I broke out of NERF. Maybe, in the back of my head, I thought if I didn't ask . . .

"How long was I out? I remember, it was barely getting light."

"It's almost two. You slept the whole day. Ranted and raved a good deal of the time. Who's Loreli, hon? Sue Jean? Yvette-Marie?"

"I guess Phil knows what happened by now. He told me last night, he's decided to stay. I didn't have a chance to tell you that."

"No. I didn't know, dear."

"He smelled real bad. Talked too much. I guess that was in his makeup, though. Someone built a bair that smells and talks a lot. I'll miss that truck. It'll be handy, if Phil wants to go anywhere."

Betty Louise didn't answer. In a moment, he heard her snore. It occurred to Asel she had stayed up all day, looking after him. That was a nice thing to do, he thought, and soon dozed off himself.

In the late afternoon, Larry Bill said if they looked to the left, they would see an awesome sight.

Awesome was as good a word as any, Asel thought, if words could do justice at all: *Menacing, tacky, vile,* came to mind, words that would do for a start.

The figure rose in granite splendor, from the mammoth legs to the chest, the shoulders, to the dark and brooding face, over half a mile high. Low clouds shrouded the features, but Asel knew them as well as he knew his own. There was no mistaking the stern and somber visage, the stubborn, challenging thrust of the jaw, the heavy, brooding brows, the grim look of constipation and despair.

He had watched the cheap statuettes roll off the line by the hundreds, by the thousands, every day at NERF. He and Sylvan McCree. The Duke of Sexxon-Apple, the twin Lords of Wrigley-Keds. Poor Hank Jockey-Visa had fallen in a vat, his vitals boiled, spoiled, stamped into replications of the massive figure Asel was gazing at now. Maybe, at this very moment, a tourist was buying a bit of Hank . . .

Maybe I hit my head harder than I thought.

"Lord, that is downright scary," said Betty Louise. "It gives me a chill, Asel. I'll have a bad dream tonight."

Asel said he thought he would too.

They were still far away from the great work itself, far from the base of San Clemente Shrine. Yet, there were inns, taverns, by the dozen, as far as one could see. Endless rows of shops, roadside stands, all selling clocks, souvenir socks, bad statuettes, each item bearing that glowering face above.

Just past the mist-shrouded head, Asel saw an old, steam-driven flyer clatter by. Rods pumped and thrashed, driving eight bat-wings in partial accord. Streamers flew from the tail. The fancy, elegant gondola, adorned in faded gold, hung on tattered wires and struts.

Asel had seen pictures of these ancient craft, knew they were designed by a famous Sherppa engineer. Now, tourists rode about in this shaky device, risking their very lives.

As Larry Bill turned to the north, slate-gray clouds rushed in from an invisible sea. Rain slashed at the giant structure; lightning sizzled against the growing dark. Asel leaned out to sniff the air. He hadn't seen rain since he'd left America East.

Betty Louise tugged at his shirt, shouted with joy, as she watched a long, silver dirigible flee from the path of the storm. Tears welled in her eyes, and Asel knew she was thinking of her mother, a famous pilot of the rigid airships.

Before the rain came down in a fury, pelting the roof and the windshield of the truck, Asel caught a glimpse of three more modern craft, fleeing overhead, heading due east. He couldn't see them close, but he knew that silhouette, knew these deadly machines bore the symbol of Disney-Dow, the leaping vole with fiery eyes.

Betty Louise was lost in thoughts of her own, and Asel didn't tell her what he saw. No need to worry her with that. She knew where they were: in the heart, in the belly, in the very bowels of the powerful West. Califoggy State. Where the almost Prince of Christler-Coke had never, ever imagined he would be. . . .

~ FIFTY-ONE ~

"I gotta turn here," said Larry Bill. "I'll let you folks off at the crossing up ahead."

Asel peered at the pitch-dark night. "I don't suppose you're headed east."

"East is where we came from, pal. This load's going to Mallyboo. I don't think you want to go there."

Asel didn't ask why. Larry Bill's eyes said enough.

The trucker offered a set of clean clothes. With some regret, Asel politely declined. His own clothes were wretched, but Larry Bill's were black, with shiny studs. Even if they caught him, Asel had the Iacola name to think about.

Larry Bill gave them foxx and fysh sandwiches, and water in a can. Gave them a handful of colorful bills. Asel had seen paper money, once, when he was six. Father had brought a sackful home from Frants.

"I got advice you don't likely need to hear," said Larry Bill. "Lay low awhile. Steal an ordinary kar. Consider a simple disguise. It's been a pleasure knowing you folks." He winked at Betty Louise. "You, I mean. Not him."

Asel watched the trucker pull away, watched until his lights disappeared. Watched with some regret. Larry Bill was a common fellow, crude of manner and socially inept, but Asel was getting used to that. Once again, he was learning there were exceptions to the rule in every class. Betty Louise had grown up in Trench. Ducky's people went back to Wall-Mutt. And look how *he* turned out.

"There's a lot of lights over there," said Betty Louise. "Maybe we ought to head for that. We'll be out of sandwiches and water before it gets light."

"Maybe we ought to not," Asel said. "Maybe we don't want to socialize a lot."

The grove of trees was well off the road, close enough to watch the kars go by, far enough to keep from being seen. Betty Louise said the trees were pahms. Asel said they didn't look natural at all. Just what you'd expect in Califoggy State.

"I don't want to seem ungrateful, Betty Louise, now understand that. I'd just like to know what good it did to get a ride west. Maybe I shouldn't ask. Maybe you'll get upset, but I am asking anyway."

Betty Louise sighed. "Now how did I know this was coming? Just a wild guess. You were hurt, Asel. I can't drive, you're aware of that. Wasn't anyone but Larry Bill to help. Which I thought was nice, seeing as how you tried to knock him down.

"He didn't *say* 'by the way, we're going west,' and I didn't ask. I thought you were dying, you stuck-up, selfish prick. I'd shut up and go to sleep if I were you. . . ."

They kept to the trees, in sight of the road. The foxx and fysh sandwiches were gone. The water ran out at noon. An hour after that, they ran out of trees. The busy highway veered to the right. An older road, cracked, overgrown with weeds and brush, wandered off to the left.

It was open ground, and Asel didn't care for that, but the highway seemed more dangerous still. It was clear that people didn't walk out here.

There were structures, vague and indistinct, in the distance, hidden behind a heavy growth of trees. Lights had glowed in that direction the night before.

Asel kept one eye on the sky. He expected black choppers to appear any moment. Or aero-machines whining down to pepper them with lead. The sky remained clear, a stark, unnatural blue.

As they walked, rusted signs appeared. Many had fallen to the ground, or teetered on shaky metal stems:

▼ LESSER LOST ANGELS
☐ WEST HOLY GOOD
☐ SANDY MONIKER
☐ CLEVERLY HILLS

"I don't like it," Asel said. "Sounds like too many people to me."

"People have water. Bir, pyes, and chikun-fried steak."

Asel gave her a wary look. "You haven't tasted the cuisine at the National Executive Rehab Facility, Betty Louise. You've never eaten at Our Lady of Reluctant Desire."

"I haven't eaten much of anything since I met you."

"Just what does that comment imply?"

"It implies starvation, thirst, a shitty attitude. What do you think?"

"Let's get out of the open. We're totally exposed out here."

"That National what's-it, it was really that bad?"

"NERF? Betty Louise, it was *cafeteria style*. You don't want to know."

Asel felt a deep sense of relief, as buildings of a sort began to appear ahead. They were hard to make out, for they were masked by the trees Betty Louise called pahms. There were hundreds of them, jammed together in a dense, unsightly grove. Most of them, Asel decided, were dead. Many leaned wearily against their neighbors, tufted crests sagging in brittle veils.

As they made their way through, Asel heard a constant scuttering in the dry foliage overhead.

"Voles," he said, with great disgust. "Wouldn't be surprised Califoggy's full of the nasty beasts. About what you'd expect out here. Damn it, Betty Louise, would you please not run ahead? If I get lost in these tacky trees—*Betty Louise?*"

She was standing there, rigid, arms stretched wide, rooted, frozen, as if some dread affliction had struck her on the spot.

"Oh, Asel," she said, her voice lost in laughter, overcome with joy. "I *dreamed* about this, every night when I was growin' up in Trench. It's prettier than Heaven could ever be!"

Asel was wary, cautious as he took in the sight. It wasn't Heaven, he'd seen it all before—the glitter, the shine, the perfection that marked the fashionable shops, the haunts of the very rich.

Only this broad avenue of rare and fabulous goods was somewhat gaudy, garish, clearly overblown. It was Califoggy, not America East. And, Asel noted with some alarm, there was not a human shopper to be seen. The street was full of elegant, smartly dressed Mechs. . . .

~ FIFTY-TWO ~

There were three distinct fabrications shopping the avenue: Imitation males, females, and those not clearly defined. Each had a shiny chrome head, a narrow face that shrank to a sharp and pointy chin. Blinky red eyes, focused on nothing at all. A nose, without any holes. Slightly upturned, as if they scented something inexpensive in the air. The mouth was tiny round "O." Each and every Mech looked startled, caught in a state of perpetual surprise.

Men donned natty fedoras, lemony jackets, and ice cream slacks. Women wore feathery plastic hats, perky pink sweaters, clackety heels, and faux leather skirts. Some, of each gender, were into mix and match.

The thing that struck Asel at once was the fact that all of these sleek simulations were perfect, spotless, as if they'd been shaped, shined, and set into motion that very afternoon. A far cry from the pathetic antiques he had left in the desert the day before.

"Yesterday doesn't seem yesterday at all," he said. "But then, today's a little out of whack too."

"Doesn't anyone *real* live here?" said Betty Louise, eyes growing wide at a window full of frilly underwear. "Lord, Asel, I can see me in an outfit like that."

Asel could too, but kept the vision for a more convenient place.

He watched, with Betty Louise, as a bogus lady went in the undergarment shop. Watched, as she entered, came out with pretty boxes, whirred, hummed, buzzed off to a shop across the way.

"That's what worries me," Asel said. "There must be people around somewhere. These fancy devices don't wear lingerie. They don't wear socks, they don't need hats."

"They sure think they do. They're buying everything in sight."

"They belong to someone. They're simply servants. And, just like human servants, they do whatever they're told."

"Like Phil, huh?"

"No, Betty Louise, not like Phil at all. Phil's an aberration, a bair out of control. I don't know what the hell he's for. My guess is he worked somewhere like Mellowstone Park—he mentioned it several times. Someone got careless, gave him too many smarts. What that does is lead to discontent."

He peered up the street. Studied the other side. Looked at the startling blue sky.

"We don't need to stand around here. Someone comes along, it's rather obvious we're real."

"I hope you've considered the subject of food."

"I'm hungry too, all right? Wherever there's food, there are people there too. People with posters. Pictures of me."

"Not everyone's after you, Asel. You will drive yourself crazy, you keep thinking on that."

Asel shook his head, clearly out of sorts. Turned without a word, stalked across the busy boulevard. Weaved through a herd of artificial shoppers. Paused, peered in windows, studied the displays in every place he stopped.

Betty Louise sighed. Asel moved like a man on a mission, ardent, determined, a man with purpose and intent. She wasn't fooled by that. He often appeared to know where he was going, and really had no idea at all.

She thought it was likely a habit of the rich. You didn't need to think. Things would appear, where you wanted them to be. Mechs, of course, acted that way too. She thought it best to forget the connection for now.

"You could use some new clothes, hon. Those rags of yours are getting worse for wear."

He didn't look up, though he knew she was there.

"Surely you don't think I intend to dress like a Mech? An Iacola has never worn a lemon suit. I don't intend to start now."

"I don't guess they ever looked like poor folks on the run."

"That's beside the point."

"You should've taken that nice outfit from Larry Bill."

"I am not a trucker, Betty Louise. I am not Larry Bill."

Asel gave her a curious look. "Did you think I was *shopping*? Do you imagine I would stand here in the open to gaze at tacky clothes?"

"You're upset with me, right?"

"No. I am not upset with you. I am trying very hard to think what to do next." He nodded toward the shop. "You see this place? It has a door. Like every shop on the street. It opens, when a Mech stands there. It doesn't open for me. A real person can't get in.

"I thought Mechs shopped here for people. They don't. There is nothing in these windows except those ridiculous garments *they* wear. And that doesn't make a lot of sense. Mechs don't shop, Betty Louise. If they did, why would they buy the same tasteless clothes they already have?"

"Well, a simulated man might. A woman wouldn't. Even a woman made of gears. A woman's not about to do that—don't you give me that look of yours, I'm not done. If they don't *buy* anything, why do they walk out with boxes all the time? I would like to hear your—your stuffy, know-it-all explanation for that."

"I don't know, I don't have an answer." He reached out and took her hand. "I was born to the stuffy persuasion, I can't help that. I don't mean to be short and impolite. I just know something isn't right. I feel uneasy. On edge. Uptight."

"I hope it isn't that head."

"No, I thought about that. It's some kind of inner perception, beyond our ordinary sense."

"There's a lot of that on Daddy's side."

"My mother might have had it too. She didn't seem conscious all the time. Father always said—"

Asel froze. Inner perception was coming to pass. He caught the sudden motion in the corner of his eye. Turned, startled, found two figures, where nothing had been before. A woman, a man, both were so spare their gender scarcely showed.

"You folks dimwits, or what?" the man said, as if he were speaking from a hole. "You ain' suppose to bees out here, don' you know dat?"

"I think they bees from afar," the woman said. "Sound kinda southerby to me."

The man showed a baleful eye. "She right? You ain' beacher trash, are you? Some of dat Dee-eggo bunch?"

"We're not, honestly," Betty Louise said, in the kindly manner she could bring to bear if she tried. "We are from afar, as you say, and we are terribly lost."

"Huh." The man looked Asel over, sidewise, up and down. Lingered somewhat on Betty Louise.

"Whoever you bees, you best get off the street. These tin bastards is dense, but they can see us in their own devil's way."

"You folks ate supper yet?" The woman smiled at Betty Louise.

It had clearly been awhile since someone had spoken to her nice. "Supper?" Betty Louise blinked. "Uh, no, I don't believe we have."

"I don' recall handin' out a invitation," said the man.

"You didn't. I did," the woman said. "I'm Amelia Jean. He's Uncalew. Not too big on manners, but he's right good otherwise."

"Uh-huh. All right, then." Uncalew spat on the ground, close to Asel's foot. "But you better not bees no coaster types, you hear?"

With a cautious look up and down the street, Uncalew turned, pressed a grimy hand against the wall of the shop. For a moment, nothing happened. Then, a portion of the wall slid back, with no sound at all. A narrow corridor appeared, and Uncalew vanished from sight.

Amelia Jean grinned at the newcomers' obvious surprise. "Y'all get on in. 'Less I'm mistook, it's ottir stew tonight."

"Lord, I can't recall when I had ottir last," said Betty Louise. "That's holiday fare for me."

Asel didn't hear a word she said. He was stunned, shaken by the great profusion, by the dizzy confusion of the sight that assaulted his eyes the moment he stepped through the door. The presence of this passage was incredible enough, but what it revealed was more boggling still. . . .

~ FIFTY-THREE ~

The store at his back was really not a store at all. It was no more than a flat, a sham, a clever set, built to deceive the unknowing eye, a stage for players to strut and say their lines.

In this drama, though, only dumb Mechs appeared, and the plot was quite inane. Simulated shoppers whirred, buzzed, into a phony store, snatched up a package from a plentiful supply, headed for the avenue again.

Now that he knew what lay behind the scenes, Asel was more baffled than before. Why? What did this useless exercise achieve? Why go through the farce again and again?

"There is more fakery and fraud in the world than we dream of, hon. I can't make any use of plastic underwear."

"I thought you folks bees hungry," said Uncalew. "Don't make me sorry I brung you along." He glared impatiently at Asel, nodded to the woman, stomped off into a stand of dead trees.

"He don't mean nothin' by it," said Amelia Jean. "We been through some hard times."

"Right," Asel said, following along behind the pair. "I can see that. Look, what's this sham, this falsity all about? It simply doesn't make sense."

"We tend to our business, mister. Machinery is no concern of ours."

"It would be of great concern to me, ma'am, if I lived next door to those things."

"You bees in Califoggy, friend," said Uncalew. "Folks like us don't live anywhere at all."

Before Asel could puzzle the fellow's meaning, the pahms gave way to a clearing, and a most astonishing answer appeared.

There were hundreds of them, at least, a near uncountable mass. Gaunt, sallow reflections of Uncalew and Amelia Jean. Leftover people, people left out, a grim and miserable clot. Asel had not forgotten that frightening horde in the desert, people who clawed out holes in the ground, people who would have devoured Sylvan, Goodtime Bob, and himself, if they'd taken the truck. The people in the clearing were a step above that, but not a lot.

"Could we go now, hon?" said Betty Louise, gripping Asel's arm. "I'm not real hungry anymore."

"Go where? I can't think of anyplace we haven't been."

"That don't smell like ottir to me. I think that's goddamn pijun again."

The clump, the knot of human debris, began to shape itself into the semblance of a line. Each of these creatures held a rusty pot. Some had a spoon. Amelia Jean found spare pots for Asel and Betty Louise.

"Keep moving," said Uncalew. "Folks behind gets nervous if you stop."

"It's best to kinda smile, if you can, when they fillin' up your pot," said Amelia Jean. "I feel they gives you more that way."

"That bees in your head, is where it is, woman. They don't care shit if you're smilin' or not."

"Oh, I believe they do, Lew."

"I am guessing this is a communal effort," Asel said. "Everyone gathers, everyone shares sort of thing? I am not familiar with helping others. I suppose it might work."

"That's not ottir. Ain't pijun either. Don't know what it is."

"Keep it moving," someone said.

"Watch your mouth," said Uncalew.

The kettles were enormous. Things bubbled to the top, things quivered and popped. Whatever was in this gray and lumpy mass, it was exceedingly hot.

The men behind the kettles ladled out a portion to every pot. They ladled, poured, and never looked up. Asel's nose had ceased to function as it should. The mess in the kettles smelled good.

"Where should we sit?" he asked Uncalew. "I don't see any tables anywhere."

Uncalew gave him a curious look. "You don't *sit* anywhere, friend. Just keep walking. Eat. You don't want it, give it to me."

"They're not from here, Lew. No need to be talkin' like that."

"I'll talk anyhow I please. Don't need any womanly help."

"Men frequently feel they don't," said Betty Louise, as if she were speaking to the sky. "That is *their* loss, but you can't tell 'em that."

"I wish I could sit," Asel said. "I am not accustomed to supper standing up."

"What you figure's in this, hon? I never made anything like it at Buckstop, I can tell you that."

"Step lively, folks, move it on along."

Asel was surprised when the man stepped out of the pahms. The path had begun to narrow. He seemed to come from nowhere at all. A bald-headed fellow with bushy brows and good teeth. He looked unusually clean. Likely, Asel thought, he worked on the kettles as well. The men there were neater than the shabby bunch they served.

Asel was appalled to find he was getting used to dirt. Who would have dreamed someone had cleaner socks than the heir to America East?

"You. Watch where you're going, heads up!"

Asel blinked. The harsh voice brought him back. The man with good teeth glared.

"You don't hear good? You're holdin' up the line."

"I don't care for your rude attitude," Asel said. "I feel you should—"

He stopped, puzzled. Confused and out of synch. Something was wrong, the line wasn't right. The line was moving, all right, but *up* . . .

Someone pushed him, shoved him from behind. Asel tripped, lashed out, tried to stop his fall, hit something hard. Felt the rough corrugation, the rusty floor beneath his hands. Knew he'd felt this surface before, knew, with a terrible certainty, where he had to be. Knew why everything was suddenly *up*.

Before he could come to his knees, the press of odorous bodies overwhelmed him, sent him down again. The big door behind him slammed shut, left him in the dark, on the gritty floor of a truck. . . .

~ FIFTY-FOUR ~

Someone cursed him, scalded him with stew. He lashed out blindly, knocked someone against the wall. Someone grabbed him, wouldn't let go.

"Shit, I knew you was trouble," said Uncalew, "settle down 'fore one of these fellas puts a blade in your ribs. I brung you in, they'll likely stick me too."

"Let me go this instant. I know a crippling move or two."

"Have at it. I been crippled before."

Uncalew eased his grip. Asel shook free. There were people packed against him, he couldn't move an inch.

"Betty Louise, are you harmed in any way? Where are you, are you there?"

"I'm standing right here, Asel. That's me, jammed up in your back. I am somewhat frightened, hon, will you get me out of here?"

"Stay calm. Stay by my side. I'm working on this, we'll be out of here soon."

He wasn't that certain this was true, but it seemed the thing to say.

The sides of the truck were peppered with holes. As his eyes grew used to the dim surroundings, he could pick out faces in the dusty beams of light. People were jammed in tight, one foul body pressed against the next. Still, no one spoke, no one complained. Those who'd kept their bowls, finished off their stew.

"I need to know exactly what happened," Asel said quietly to Uncalew. "Clearly, this whole thing is a trap. Food is offered to lure us into line, and thus inside the trucks. What I cannot fathom, cannot understand, is how you could let this happen?"

"Damn it all, you knew about the trucks, knew it was a sham.

Yet you walked right in like—no offense, you understand—like a pack of dullards, a herd of witless fools."

"It's supper," said Uncalew. "Even when they're outa ottir, it ain't half bad."

"Thing about your ottir," said Amelia Jean, somewhere at Uncalew's side, "it tends to the chewy side, seems to me."

"I knew you bees a coaster right off," said Uncalew. "I ain't surprised at your uncivil tone. We was lucky today, better be thankful for that. Sometimes there isn't no work. They don't bring nothing then."

"Damn straight," said someone Asel didn't know.

"Go without eatin' for a week," said someone else. "See how you like that."

"He wouldn't like that."

"Bees a hollerin' then, I bet."

"Beacher folk don't bees working at all. Eatin' klams, shit like that."

"Wait a minute," Asel said, wishing he could back off, wishing he had a little room. "I am *not* from—wherever you said. If I seem uncivil, it's because I abhor the thought of giving up my freedom for a bowl of ottir stew."

"Had pijun today," said Amelia Jean. "That, or a similar fowl. Not the same as ottir."

"Not even close."

"No sir, it's not."

"All right." Asel fought for breath. This crowd was using up atmosphere fast. "I just want to make it clear. I'm not a beacher. I am not even from Califoggy State. I'm from the East."

"So you say, mister."

"Doesn't make it true."

"Coaster might bees sayin' whatever comes to mind."

"He's not," said Betty Louise. "I know Asel well, and I can say he's not from the West, not even close."

"*I* know him too. Man's not from anywhere at all. What the man is, is flat fucking lost. . . ."

Asel gave a start. He knew that voice, knew it very well, knew the man before he stepped out of shadow, into a path of sulfur light. Knew those rugged features, that off-center nose, the stubborn, irritating thrust of the jaw.

"I never thought to see you again," Asel said, and, without thinking, took the fellow in a manly embrace. "To tell the truth, I thought you were very likely dead!"

"So did I," Sylvan said. "Check every morning, make sure I'm not. . . ."

~ FIFTY-FIVE ~

It wasn't easy, but Sylvan shoved his way through the crowd, ousted three bodies from a corner, made space for Asel and Betty Louise. Asel barely had time to tell his old companion about Tom Micks, the Buckstop, and Phil, the great enormous hole, and the Mechs who dropped their parts.

He had scarcely started on Larry Bill when the big engine roared, and the truck jerked to a start.

Sylvan caught the alarm in Asel's features, saw the woman's eyes go wide. Thought Asel's lady looked fine, hoped he got a chance to know her well.

"You've got a lot of questions, Ace, I know that. I've got answers to some, none of which you're going to like."

"Who's running this sham is easy, I guess," Asel said. "Disney-Dow's behind everything in Califoggy State. And you're right. I doubt I want to hear where they're taking us now."

"Mally-boo Pharmaceuticals, man. Past Lost Angels, up the coast a bit."

"Oh, dear." Betty Louise looked at Asel. "Larry Bill. He was headed up there."

"The trucker who gave you a ride?"

"Wore tacky clothes, Sylvan. Leather. Chains and lots of studs."

"Real bad taste, but he did you a favor not taking you there. Not that it matters, seeing how that's where we're going now."

Sylvan shook his head, ran a hand across his face. "That place is something awful. Like you guessed, part of Disney-Dow. All they make is drugs. Methaphane, Hellbane, Choco-mane, Chillbane, and Klots. More drugs than you can name.

"That's what they got these people here for. Fumes from that shit screw up circuits in the Mechs. Damn things cost a bundle. Can't have 'em conking out."

Some of the things Sylvan told him, Asel knew. The rest he was appalled to find out. Certainly, he knew the Houses in America East, and Sylvan's Greater South, imported servants, flunks, ordinary workers from places overseas. Mechs were a lot of bother—people were extremely cheap.

"What we should have been doing, Asel, is pay heed to what these dudes were up to in the West. We've been looking in, instead of looking out. Manipulating, copulatin', merging this and that, while these folks are cutting our throats on the sly."

The rest of the country had paid no attention, Sylvan said, while the West quietly grew by leaps and bounds. Everyone knew they made Mechs, but who cared? The East and South had all the labor they could use.

"Mechs and drugs," Sylvan said. "Disney-Dow's got the Aisyaticks, the Filypeens, the Rushins, up to their asses in dope and machines. Got that tourist shit, too. I saw that thing, same as you. Gave me the shakes. Told myself they'd never get me back in NERF again.

"That little charade back there? That's part of the game. They're training those Mechs for export overseas. How to shop, do what your owner tells you to do. There's setups like it all over the place. How to drive, how to clean, how to do this and do that. . . ."

Sylvan paused, ran a hand across his face. "There's something you've got to know, Asel. Something I want to get said. What I did I thought was right. Seeing those young ladies on their way.

"That's true, and it's not. I was taken by the charms of that tall one, Linette. The one with the neck. I could see her safe, go back and find her when I could.

"Ace, I was coming back. I figured no more'n a day or two. You and me, we'd catch up with them in the truck."

Sylvan looked pained. "I thought I could work it out right, didn't happen that way. Don't guess I have to tell you that.

"Soon as it was light, we stopped to get some rest, keep out of sight. I wake up, it's late afternoon, everyone's gone. Took the water with them. Left me without a fuckin' drop.

"I got used, Asel. Isn't the first time I've been fooled by feminine wiles. No offense intended, Betty Louise. I have a weakness for the gender, that's all."

"I see that you do."

Asel wanted to say that in his experience, taller persons were no more sincere than the medium or the short. He decided to let it pass, for Sylvan hadn't brought up Cele.

"Maybe I shouldn't have doubted you, Sylvan. I have to say I did. Still, I am glad to see you again. I am sorry it had to be here."

Sylvan glared at a shabby fellow who was taking up too much space.

"I was getting tired, wasn't real alert. Didn't have anything to drink. Stumbled right into this bunch, all of 'em armed with warty-lookin' guns. They were rounding up the poor. Making 'em build tennis courts. Stuck me in a chopper with some of these louts, took us out here. Next stop, Mally-boo . . ."

"No, damn it all," Asel said, in a burst of anger, necessarily confined. "We've come too far to simply give it up now. Look at these witless fellows. They let themselves be duped for a—for a final bowl of stew!"

Sylvan raised a brow. "I guess I didn't tell it right. Some of 'em die, a lot of them don't. They work with that shit at Mally-boo. Get hooked on the fumes. Don't want to eat, don't care. Get to looking bad, Mally-boo ships them out again.

"What I'm saying is they *know* what they're doing, man. It isn't food they're hungry for. They've got to get *back*, got to be sniffin' again. . . ."

~ FIFTY-SIX ~

" 'It's a game, son. The grandest game there is.' That's what Father always said. I wouldn't know, I never got a chance to find out.
"You were right, Sylvan. We all went to sleep and those thieves stole everything in sight. We never even noticed they were there."
"Being a business czar was real fine," Sylvan said. "I wish you'd had a little more time. You have a princely mien, Ace, I've got to say that."
"I appreciate the thought."
"Not just saying it. I'm sincere as I can be."
"You boys have had a run of bad luck," said Betty Louise. "I feel that's got to change."
"Where? At Mally-boo? Making dangerous drugs for persons overseas? I—My God, you know what I was thinking just now? We have this enormous country, with a great many states—I don't know all the names but I'm certain that they're there.
"There's an East and a West and a middle in between. We have seen that middle, the three of us here. It is writhing, boiling with the wretched, the hungry, the common people who are actually poor. Alone and afraid, lost in a world they never made.
"And they are not *all* lacking in spirit, such as this miserable bunch in here—helpless, doped up to the gills. We saw what happened when they jumped the Rangers' camp. I have a lasting image of that. What they did, how they—well, I find that of interest, don't you?"
"No, Ace. Can't say as I do."
"Were you listening at all? Uh, Betty Louise?"
"We're stopping."

"What's that?"

Sylvan look startled. "Can't be. Haven't gone that far."

"We're somewhere though. Oh Lord, hon!"

Her words were lost as the big double doors at the rear opened wide. Harsh light assaulted the pale, wasted faces inside.

"Aw'right, you clods, lackwits, fogheads, anyone I missed, get your skinny asses outside. NOW!"

The packed-up, stacked-up odorous mass began to rumble, grumble, and howl. Shuffled, scuffled, shoved one another, eager to get out. The weakest of the lot never made it down the ramp. The poor louts who did staggered dizzily about. Those who were able, dropped into a squat. Fouling every bush, every stone, every patch of grass. Some simply did it where they stood.

"Betty Louise, don't look. Hold it if you can."

"Well I can't. You better turn around."

No one had to tell Asel this was not Mally-boo. A broad, well-kept highway ran north and south. To the west, he could see a distant cluster of sun-bright houses with red tile roofs. Pahm trees abounded, the first he'd seen that were not completely dead. Someone lived well in Califoggy State.

Several of the truckers stood around with guns. None of these fellows seemed overly concerned.

"Sandy Moniker, I think," Sylvan said. "There's an ocean somewhere. I believe it's to the left."

Asel looked at the motley crowd. Picked out Uncalew. Didn't see Amelia Jean.

"How far is it, Sylvan, do you know?" He didn't want to hear, knew he had to ask.

"If we're where I think? Too fucking close."

"Then why stop here?"

"I owned pharmaceuticals once. Just recreational stuff, nothing like this. They keep those places clean."

"You boys bees in for a treat," said Uncalew, pulling his trousers up tight. "Get a free shower, a good, hot meal. Won't let us work, though. Not the first day."

"We shall look forward to that," Sylvan said.

Uncalew hobbled off. Asel turned his back to the nearest guard. "You know what we have to do, Sylvan. Once we get to Mally-boo we haven't got a chance. We've been captives before, we came out of that."

"We had a little help that time."

"You'll be like *them*, Sylvan. A hopeless drug fiend. You want to live like that?"

Sylvan blew out a breath. "Betty Louise . . ."

"She'll have to agree. If she doesn't want to try it, of course I'll stick it out."

"I heard that," said Betty Louise. "You ought to know you don't have to ask."

Asel felt a burst of great affection, coupled with regret. Their time together was coming to an end. Her steady stance, the courage in her eyes, told him some highborn stranger had graced the family lines.

"The way I see it, we mingle with the crowd. Make our way over there, where the weeds are rather high. The guards can't watch us all at once. We pick our moment. Drop to cover fast. I don't think they count. When the truck is out of sight, we break for the trees. What do you think?"

"Good idea," Sylvan said. "We haven't got a chance."

"I'm glad your family can't hear that."

"No problem. Family's dead."

"So is mine. Honor knows no quarter, my friend. It lives beyond the grave."

"I never heard that."

"Betty Louise, try not to stop. Watch the way you walk. Your feminine manner might attract the guards."

"Don't you tell me how to walk."

"I assure you I'm not. I'm just saying—"

Somebody shouted, somebody howled. A groan swept through the crowd.

Asel looked up, saw them coming swiftly, out of the northern sky. Five, six in a dark and ragged V. Squat, ugly choppers, graceless as predatory flies.

He counted, drew a breath. Five seconds, four, they would pass directly overhead. For an instant, every gaunt and shaggy wretch was gripped by the sight.

He glanced at the guards. Knew what he'd see—they were looking up as well.

Three seconds, two . . .

"Now," he said, "go. Run, *go!*"

He didn't need to ask. They were gone, darting through the mob. Sylvan knocked a lout aside. No time for sly deception now.

Two, one . . .

Asel felt the deep pulsation, the thrum of engines overhead.

Felt it in his belly, the *whup-whup-whup!* of the blades as they pounded air to the ground.

The crowd was behind him, high weeds ahead.

Keep low, race for the trees—

"Hey, where you think you're going, dumbhead!"

Asel saw the trucker's surprise, saw him jerk the weapon up. Sylvan hit him low, sent the fellow sprawling, sent his weapon spinning out of sight.

Asel didn't stop. Caught Betty Louise in the corner of his eye. Heard her gasp, stumble, catch her stride again.

Sylvan shouted, his words lost forever in the wind that thundered from above. Shadows blotted out the sun. Dark shapes descended—one, then another, like drunken spiders on a string.

Grit, shit stung Asel's eyes. Black-clad figures came at him in a crouch, men in armor the color of night, men in helmets with sharp and pointy ears, grim reminders of the dreaded leaping vole. Each man carried a weapon of coppery hue—weapons with pocks, cankers, wicked metal sores.

Every man was hidden beneath his bulky gear. Asel could only see their eyes, knew those eyes stared directly at him. They hadn't come for this motley crowd. They had come here for him.

Two dark figures stepped forward. Another, the biggest of the lot, swept the pair aside. Stalked up to Asel with fierce and pitiless eyes. Drew a massive pistol, poked it in Asel's face.

"There you are, then," said a coarse and friendly voice, muffled behind that ugly mask. "Just hold still, lad, this won't hurt a bit. . . ."

~ FIFTY-SEVEN ~

He dreamed about voles . . .
 . . . voles big as dawgs, fatter than frawgs . . . voles with blind and colorless eyes . . . wet and horrid voles with pink and hairless hides . . .
 . . . they shuffled, snuffled till they found him, clawed him, pawed him, dragged him down, down in their burrows as far as they could go . . .
 . . . started on his toes, gobbled up his ankles, feasted on his bones . . . squealed with delight as they munched on his tummy, eager to get to the goodies down below . . .
"no—
 no—
  no—*no*—NO—!"
"All right, it's all right, hon."
"No it—is—NOT!"
"Stay down, don't try and get up."
Asel stared. "I know who you are. I've seen you both before."
"That's a good sign," said Betty Louise. "He'll be just fine."
"No I *won't*."
Sylvan tried to push him down. Asel shook him off, pulled himself erect. Light mottled canvas overhead. A canopy, a tent.
"All right. I guess I'd better ask. Where am I? What happened? I'm awake, I'm certain of that."
"They got us at the truck," Sylvan said. "You remember that? Good. Knocked us all out. Some kinda gas. Dumped us in a chopper, brought us up here."
"You got a pretty big dose," said Betty Louise. "You've been out all night."

"It's morning again," Sylvan said. "Tomorrow, I suppose, since you didn't do today."

"Where?" Asel tried to clear his head. He was cold, hot, couldn't say which. "They brought us here, where's that?"

Sylvan looked away. "I'm not even going to try, Ace. You got to see this one for yourself."

"There's no big hurry," said Betty Louise. "You rest awhile."

"No, I don't think so." He came to his feet. A little dizzy, the first few steps. Ducked, opened the canvas flap. Stepped out, blinked in muted light from the canopy of green overhe—

Asel gasped, stared in wonder, in utter disbelief. It had to be an illusion, a clever deceit, a trick of some kind. He couldn't imagine such a thing could be real.

The great tree towered out of sight, two, three hundred feet, lost in green light that filtered through the branches overhead. In the mix of shadow and pale illumination, he imagined spidery webs up high, a tangled filigree. Saw, in an instant, he had watched the dance of morning light.

The trunk of this wonder was a mammoth wall, seemingly endless, stretching away on either side, like a mountain come to rest. Without a conscious thought, Asel stepped quickly away. He felt as if its power, its oppressive weight, was drawing all his strength. It wasn't right to approach such an alien thing.

As he moved, retreated from this overwhelming sight, he saw there were others as well, hazy in the early morning light, massive columns that might shoulder the sky itself.

"Something to see," Sylvan said. "You could build a lot of furniture with that."

"I suppose they're real. One has to wonder in Califoggy State."

"One of those louts in black brought us supper last night. Told us it's Sekwoyah Heights. Biggest trees there ever was. Three, four thousand years old. *He* says. I personally doubt the whole world's old as that.

"I hope your head's on straight now, Ace. You likely guessed we're in very deep shit. Look real high? The big man himself hangs out up there."

"What?" Asel was a lap or two behind. "Jackie Cee? Jackie Cee's up there?"

"You've mentioned the name a couple times. Him and that duck."

"Ducky. The man who stole my heritage. On my wedding day too. Shit, Sylvan." Asel let out a breath. "That odorous fellow,

Uncalew. He said the Mechs are dense, but they can *see* us. I paid no heed at the time. I expect my picture's in every tin head. That's how they did us in."

"Don't blame yourself. I'm a wanted man too. Not as much as you, of course. Hard to top that . . ."

Asel stopped him, nodded to the right. Four large men in black strode toward them across the mossy ground. They strutted, swung their arms about. Marched in time, as if they were on parade. Their uniforms were shiny, lavishly adorned with silver piping, silver buttons, silver this and that. Boots with silver buckles, silver on the toes. Peaked, silver-billed military hats, a silver leaping vole emblazoned on the front.

Three stood back. Spread their legs at rest, hands behind their backs. The leader was taller, broader, with more gilt than the rest. He took a step forward and stopped.

"Well, now, this is a pleasure indeed. Both of you together, that's an extra treat." He looked at Asel, his gaze hard as stone. "We met yesterday. Didn't have the time to talk . . . Ah, fine. The young lady as well."

His blue eyes flashed with mischief, his grin so wide it stretched every feature out of place.

Asel didn't look back. Knew she was there.

"You stink a bit, boys. We'll get you bathed, shaved, gussied up good. Get you out of those rags. You too, miss. I shall personally see to your care."

Asel felt the heat rise to his face. Clenched his fists at his side.

"Easy there, son," the man said. "Save your kind words for himself. I know he's looking forward to that. . . ."

~ FIFTY-EIGHT ~

Asel vowed he would not enjoy the steamy hot shower. Swore he'd not yield to the pleasure, the delight, of frothy suds against his skin. The officer watched, never let them out of sight. Betty Louise pretended he wasn't there. Asel pretended he shot the fellow through the eye.

 The walk from their tent had taken some time. Asel guessed the small building served as barracks for the troops. Everything was neat, tidy, perfectly in line. The three were given robes, herded into yet another room. Asel refused to take comfort in a haircut, a shave.

 His resolution failed before wudchuk soup and tasty black bred. He looked at Sylvan. Exchanged a weary smile with Betty Louise. They all knew what this attention, this favor was about.

 After the meal, they were given clean clothes. Loose shirt and trousers of a citron-yellow hue. A billed cap to match. Sandals, no socks. Tacky at best, but Asel was used to that.

 Troopers led them down a narrow hall. Through a wooden door, far from where they'd come in. Outside, into the open — thrust, of a sudden, into a bustling sea of life beneath the giant trees. Mechs darted this way and that, in the manner of their kind. Black-clad troopers kept watch over human and artificial traffic alike.

 Troopers cleared the way for a swift electro cart. Asel and Sylvan exchanged a furtive glance. They knew their own kind — corporate dukes and earls, unsmiling fellows, earnest and intent.

 Now, Asel could see into the heights of the towering trees. Light pierced the thick greenery, turning the illusion of the morning into something quite real. Those illusory webs were bridges, a maze of graceful structures that linked one tree with the next. Asel saw that each bridge led to an entry *into* the tree itself.

Canopied balconies offered a breathtaking view of the world below. Sheltered paths, a network of steep, winding stairs girded the tree, and vanished out of sight.

In spite of his deep, abiding hatred for his vile and ruthless foe, he could not dismiss what had been accomplished here. What an arduous labor it must have been! The minions of Jackie Cee had carved, chopped, bored through solid wood to create these palatial estates. And all to please the vanity, the pride of the Lord of Disney-Dow.

The arrogance of such an act was rivaled only by an even larger conceit—the gloomy figure that loomed above San Clemente Shrine. It struck Asel that, on the one hand, that vulgar display had surely inspired Jackie Cee—and, on the other, that Jackie would love to see it topple to the ground.

"They'll kill that tree, poking holes in it," said Betty Louise. "That's the quickest way to kill a tree."

"I've got to agree," Sylvan said. "Nature doesn't need any decorating tips. Something like this, you need to let it be."

"Write them a letter," Asel said, "they'll appreciate that."

"Shut up, the lot of you," the burly officer said. "Move along, step lively there!"

Another surprise awaited them at the base of the giant tree. At the officer's touch, a panel of ancient wood slid noiselessly aside. Three troopers ushered Asel and his companions inside.

Asel was duly impressed. Uncle Hal had installed an elevation device for Mother, the only one in Iacola Keep. That machine carried Asel's mother three stories high. This one, clearly, would rise to a greater height still.

"Do not get any foolish ideas," the officer warned Asel, as the device began to hum. "That goes for you too, darky lad."

"You want to see *dark*," Sylvan said, "let's you and me have a private chat somewhere."

The officer's jaws clamped shut. His face flushed a violent red.

"My, my," said Betty Louise, smothering a grin behind her hand.

The device continued to ascend. There was no way to tell how high they had gone. Father had always told Asel to count off the seconds: stocksandbonds one . . . stocksandbonds two . . . Carry your six.

Cogs and chains rattled, the machine came to a stop. The door slid back. Asel had not imagined he would see the signs of wealth, opulence, the trappings of the privileged again. Here, in the lair of the enemy, he was in such surroundings once more. For a desperate moment, he prayed some higher power might whisk him up and set him free among the middle-class poor. Betty Louise would help him think of something to do.

"Let's go," said Asel's captor, poking a pistol in the small of Asel's back. "The chief's a busy man. Got important stuff to do."

The passageway was long and narrow. The floor was highly polished, the wood of the tree itself. Rich, black velvet drapes hung with fringes, tassels and swirls lined the hall's inner curve. Large oval windows dominated the outer wall. Another giant loomed not far away.

The officer came to a sudden halt. Asel's heart nearly stopped as well. Two dark-clad guards stood beside a wooden door. The door was immense, carved in a convolution of leaves, branches, and a herd of leaping voles.

The guards snapped to rigid attention, quickly stepped aside. The officer tapped very lightly—twice, once again.

The door opened without a sound. Asel wasn't sure just what he expected to see. More velvet walls, carpeted floors, lavish décor. Instead, the room was small, nearly bare. A window. A door in the rear. Straight-back chairs. In the center of this Spartan setting, a table with a glass of wyne, a saucer of graypes, an appul, nothing more.

Asel was startled, taken aback. This couldn't be the sanctum, the retreat of Jackie Cee. Frounces, frills, vulgar display all about, but not here. It was wrong, it didn't go together, it simply didn't fit—

The door at the back swung open, laughter spilled into the room. Asel froze. He was taken with a fever, with a rage he could scarcely contain. There were no counts or baronets here, no courtiers eager to scrape and bow. Only a dozen lads and maids—merry, chipper, birthday party clean. All of them dressed in the very same citron-yellow costume Asel wore himself.

Domestics. Lackeys. Ready to serve their master's every will. This was Jackie Cee's message to Asel Iacola, the former Prince of Christler-Coke, one-time heir to America East. This is how he showed his scorn, his contempt. Strip a noble of his rights. Dress him like a flunk from overseas.

As if some signal had occurred unseen, the troopers on either side of Asel grabbed him, held him in a crushing grip.

"Asel, Asel," said Jackie Cee, with a handsome bow from the door, "I earnestly *prayed* we'd get a chance to talk again. . . ."

~ FIFTY-NINE ~

"You were rude to my mother," Asel said. "I have not forgotten that."

"Oh, pooh. Who cares?" Jackie raised a pinky twice. A perky little flunk poked a graype in his mouth. Another after that.

If Asel hadn't been seized with anger, he might have laughed aloud at Jackie Cee. The Lord of Disney-Dow was stubby by nature. Not exactly stout. Closer to squat. Nose mashed flat. Bull-frawg eyes, ever in a state of surprise. Unruly tufts of auburn hair.

These bodily charms were stuffed into garish gahlfer wear. Polo shirt with leaping vole. Baggy knickers in a lurid Scodish plaid. Tick-tock socks. Shoes with tassels and flaps. Cap with a fuzzy on top. Clearly, a bad fashion gene lurked in Jackie's line.

"I did not bring you here to talk about your mother," Jackie said. "Or your father, or your cousins or your ants."

"Do I have any left?"

"Do you?" Jackie raised a brow. "I'm not certain. I'll have somebody check. No one we desperately *need*, I know that."

Asel fought, strained to break free.

Jackie grinned at that. Knew his words had struck home. Perched on the table, picked a goodie from his teeth. Flicked it somewhere.

"I have followed your exciting ventures, Asel. You have led me a merry chase. You and your—Southern companion, here. I don't believe we've met, McCree."

"Didn't catch the name," Sylvan said. "Who are you supposed to be?"

Jackie didn't blink. He was confident, secure. Clearly in

charge. Raised in the proud tradition of intrigue, bribery, and strife. Emotions were tools. Daddy Cee said that. Tools you could build with. Or tear something down.

"I should thank you for some very nice holdings," Jackie said, with a smile. "You built Datadog into a fine enterprise. I am most delighted with Eata-Fajita. *Not* so pleased with Pan Electric-Goat. Not my kind of thing. You're awfully dark, you know."

"Wondered when you'd get around to that."

"I'm sure someone's mentioned it before. A*liciya.* I *hate* this kind of appul. Do not let me see it again."

A wide-eyed flunk grabbed the offending froot, hurried it away. Not for the first time, Jackie let his gaze wander to Betty Louise.

"You would be the common person. Conceived in Trench, I believe. A serving girl and cook. Is there more? No, I think not."

"Listen, chubby—"

"Don't," Asel said. "Leave it alone, Betty Louise."

Jackie slapped his knees. "This is delightful. I must take more time off for fun. Now. The rest of it, Asel. I am missing parts of your droll adventure. Do fill me in."

"Fill it in yourself."

"Oh, dear." Jackie feigned sorrow and regret. "You simply won't quit, will you? What did you expect, Asel? Really? What did you think the world was all about? You may not believe it, but I had great respect for your father. He must have taught you *something* while he still had his wits.

"It's business, is what it is. If he'd been in good health, he would have done the same to me. The East was weak. That's why it fell. The South too."

Asel heard the familiar thrum of choppers overhead. Jackie heard them too, rolled his eyes in irritation, paused to let them pass.

"These are times of change, you see. We cannot dilly-dally, merging this and that. It slows *every*thing down and completely wears me out. I—What?"

A flunk whispered in his ear. Jackie Cee grinned.

"Good. Fine," he said, and waved the fellow away.

"I sent for someone, Asel. Someone I know you'll want to see. And he's just *dying* to see you again."

Flunks turned to watch the inner door. Jackie watched Asel, eyes bright with unrestrained joy, malicious intent.

Asel drew a breath. Knew who it had to be. He had never hated anyone, despised anyone, felt murder in his heart for anyone except Ducky Du Pontiac-Heinz. Now, the man who'd plotted, schemed with Disney-Dow to bring his family down—steal his title, ruin his wedding, fuck up his life, stood before him now.

Violence, vengeance, homicide still raged within, but Asel also had to grin. Ducky wore a citron-yellow suit exactly like his own. Like every other wretched flunk in the room.

"Ducky, my word," Asel said, with joy and contempt, "things not going well? Jackie take all your toys too? Say, I'll wager he stole the lovely Loreli, after he *promised* her to you."

"I wouldn't know about that." Ducky looked at the floor, away from Asel's glance. "Everything's—different now."

"Ducks, Ducks, Ducks." Jackie Cee sighed. "I gave her to some worthy fellow, can't remember who. Ducky knows that, don't you, old boy?"

He wagged a stubby finger at Asel. "Too many nobles spoil the soup, as they say. A highborn fellow yearns to climb higher still. Greed is the creed, there's nothing wrong with that. But you have to watch your back. That's what NERF is for."

Jackie winked. "Surprised? "Yes, that's mine too. Daddy's idea. Only NERF doesn't always cut it. You and McCree are naughty examples of that. Sometimes I have to take sterner measures. Don't like to, you understand, but that's my job. It is awfully lonely at the top. Your father should have told you that. Mine did. You can be certain of—"

The *shup-shup-shup* of choppers drowned him out again.

Jackie looked at Asel. Past him somewhere, a blank and distant stare. For an instant, Asel thought Jackie had simply stepped out. As if some portal behind his tiny eyes had slammed shut. Then, with a blink, he was suddenly back.

"I wish I could find a place for you, Asel. You and McCree. I do, really. I can't do that. A prince and an earl. No, I've learned a thing or two. A man of gentle birth is never satisfied. I am not unkind. You won't have to worry or wait. We'll do it right now. . . ."

~ SIXTY ~

Asel felt the hairs rise up the back of his neck.
Betty Louise made a sad little sound that tore at his heart.
"You are a vile and wicked fellow, Ducks. A man of no merit at all. You're a coward, though, and I do enjoy that. Having a fellow around who's afraid to do me harm."
Without taking his eyes off Ducky, Jackie reached behind him and came up with a pistol in his hand. Took the Duck's fingers, wrapped them around the grip.
Ducky's jaw fell. All the color drained from his face.
"I don't want to, Jackie."
"I didn't *ask* you, Ducks. Do what you're *told*. Asel first. He's got the rank, he's entitled to that."
"You are a sorry-looking man," said Betty Louise. "I expect your mother told you that."
Jackie took a step forward, slapped her soundly across the face.
Asel tried to jerk free. Kicked the trooper behind him, earned a blow to the head.
"Slap me, man." Sylvan showed Jackie a terrible grin. "See if you can handle that."
Jackie looked pained. "Ducky, what are we waiting for? You want to get me upset?"
"I don't know—how. Never did it before."
"Well *try*."
Ducky struggled to raise the weapon. Couldn't bring it up. Dortmunder-Gucci. Forty-two or .46, Asel noted. Avycado green. Extended magazine. Light enough, but weight wasn't holding Ducky back. Ducky was patently stressed, coming unraveled at the seams.

"Ducky, *now*."

"Nu-nu-nuh," Ducky said. A twitch and a jerk. He held the thing out stiffly, shrinking from it as far as he could.

"Don't be a fool," Asel said. "This isn't real, you surely understand that. It's another humiliation, Ducks. My God, do you think he'd give you a loaded weapon? After all he's done to you?"

Jackie glared. "You will have to go in that *room* again, Ducky. You don't want to do that."

"Huuuuh," Ducky said.

"Go ahead," Asel said. "Shoot. Watch him laugh at you again. That's what he'll do, you know. Go on, you silly fuck, do it!"

"Asel . . ."

He heard her, but didn't take his eyes off the Duck.

"I've got an idea," Asel said. "Shoot *him*. See if that thing's really loaded. Then shoot me, all right?"

"Man's turning whiter than you, Ace. That's about the whitest man I've ever seen. He's going to wet those pretty pants, is what he's going to do."

"Don't—talk to me—darky person!"

"I think you're right. I think he might do that, I think he—"

"DUCKY, YOU ARE DEFINITELY GOING TO THE ROOM!"

"Nu-nu-nuh—" Ducky trembled, Ducky shook. Jerked the trigger, jerked it again and again and didn't stop. . . .

~ SIXTY-ONE ~

Lead singed his cheek
    whined past his shoulder
        plunked into wood
            tore the silly cap from his head . . .

Asel felt an odd, uncanny sense of calm, unconcerned, perfectly at ease. Time seemed compressed into orderly scenes, a gallery, pictures on the wall.

Sluuuuup. A bullet struck the trooper on his left. Very good shot, Asel thought, considering Ducky never opened his eyes.

Duck was a dancer, a tapper, a drunken sprite. Duck hopped dizzily about, as he sprayed the room with dread. Didn't, truly, fire the weapon at all. Held on tight while the weapon fired him.

The trooper took forever, floating to the ground. The sound of Ducky's weapon was a deep and distant groan in Asel's ears. Still, he couldn't believe a forty-two could shake the mammoth tree. Doubted a sixty-six could cause a tremor like that.

Ducky's gun chattered
    bullets sang about
        trooper dropped dead
           other fellow swung at Asel's head
                Asel kicked him in the gut . . .

Sylvan moved in the corner of Asel's eye. One of his captors was down, the other on the way. The hefty officer went for the Duck. Head tucked low, pistol in his hand. Sylvan hit him low. The weapon spun lazily across the polished floor. Asel tried to reach it, had hours, plenty of time. A trooper beat him there. Asel was annoyed. He'd downed the fellow once, that seemed quite enough.

The trooper came to his feet. Clumsy. Kicked the weapon out of sight. Reached behind him, came up with a knife. Asel watched. Time dragged by. Betty Louise struck the fellow with a straight-back chair.

Ducky's weapon chat-chat-chaaaaatered to a stop.

Another muted roll of thunder shook the tree—

—*Ducky jerked the trigger, jerked it again, and again and didn't stop—three, four, five long seconds winked past — Time yanked Asel to his feet, raced along at its ordinary pace* . . .

Asel gasped. Scared out of his wits. Grabbed the loose weapon. Watched Sylvan bound across the room for Jackie Cee. Watched him leap over wyne, graypes, terrified flunks.

Jackie crawled for the door, lost his cap, lost a flappy shoe.

Asel looked for Ducky. Ducky was gone. Asel smelled smoke. Another quake shook the room.

"Sylvan, leave him be. Something's amiss. Got to get out of here now."

The burly officer was dazed, clearly out of sorts. Three troopers had survived. Asel gave them a glance, stuck his weapon in his belt, headed for the door. Betty Louise found a Steuben thirty-six. Sylvan cherished the Dortmunder-Gucci, but Ducky had emptied it out. Grabbed up whatever he could find, raced after Asel and Betty Louise. . . .

~ SIXTY-TWO ~

There was no one in the long and narrow hall. The guards had scattered. Smoke poured up the shaft of the elevation machine. Sylvan checked the hall, found an entryway. The open arch led to a porch, hanging over empty air.

Betty Louise looked down. Then up—across the narrow bridge that swung from a network of cables and ropes.

"Huh-uh. No way. I'm getting sick just standing here."

"I don't think we have a choice. There's no place else to go." Asel glanced back. Maybe they should have shot the guards. Being nice was a burden sometimes.

Asel joined Sylvan at the railing. Gunfire echoed from below. A small war was raging down there. Black-clad troopers were thick as flyes. They had clearly been caught unawares. For the moment, they were somewhat confused, unsure who they had to fight.

A number of troopers were dead. An electro cart had overturned, spilling its passengers out. Someone had set the tree afire. Another was burning, off to the right.

Asel looked up as a chopper screamed by, tumbled, and exploded in a ball of fiery red.

"Someone is severely pissed at Disney-Dow," Sylvan said. "I applaud this vicious attack."

"Asel, I *will* throw up, you don't get me off this thing."

"From here you throw down."

"That's some of your Eastern humor there."

"They're big on that," Sylvan said.

"Let's go," Asel said. "Those fellows won't thank us for taking their guns. I expect they'll want them back. . . ."

✻   ✻   ✻

The first few yards were terrifying. The next were even worse. The bridge reeled, shook, swayed dizzily about. The maze of ropes squeaked with every step.

Asel led the way. Betty Louise in the middle, Sylvan in the back, keeping a wary eye on the tree they'd left behind. Asel was tempted to run, race to the other side, get it done as quickly as he could. The first time he tried, he learned the bridge wasn't built that way. It would stand for a steady rhythm, a cautious pace, no more than that. Any faster and it buckled, teetered, threatened to toss him over the side.

The battle raged below. No one paused to look down. The clatter of weapons told the story well enough.

Asel knew they'd been lucky so far. No one had appeared in the entryway behind. Maybe the troopers had other things in mind. There was surely another way down. Getting his hide out safely would be first on Jackie's list. He wouldn't be pleased with Ducky. He'd send someone to handle that . . .

The sharp crack of a rifle sent him sprawling, shouting at Betty Louise. Bullets stitched the wooden slats, inches from his head.

Betty Louise didn't answer. Asel couldn't turn and see. Sylvan called out. Said they were both all right. Asel raised up head and risked a look. There were three of them, maybe four. Troopers in black. Full armor, glossy helmets, pointy ears on top.

Asel edged a hand across the flat of his back. Showed the others a count. One-two-three . . .

Came to his knees and fired. Three quick shots. Ducked, as Sylvan and Betty Louise loosed a volley over his head. Somebody howled. Good. Go away, you bastards, leave us be.

Five, six rapid shots came back. A rope snapped above Asel's head. Another after that. A row of slats vanished, spraying splinters in his face.

Asel's heart nearly stopped. The last fusillade had done the job. A good eight feet of the bridge had disappeared. The troopers could finish them off—or wait until they stood, tried to make it back.

Someone touched his foot.

"It's me," said Betty Louise.

"I know who it is. What are you doing up here?"

"Coming to see you."

"I appreciate the thought. It would be a lot better if we didn't move around. They can tell where you are."

"My, I didn't know that."

"It's all right. You're here. Do you have any ammunition left?"
"Four. I don't know if I hit anyone or not. Sylvan has two."
"So do I. That's not good."

Another pair of choppers whirred by. Something blew up down below. Black smoke thickened the air.

The troopers opened up again. Bullets whined overhead. Another struck the bridge. Asel knew what had to be, knew it right then. Didn't hesitate, didn't have to think.

"Give me the shells you've got. Try not to move about."
"Why? What are you going to do? I don't like it, I can tell."
He held his hand behind his back. "They'll fit. These louts all use the Steuben thirty-six."
"Asel . . ."

Another shot rang out. Behind him this time. Maybe they could see Sylvan. Maybe they got him—maybe Sylvan had the sense to keep down.

He added the shells to his own. Slipped the weapon in the small of his back.

"Betty Louise?"
"I'm here."
"This won't take a minute. Maybe half of that."
"To do what?"

Asel didn't answer. In one swift motion, he came to his feet, dug his heels in, ran, came to the gap where the bridge played out, leaped into space—had ample time to see it was farther than he thought. . . .

~ SIXTY-THREE ~

Don't look, don't watch,
   as Uncle Hal would say.
      Close your eyes
        and
          kiss your
            ass
              goodbye . . .

Something solid, something real, something harder than air. Grab-it-hold-it-hang-on-tight.

His body kept going. A jerk, a jolt, a bone-jarring stop. Asel shook. He was there, across the gap. Dangling on a frail, wooden slat. The ropes that held the thing groaned beneath his weight. Thought he heard Betty Louise, couldn't turn and look.

A bullet sang past his shoulder. Another parted his hair. The next one ate wood. A rope snapped, dropped him half a foot.

They opened up, then, a volley, a barrage of withering fire. "Shit, there's more than four or five, there's an army up there!"

"When you die," Mother said, "do not be expectin' anything grand. We do not believe in them. I rathah doubt they believe in us . . ."

Asel squeezed his eyes shut. Tried to look small. One shot was lost in the next, in a thunderous din—

—then everything stopped.

Silence. So sudden, so abrupt it became the sound itself. Someone walked onto the bridge. The planks sagged with every cautious step.

The walker came to a halt. Strong hands reached down, seized Asel's wrists. Began to draw him up, with scarcely any effort at all.

"What the hell you doing? That's a safety hazard, I ever saw one, friend."

"*Phil?*" Asel stared. "What—what are you doing here?"

"We going to start that? I thought I was asking you. . . ."

He watched them work. They tossed a stout rope to Sylvan and Betty Louise. Linked another, and another after that. Wove a net to bring the pair across. The war continued down below.

Betty Louise rushed into his arms. Held him close for some time. Broke her cardinal rule: Never hug a bair.

Asel looked away as Phil's crew tossed the bullet-torn bodies of troopers over the side. There were only four, as Asel had guessed.

Asel heard a shot, turned to see the heavyset officer and two of his men firing at them from the other side. Phil's men answered. The troopers scurried back.

Sylvan shook his head in wonder. "You said you knew a bair. I see that you did."

"I wouldn't lie about a bair."

"I've seen the Floriday Dragoons. A most peculiar bunch. Set their hair on fire when they go into the fray. Tie ribbons to their parts. It rattles their foes, I hear. I'd put this crew up against a horde of Nones any day."

"I don't want to hear about Nones," said Betty Louise. "Or semi-clad girls either one."

Asel wished Sylvan would confine himself to Floriday Dragoons. He was right, of course. Phil had a most unusual band. They were fierce, savage fellows, gaunt and hungry men with fury in their eyes. He and Sylvan had tangled with their kind at the Oklahomer Wall. Any lout among this crew could have served with the TechsMechs Rangers—or the wretches who'd attacked them that day. Nearly every one was lame, partially unfit, attached to artificial parts.

Asel was amazed to see a squad of Mechs among the group. Wobbly, unsteady creatures with limbs that didn't match, heads that jerked about. Nothing like the finely crafted Califoggy Mechs. These were cousins to the gamblers of the desert, and Mr. LaGorse's crew—janitors and waiters who had no purpose, and no hotel.

Asel, Sylvan and Betty Louise had a hundred questions, but Phil had no time for that.

"We'll talk when we're finished up here. Got to get down fast."

"Good," Asel said, "I'm relieved to hear that. I shall cherish every foot on the ride back down."

Phil shook his furry, simulated head. "If you're referring to that liftin' thing, forget about that. Those crafty fellows cut it loose, soon as we got up here." He turned a big thumb straight down. "That way, friends, 'less you'd care to settle in here."

"Oh, Lord," said Betty Louise.

Asel tended to agree. The route was a shaky tumble of wooden stairs that wound about the giant tree. Portions were shot away. Railings were shattered, or no longer there.

Still, there was little else to do. Asel decided he had cheated death often in the last week or two, and might even do it again.

He looked up, then, aware that a sudden quiet had stilled Phil's crew.

Betty Louise held his hand. "Great Gods," Sylvan said, "what on Earth, or under it, is that?"

Without a conscious will, Asel took a step back. The creature who had hushed this fierce brigade was immense, a giant of a man, two, three heads taller than any fellow there. He was solid, a block, with scarcely a difference from his shoulders to his thick and sturdy legs.

His size alone was frightening indeed, but great dimension scarcely did him justice at all. For he was not wholly man anymore, but a mix, a fusion of man and machine. His body was patched, welded, hammered into place. Plates of iron armored his chest. His legs were pistons of steel.

Yet, there was part of a human in there—skin, gristle, and extrusions of bone appeared, bits of weathered flesh between more stable parts. One great arm was formed of cable, tendon, and steel. The other was a weapon, a ball of iron studded with ugly spikes. His head was a ruin—ragged striations, scraps of bronze, corrugated tin. A silver nose, a very human mouth. One piercing blue eye, another blinking red.

The strength, the power of this fellow was a near visible aura, a mantle cloaked about his massive form.

"You might want to take a care," Phil said under his breath. "BIG BUGG, he's kinda sensitive 'bout his appearance. I don't think I'd stare. . . ."

~ SIXTY-FOUR ~

Asel didn't throw up, didn't look down.
    Hugged the rough bark of the tree. Prayed the narrow, precarious stairway wouldn't give way. Now and then, shots rang out from below, spanged against the tree. The raggedy bunch fired back. Asel, Sylvan, and Betty Louise had weapons—but a pistol required one hand to be free.
    Asel could see the giant leader a level below. For all his size, he was neither ponderous nor slow. Logic said if the stairs would hold him, they would surely hold anyone else. Logic didn't help Asel a bit.
    He smiled up at Betty Louise. She didn't smile back.
    He could not get the first astonishing sight of BIG BUGG out of his head. And, with that image came another—the mounds of rotting corpses, the bones of enemy dead—BIG BUGG'S bloody message scrawled on stone, a grim and vivid warning to those who passed by. At the time, Asel didn't know that BIG BUGG'S foes were his enemies as well.

A small, fierce battle was still broiling below. Clouds of smoke obscured the field, but BIG BUGG'S horde had nearly cleared the heights, and Asel could see the troops of Disney-Dow were giving way. They poured from the trees, fled through the grove—desperate, defeated hornets deserting their ruined hives.
    Ducky and Jackie Cee . . . Asel wondered if either of the two had made it down alive. If they had, they'd find little comfort below, for the earth below was a hellish place to be—
    —and, of a sudden, no safe haven for BIG BUGG'S crew. As Asel and the others reached the surface, they ran headlong into a

swarm of troopers fighting to break free. They came on swiftly, nearly broke the ranks of the men who'd just reached the ground.

The giant leader roared his commands. His crew stood firm, meeting the black-clad soldiers with a fearsome clash of arms.

In an instant, Asel found himself in the forefront of the fray. Fired into them until his gun was empty—saw a man shot through the middle, saw a trooper's face explode. Threw his weapon aside, grabbed a broken rifle, battered a trooper down, kicked another in the head.

A man beside Asel clutched his chest and fell. A wiry fellow took his place, dropped dead, sprawled atop the first.

Asel saw lead bounce off a Mech's face. The Mech took a jerky step back. Forward. Left. Right and back again.

Sylvan was just ahead. Couldn't see Betty Louise at all.

A squad of troopers broke the line. Knew they had little chance to survive. Still, they were hard, disciplined men, deadly in their retreat, men who had nothing to lose.

"Asel—look up, man!"

Asel turned at Sylvan's shout. Saw the trooper bearing down, a man with blood on his armor, blood that was clearly not his own. Asel ducked, caught a numbing blow to the shoulder. Stumbled, went down. Brought himself back to his knees. The trooper struck him with an iron fist. Asel staggered back, shook his head to clear his eyes.

The trooper showed him a toothless grin, saw his foe was shaken, saw he could quickly take him down. He came straight at Asel, both fists together, hit him a punishing blow. Took Asel off his feet.

Asel tried to stand again. Knew he wouldn't make it, knew he was done.

The big man kicked him with his boot. Asel grabbed it, twisted, brought the fellow to ground. The trooper rolled to his feet, came at Asel again. Asel answered with a feeble chop to the head. The trooper didn't move. Asel hit him again. All he had left. The trooper caught him with a looping right, slammed him to the earth.

Once more, Asel came to his knees. Looked for the trooper, saw him swallowed up in the battle raging by. Sensed a figure behind him. Ducked as he turned, knew the man at once—the burly officer from Jackie Cee's lair.

The big man smiled. "It's a blessing it is, lad, to see you one more time. . . ."

With this cheery greeting, he raised a pistol to Asel's head. Gluck-Godiva thirty-nine. Not the new model, the one with the fancy grip.

What a useless fact to take to the grave—

The officer's eyes went blank. He folded, dropped like a stone.

"For a person of the noble persuasion, you don't do bad," Phil said. "Another round or two, you'd have had the fellow cold. . . ."

~ SIXTY-FIVE ~

"You and me, we had it all wrong," said the bair. "Those choppers at the big hole? They weren't after the Sue. They weren't from your SEC friends, or Califoggy State either one.

"B𝕚G BUGG, he'd already taken 'em, farther down south, the day before. What he was doing, was wiping out a bunch of troopers on the north rim of the hole."

Phil stopped to finish off a bir, wipe his faux muzzle with his hand. "I met up with his crew when they stopped in Less Vaguest, where you an' Betty Louise took off with your trucker pal."

"I would like to comment on that. We were, indeed, with a trucker. One Larry Bill. But I assure you he was no friend of mine. What a vulgar term: *Pal.* I suppose that's a mechanical word of some sort."

"There you go again. An' I thought you were coming along. You can't shake off that highbrow shit."

"He can't help it," said Betty Louise. "It's inbreeding causes it, I think. They all do that."

"You don't know what we *all* do. You don't know any high-born persons but me. And Sylvan, course. He's one, too."

"Thank you," Sylvan said. "I am one indeed. Though I don't know the point of it now."

"Good thought," Phil said, scratching something on his simulated hide. "You're the darkest human I ever seen, but your head's on right. . . ."

The edge of the grove was pleasant. Almost eerily quiet, now that the war was over and done. B𝕚G BUGG'S irregulars had lost too many men, but their foes had been badly mauled. Many had gotten away. Those who hadn't likely wished they'd perished in the fray. BiG BUGG was not a forgiving man.

Phil had told them he'd joined up just in time to attack Sekwoyah Heights, riding in a captured chopper to join the brigade BiG BUGG had sent to await him in Califoggy State.

"It's hit and run now," said the bair. "But there's no lack of poor and hungry fellows in the Midlands, itching for a chance to eat and fight. We'll haul out of here fast. Hit the fuckers somewhere else."

"What then?" Sylvan asked. "After that. Where does all this go?"

Phil pondered on that. "I don't rightly know. Maybe there's something. Maybe there's more of the same. . . ."

"I would say East, because I came from there. But it's useless to think about that. There's nothing there for me now."

Asel paused, looked past the grove. The great trees were lost in the fading light, but he could feel their mighty presence, even from afar.

Betty Louise had loosed her anger on the raggedy crew for setting trees afire, had even faced the leader himself. BiG BUGG had simply smiled, patted her gently on the head, told her it was smoke, not fire. Assured her he would never harm a tree. That he had a weakness for nature himself.

"You know, don't you," Asel said, "this rowdy bunch has no chance of winning this fight, no matter how many scarecrows they throw into the fray. It doesn't matter if Jackie Cee's alive or dead. Someone will be quite willing to step into his place.

"Disney-Dow is a power. Not just in Califoggy State. They have markets overseas. They have Mechs, dangerous drugs, aero-machines. They are gobbling up America East, and the Newer South as well."

"That's sort of what you had in mind, if I recall."

"What?" Asel was appalled. "The Iacola family served America East quite nicely, thank you. Our corporate structure was sound. Dividends. Top personnel. Sound and steady enterprise."

"I expect that's true."

"Father had respect. Ask anyone. Of course, he wasn't himself at the last. He couldn't help that."

"We could go north, hon."

"What? What's that?"

"I've been talking to BiG BUGG'S men. The Sue have got a fierce reputation, but they're not unkind, unless you get 'em riled."

"I have some cousins in Frants. Father had investments there."

"Frants? Are we talking overseas?"

"Well, that's where it is."

"Tom Micks knew someone went to Frants. They're into peculiar food and drink."

"What do the Sue eat? Spyders? Weeds?"

"I'm certain they eat like anyone else."

"Not like me they don't."

"Everyone but you."

"But you see, don't you, that's the very thing, Betty Louise—"

"Aaaaaaasel—!"

He wished she wouldn't make such a terrible sound. It was most unpleasant, and she simply wouldn't stop. He turned, quickly, but there was nothing he could do, it was over, it was done. Poor Ducky just appeared—bruised, bloody, out of it, totally whacked, and

Sylvan was coming as fast as he could, but nothing was faster than the fire so bright, so terribly white, from the mouth of Ducky's gun. It blazed again and again and wouldn't stop. Ducky was doing so much better than he had the time before and Asel was quite amazed at that.

And, even more astonished, more totally surprised, that nothing, absolutely nothing, seemed to hurt at all. . . .

~ SIXTY-SIX ~

He kept a ledger by the bed. A ledger with a dirhide cover, and his favorite pen. The ledger was to set down things he had done. Write about the people he had known, the places he had been. On the cover it said:

ASEL IACOLA, PRINCE OF CHRISTLER-COKE,
HEIR TO AMERICA EAST

When he first got the ledger, Betty Louise would ask how it was coming along. Asel would always say fine. After a while, she stopped. She knew he hadn't written anything at all.

Early every morning, he sat on the porch and waited for the kaufee to boil. Sometimes he'd smoke a pype. He had learned about pypes from the Sue. They had a trading place south of the river. Betty Louise got along with them fine. They didn't care for Asel. He didn't care for them. It simply worked out that way.

From the porch, he had counted thirty-seven different kinds of trees. Sometimes there were only thirty-six. He didn't know their names. He knew what their leaves looked like: They were narrow or broad, they were short or they were long. All of them were different shades of green. He liked them best in the fall, when some of them looked like trees from the East.

There was a settlement to the south, another to the north. BIG BUGG'S irregulars lived there with their families, when they weren't off to war. They would drop by and visit when the weather was good. He didn't enjoy these times. He had learned there was good in the common folk, but the gap was always there. He seldom thought about the fact that he was poor as well. If it ever came to mind, he set it swiftly aside.

"We are very lucky," Betty Louise would remind him. "We have all we need and we're together. We came through some very hard times."

"I guess we did," Asel would say. And, in truth, he was mostly content. He would never say it aloud, but he was getting used to the life he had now. Even the food sometimes.

He was watching the trees, checking out the leaves. The day before, he'd been almost certain he had spotted a tree he'd never seen before. It didn't seem likely, but nature was cunning at times.

His pype had gone out, and he turned to call Betty Louise. Turned, then stopped, for he sensed that something was different, something had changed.

He listened. Watched. Suddenly understood. *Byrds.* The byrds had gone silent. Except for the sigh of the wind, there was nothing to hear.

He reached for the Oolong-Rolls forty-six he always kept by the chair. Turned to call quietly to Betty Louise, saw she was already there. Holding the long Beluga, quietly chambering a shell.

"Could be anyone," she said. "Someone from the south."

"They'd make a little noise, let us know they're here."

"We'll get inside. Wait and see."

Asel didn't move. In a moment, the brush by the spring began to stir. Stopped, stirred again. Asel clicked his safety off. Betty Louise did the same.

A stick poked out of the brush. A stick with a ragged red flag. The flag waved back and forth.

Asel laughed aloud. "Whatever you're selling, we don't want it. Get your sorry ass out of here."

"What if I was sellin' bir? Dolfen dick pye? Perch ice cream?" Sylvan stepped out of the brush and stalked up to the house. Betty Louise ran out, met him halfway, gave him a hearty hug.

"Come on in the house, dear. The kaufee's still hot."

"Why not?" Asel said. "We'll let about anyone in. . . ."

The war was going well in South Califoggy. Not so well anywhere else. The irregulars had taken San Frisky, lost it, taken it back again. The Sweeds were bringing in arms, but they weren't any good.

"We still rely on what we take," Sylvan said. "And that's chancy at best. The Aisyattiks are supplying Disney-Dow. No big surprise in that. We lucked out. Sank a ship in Hokelan 'cross the bay."

"They won't like that," Asel said.
Sylvan was different. He had always been strong. Now his arms, his shoulders were hard as stone. He had let his beard grow. Gathered his hair in back, tied it in a knot. He was never at ease. His eyes flicked back and forth, searching for anything different, before it found him. He was Sylvan Lee McCree, but not the same man that Asel had known before.

He waited till after supper. Waited till Betty Louise had yawned and gone to bed. Asel knew something was coming, but didn't know what.
"BIG BUGG'S dead. They jumped him down south near Tio Whana. Killed him, and twenty-six men."
"Shit," Asel said. "I can't believe anyone could bring him down."
"Just be glad they didn't get him alive. Phil's in charge now, Ace."
"Phil." Asel shook his head.
"He's good. Sends his best."
"An imitation bair. Imagine that."
Sylvan paused, looked out at the dark. "We think we found him. We think we've found Jackie Cee."
Asel closed his eyes. Let the words sink in. Heard the insects buzzing in the trees. He thought about Father, Mother, Iacola Keep. All that seemed so far away, now. Another world, another life. Not his life any more.
He thought about Betty Louise, what it would do to her, how angry she would be. He hated to see her like that, didn't want to hurt her in any way.
He stood, making it look real easy for Sylvan Lee McCree. Walked across the porch for his pype, came and sat again.
"You showing off or what?"
"I don't need to, Sylvan. It works just fine."
"That's good."
"Before you ask, it's a leg and a hand. One fucking ear, a very small piece of chin. All the other vital parts are real."
Sylvan grinned. "I guess I could check with Betty Louise."
"I guess I could gun you down right here."
"You don't need to prove a thing, Ace. Nobody thinks you do."
"Maybe nobody but me. You can sleep in or out. Whatever you please. What time do you want to leave?"
"What you going to say to her?"

"I think that's up to me."
"I'd say it is."
"Phil told you to come."
"I could lie and say no."
"You don't have to do that."
"I'll find me a place in the woods. I'm more used to the outdoor life."
"You're a highborn fellow through and through."
Sylvan shook his head. Picked up his weapon and his gear, stepped off the porch and into the dark.

Asel lit his pype. Listened to the nightbyrds, the sound of the wind. Felt his heart would break in two. Knew it would for sure. Knew what he was doing was wrong, knew it was somehow right too. Knew he didn't ever want to go inside, knew that's what he had to do. Get up, go in, go up the stairs and get it done. . . .

Three thousand copies of this book have been printed by the Maple-Vail Book Manufacturing Group, Binghamton, NY, for Golden Gryphon Press, Urbana, IL. The typeset is Electra, printed on 55# Sebago. Typesetting by The Composing Room, Inc., Kimberly, WI.